WATER IN A BROKEN GLASS

WATER IN A BROKEN GLASS

odessa rose

LA CAILLE NOUS
PUBLISHING COMPANY, INC.

Cover photo by Al-Khabir Richardson
Cover layout & design by Amiyr Barclift
    for A-Train Studios

Edited by Marie Michael and Judy Salcedo

Rose, Odessa 1966-
    Water in a broken glass/ Odessa Rose.
        p. cm.
    ISBN 0-9647635-7-5
    1. Women sculptors--Fiction. 2. Identity (Psychology)--Fiction I. Title

PS3568.O764 W38 1999
813'.54--dc21

                                00-35206

P.O. Box 1004
Riverdale, MD 20738
www.lcnpub.com

Media contact:
328 Flatbush Avenue
    Ste. 240
Brooklyn, NY 11238
212-726-1293

To Odessa Roberta Southers Miles, 1912-2000
We miss you, Grandma.

For my husband, Michael, who has been encouraging,
inspiring, supporting, and carrying me home since I was 12 years old.

For my little fussy man, Brian, who has given me love, strength, patience,
courage, joy, and laughter beyond my wildest beliefs.

For my father, Al, who believed in me enough to think that one day he'd
see me on TV competing in the Olympics. I hope this will do.

For my mother, Adelsia, who sat on the front porch one warm summer
night and told her 9-year-old daughter to write.

Acknowledgments

Many, Many Thanks:

To my best friend, Linda, who has been here, there, and everywhere for me and with me whenever and for whatever no matter what for the last 22 years; Beaver (Karen) for reading every single draft and telling me what I missed and what I hit right on the head.

To Ann Cobb for caring enough to expect, listen, read, and play music over the phone, Rebecca Rose for giving me the title during one of our many heart-to-hearts.

To my family: Rachel, Sidney, Mark, Tyshmia, Ann Jackson, Paul, Claudette, Vicki, David, Arthur, Clinton, Melodie, Jo-Jo, Sandra, Jamal, Johnathan, and Amber for giving me a reason to do this again and again.

To Austin Housen, Ann Steinecke, Terry Branch, and Jenny Smith for reading the first draft and, instead of telling me how horrible it was, told me that it was a good beginning. To Cynthia Johnson for reading, giving me pep talks, and believing that I could do it.

To Guichard Cadet and LCN for making an old dream of mine come true. To my editors Marie Michael and Judy Salcedo for keeping me, my story and its characters honest. To Amiyr Barclift for designing such a beautiful cover. To Koritha Mitchell for helping me get my novel out there.

To Coppin State College professors Ron Collins, Amini Johari-Courts, Robert Cataliotti, Chantal Moudoud, Ralph Stevens, and Ann Cobb for teaching me to read and listen to literature so that I could write it.

To Dr. T.J. Bryan and the McNair program and its members for helping me take my study of literature to the next level. To Theresa Maultsby for giving me a job so that I could concentrate on my writing without having to worry about how I was going to help support my family.

To Thurman Zollicoffer for being my legal eagle. To Sheila Johnson and my mother for being my secretaries, even when they didn't want to be. To Jim Ray for keeping my old computers up and running.

To The Black Writers Guild of Maryland for creating opportunities for me to share my work. To the University of Maryland at College Park for giving me time off from school to finish the book.

To Bob Godin for introducing me to Etta James, and Dr. Cataliotti for introducing me to Big Jesse. To Verna Hall, Kathy Sease, and Ron Maultsby for being with me on a day that I felt so alone.

1

It was the crack of dawn, and I was under the iron stairs kneeling in front of the woman, curiously, nervously, and eagerly running my thumbs along her inner thighs as though this were the first time that we'd ever been together. It wasn't, of course. She used to come to me all the time, when my mother wasn't around, to keep me on the straight and narrow. But when I went to high school, I had to seek her out because she wasn't there when I needed her. Then one day she just upped and disappeared as if she'd wanted to leave me for a long time. I begged her to come back, but my pleas fell on deaf ears. So I said, Screw her! I don't need her. But two weeks ago, I found myself needing her more than I'd ever had in my life. And after some coaxing and manipulating, she came back. Reluctantly. But she came.

She had legs like a dancer--long, lean, graceful, powerful. I hadn't noticed that before. They were so shaped by dance that I could almost feel the splits, leaps, and pirouettes that kept blood flowing through them at an even, hypnotizing tempo. Images of her dancing through life to beats foreign and dear to her soul flooded my mind and made me envious of the freedom she possessed. I wanted to see her dance. But dancing was out of the question for her this morning.

Through the gaps in the stairs I watched as an orange day climbed into the three tall, arched windows of my haven. Like a searchlight sweeping the still and silent grounds of a prison, the loud, harsh dawn scanned the joint, catching everything in its inescapable net of illumination except for me. Determined to flush me out, the dawn slid down the walls onto the cold cement floor and scoured my retreat. The patrolling sunlight had its work cut out for it, though, because I'd been holed up in this place for ten years. And in that time I had become a master at hiding in the light.

My hideout was a white, wide, square studio on the third floor of America's Art Institute. AAI was a long way from my parents' dark, cramped basement where I used to sculpt my thoughts while sitting on a low metal stool in front of a wooden table with three measly modeling tools and one bag of clay a month. I couldn't wait to get out of that basement and into a studio inside of AAI, but at this moment I wished that I'd never left. As unsuitable as that basement was for sculpting, I'd been seriously thinking about going back because I could be alone with her down there. But I didn't want to or even know how to explain my return to my mother and father. I couldn't even explain it to myself.

Quiet hung low in my studio and was only interrupted by an occasional graveled squeak of the stone sculpture stand rotating as I viewed the woman from different angles. The field of fluorescent lights was off so it was dark even with the incoming sunlight. It was cold and uncaring, this sunlight. It searched all around, and when it couldn't find hide nor hair of me, it interrogatively beamed into the faces of the white men drying on shelves and staying moist under clear plastic bags atop sculpture stands. My accomplices, as I now called these clay portraits, seemed to squint their eyes to close out the intense light. If I had known that the light from this time would be so blinding, I would have turned their faces toward the wall. But that was to assume that I knew that this time would come. It hadn't come in nine years. So, for the life of me, I couldn't figure out why it was here now.

Nothing warned me of this time's coming. Especially nothing that happened Tuesday before last when I'd decided to clean and straighten up my studio. I'd just completed a series of sculptures that celebrated American presidents who were in office during major wars, and I was waiting for Dr. Zimmerman to bring me his next thought. You see, that was how I made my living, sculpting the thoughts and feelings of Dr. Zimmerman. And the debris from years and years of sculpting without a care or thought of my own was scattered about and piled in corners.

I wish that I could say that my sudden urge to clean was fueled by my inability to look around this studio and see my thoughts and feelings, my take on life and the world around me. But I came to AAI so that I could get away from those things. So, truth be told, I started cleaning because I just wasn't used to having nothing to do.

While I was doing this seemingly mindless, innocent chore, I stumbled upon my old table and stool up in the loft. That elevated space had been used for storage before I dragged a futon up there so that I'd have a place to sleep when I worked late and was too tired to make the twenty minute drive to my house in northwest Baltimore.

The table and stool were behind some boxes that were filled with old soap sculptures of animals and clay sculptures of my family and best friend and roommate, Nikki. I'd forgotten all about them, didn't even remember putting them up there. But after I pulled them out, sat down on the stool, and ran my hands over the table, I started remembering things that I wanted forgotten. And those things were making me feel as if I didn't know myself or my life. For a long time I was certain that if I didn't know any other truth in this entire world, I knew my truth. Then all of a sudden, as I sat there trying not to remember, my world began to turn upside down again, but I didn't know what for. All I knew was who. And in a woman's life who else but another woman would have the audacity to be behind so much anxiety, confusion, and mischief?

Not less than two weeks ago, she was no more than a faint, distant memory that I didn't even believe was mine. Now, she was weighing on my mind so heavily that I couldn't imagine her belonging to anybody but me. Ten years. That was how long it had been since I'd thought about her, since I'd thought about the last time I saw her.

We were outside of Principal Menefee's office. I was sitting straight up in a chair with my sweaty hands in a stranglehold on my lap, glaring across at her, and she was sitting with her head cocked to one side and her arms folded across her chest. The look of absolute hatred was gone from her face and was replaced with what appeared to be concern for me. And I believe that had her anger not been so delicious, she would have come over, taken my hand and said, "It ain't that bad." That was what I needed to hear. But her anger kept her in her seat and only let her glaring brown eyes say over and over what she'd said to me in the shower minutes before.

I'd done all I could to forget the words in her eyes and everything that led up to her saying them. Today, though, I remembered it as if it were happening right this very second.

May 18, 1984. Three weeks before graduation, and I was going to be suspended from school for the first time in my life. Suspended! It seemed to me that they would have gone easy on me since I'd never so much as gotten into an argument with anyone. But no! They had to make an example of me. Which meant that I wasn't going to be allowed to walk across the stage of Northwestern High School, where I'd spent four long years busting my behind for a diploma that I had to accept from the mailman. My parents canceled my surprise graduation party in order to teach me a lesson. As if worrying about the fact that my suspension may have screwed up my chances of getting accepted into America's Art Institute wasn't lesson enough.

AAI was the kind of school where you had to be recommended before they would even consider your application or your work. In my case, my tenth grade art teacher, Miss Miller, put in a good word. I was waiting to hear their decision, hoping and keeping my fingers crossed that I'd be able to walk onto the campus of AAI in the fall and officially sit in one of its grand studios to study and create sculpture. I was terrified that they would get wind of my suspension, look upon me as someone who would ruin their school's reputation, and throw my application and portfolio in the trash.

Another dream of mine was also in danger of being thrown in the trash--my dream of getting married. I'd been fantasizing about my wedding day ever since I'd marched down the aisle in my Aunt Josephine's wedding. There wasn't a flower girl on earth who took her job more seriously than I did. And as I sprinkled tiny handfuls of freshly plucked red rose petals onto the white runner that guided my way to the altar where Mr. Charlie stood in his black and white pinstriped tux, I wished that I was his bride-to-be.

Now everything I wanted my life to be was on the line, all because of a girl I'd met four months earlier.

She'd come in the middle of the year, right after the Christmas holidays. Some said that she transferred from Walbrook; others claimed that she came from Forest Park. But neither of these schools gave us the ammunition we needed to turn gossip into fact. Then one day while we were showering after gym and talking about her--it seemed that we were always talking about her--my best friend Nikki came up with the evidence we'd been looking for to explain the difference we all felt about her.

Nikki transformed talking about people into an art, but she didn't do it because she was insecure or cruel. She did it because she had a knack for it, and it was fun. Nothing interested or entertained her more than analyzing people, using their facial expressions, walks, laughs, and words to unmask them and then give us just the right tidbit that would make a rumor travel like gospel through the grapevine.

While Nikki lathered her body, she dropped on us the speculated truth that would send the girl up the river. "Na-uh," Nikki said to the list of schools. "I heard that that girl came from Western."

This explained everything and explained nothing at the same time. So it was followed by a loud chorus of long "Oooooh's!" that said, "*I see!*" and hard sucks of teeth that said, "*No wonder!*" because Western was an all girl school.

Who knows how or why rumors like these get started? But by the first week in February, the buzz at Northwestern was that the new girl, Meyoki Outlaw, was... *funny.* I never said much about Meyoki. I just listened to what was whispered about her in the hallways, cafeteria, and girls' shower. I also watched her, trying to see if any of it was true. A few times I caught myself sketching her in the pages of my loose-leaf notebook when I should have been copying something off the blackboard or taking lecture notes. She was tall (at least six feet), dark brown, and thin with two small handfuls of perky breasts. She had wide-open eyes the color of brown sugar. She wore her hair braided in rows of tight, silky plaits, and had three gold earrings in each ear and a wide gold band on her left thumb. But the thing that drew me to her the most was the wonderful tapping sound she made behind her full, saucy lips. I used to listen for it everywhere, trying to figure out how she did it.

Meyoki took gym with us, and I'd often find an excuse to look in her direction or walk past her aisle in the locker room while she was dressing or undressing. But if she looked at me, I'd turn my head and walk away as fast as anything on two legs.

Around the end of April the rumors about Meyoki started getting vicious. We had her sleeping with female teachers, cheerleaders, girls on the basketball, softball, tennis, track, and badminton teams. She couldn't walk to class without people pointing, staring, whispering, and giggling at her. Couldn't eat lunch without hearing a table of students bursting out in laughter from a joke told about her. Finally, I guess it all became too much, and Meyoki lashed out.

It happened one Friday after gym. We were in the shower, talking about Meyoki, when she stepped in the doorway. Everybody shut up and gawked at her. She stood there for a minute and stared back at us, looking from one side of the steamy, white-tiled room to the other. The shower room had never been so quiet, and was never meant to be. It was supposed to be filled with girlish giggles and jokes about who liked what boy, or what hairstyles, shoes, and clothes were in or out of fashion. There was none of that kind of talk going on. The only thing you heard was water gushing out of the showerheads and running down the drains in thick gurgles.

Meyoki shook her head as if we were the most pitiful souls she'd seen that day. After what seemed like hours of us staring at her and her shaking her head in pity at us, Meyoki curved her lips into a devilish smile then took off her towel right there in the doorway. The shower exploded in gasps. How could she do that? I wondered. I could have never done anything like that. I didn't like taking showers at school. The only thing I hated more than taking showers at school was being constantly teased for the one time that I was too shy to shower way back in ninth grade. So I suffered through it, wrapping my body in a long beach towel like a cocoon, and praying, always in vain, that by the time I reached the shower, my small breasts would blossom, my straight hips would become curvy, and my thin legs would grow long and shapely.

But Meyoki's body was just like that. I guess that's how she could walk slowly through the shower wearing nothing except the shiny, gold ring in her naval. Goodness, how that must have hurt, I thought.

Meyoki passed unoccupied showerheads and headed toward the very last one so that we all could get a good, long look at her. Girls were whispering and elbowing each other, but not one took their eyes off her. I know I didn't. I watched every inch of her body swaying and jiggling, and I listened to her perfect feet slapping on the wet tile, although they sounded more like hands clapping. That was the second time in my life that I'd heard a woman make her own music with her footsteps. I liked her sound. It was brave and catchy, just like her.

When she got near the shower that I was using, Meyoki paused then quickly closed her left eye and smiled. The blink of her long eyelashes felt like they'd kissed me on the nape of my neck, and I'd never been kissed there before.

There were no fervent, glowing, orange flames to be seen, nor was there the stench of thick black smoke stifling the air, nor was there the crackling sound of burning flesh. But my body was on fire! There I was engulfed in this invisible, odorless blaze that was threatening to reduce me to a smoky pile of black ashes, even as I stood in the shower with water running on my back. All because some girl winked her left eye at me!

When that stool and table triggered those horrible memories of Meyoki, I wanted to scream and throw them out of the window so that they and the thoughts of Meyoki Outlaw would smash to bits when they hit the ground. But screaming and destroying things wasn't how I spoke my peace to myself. I learned, probably too soon for my own good, that the tongue could only say so much, and that I, like most people, stopped listening long before it said too much of what I didn't want to hear. So when I had something beautiful or important to tell myself. Or when I really needed to give myself or someone else a piece of my mind, I'd sketch or sculpt my thoughts, my feelings, my actions, which were almost always more vivid and radical than any words that fell off my tongue and dribbled past my lips.

The thing was I'd stopped conversatin' (as I called it) like that with myself when I received my acceptance letter from AAI. But I had to do something to rid myself of these memories, or at least protest against them. So two weeks ago, I retreated under the iron stairs that led up to the loft, and sat like a silhouette on my wobbly metal stool in front of my aged, wooden, clay-stained table that had "TONYA AND NIKKI, FRIENDS FOREVER" carved into it.

2

The orange dawn promised the city a colorful spring day that it could not deliver. Two hours after it had climbed into my studio windows, the bright May morning turned gloomy. Large gray clouds smeared themselves over clumps of pale white ones, making rain just a matter of time. By three-thirty it was raining, and I was just finishing the thought I'd been working on to exorcise the thoughts I'd been having about Meyoki.

The thought began with a solid oak staircase. It had a long, unpolished banister and ten dusty steps. The woman with the bewitching dancer's legs was standing on the edge of the tenth step like an unbroken promise on her lover's hungry lips as they taste the small of her back. She was black with heavy-lidded eyes that were cast downward, but her head was thrown back in remembrance of a fresh, erotic past. She was wearing a man's shirt, which was noticeably a few sizes too big. It hung loosely, exposing her plump breasts and delicately outlining her tender round behind. The cuffs of the sleeves covered her small hands, and the shirttail lay against the middle of her thighs, which, like her face, were still hot and wet from their lovemaking.

On the first step the eager toes of a black man were lightly planted. He was naked, large, and muscular. He had tiny round mirrors for eyes that held the black woman's image like a silver picture frame, and kept her from seeing him even though she was inquisitively looking directly at his face. All of the things that she wished to know about him were behind his tight, loyal lips. But she didn't have to pry open his mouth with her feminine wiles to uncover his secrets. All she had to do was let her eyes sip from the glass of cool water that he was carrying up to her.

A lazy glance at this terra-cotta sculpture would easily give its viewer the true but superficial impression that the man in the piece was hopelessly and forever whipped. But I was looking at it with an alert eye. So I saw a beam of daylight slanting across the black man, animating the loving expression on his face, the delicate manner in which his strong hands held the glass, and the earnestness in his footsteps. And all of this revealed the black man's belief that the most manly, romantic, and, yes, whipped thing he could do for his woman after such a beautiful entanglement was bring her a glass of cool water.

The odd thing about this piece was that if you rode the gray shadows of a cloudy day up the stairs and a little to your right, you could see that in actuality it was the woman who was truly whipped, though not so much by what swung between her man's hairy legs as by what was cradled inside his rough palms.

Like I said, the woman in the piece, which I'd titled *A Glass of Cool Water*, wasn't a new thought and neither was the man. This was, however, the first time that I had put them together. But the two of them had been part of my dreams since the morning of Aunt Josephine's wedding.

Aunt Josephine came to stay with us in 1973. I had seen pictures of her before, but they didn't prepare me for the real thing. She was light-skinned with smoky gray eyes, short wavy black hair, and a sharp tongue. She mesmerized me from the moment she set foot in our house because she was so different from my mother. Aunt Josephine was easy-going and fun. She didn't have any children, and as if that wasn't scandalous enough, she often bragged about not wanting any.

My mother was gingerbread-brown, slim, and short. She had thick, soft black hair and tiny, worried brown eyes. She was strict and uptight. She'd miscarried twice before having my older sister, Elaine, and once more before having me. The losses made her overprotective. She ran around trying to prevent falls, fights, colds, tooth decay, cuts, broken bones, heartbreaks, and teenage pregnancies. My mother would have truly and easily died or murdered for us. My father said that my mother was too crazy about us. My mother told him that she just wanted her girls safe and happy.

One of the things that I really admired about Aunt Josephine when she first came was that nobody, including my mother, could tell her what to do. She did exactly as she pleased, and I wished that I could have been that free and comfortable with myself. But the thing that I liked most about Aunt Josephine was the way that she called me "Love."

"Hey, Love," she'd said when my mother introduced me to her.

She was standing, and I remember that the first thing I saw of her when I ran into the living room were her hot red pumps. She looked like a life-sized exclamation point to me, and those heels were the defining period. She walked over to me. Her heels on the wood floor sounded like two drumsticks being hit together. ClackClackClackClack! That was the first time that I'd ever heard a woman make her own music. And it was the awesome sound of that clacking and the soulful tone of "Hey, Love" that made me jingle like a bell all over.

Aunt Josephine brought chit'lins, Hoppin' John, bread pudding (my favorite), men, and blues into our house, in particular Mr. Charlie and a dark-berry blues singer named Pearl Knight, who, in 1977, abruptly walked away from the music business at the height of her career. Aunt Josephine had every album Pearl had recorded, but she used to play this song called *"When My Man Gave Me Black Satin"* the most. You could hear Pearl's twangy voice all through the house.

> *My man gave me mink*
> *And made me wink.*
> *My man gave me lace*
> *And put a smile on my face.*
> *My man gave me silk*
> *And made me cream like milk.*
> *But you should have seen what happened*
> *When my man gave me black satin.*

Charles Blackstock owned The Fish Store. He was a thin, high-waisted, ivory-black man with a small beer belly and poppy brown eyes that sat behind large eyelids that made him look half asleep. He looked like a cartoon character, but women loved him. Mr. Charlie opened his store at seven in the morning to catch the school crowd, and closed it at nine o'clock at night when most of the neighborhood kids had to be in front of their doors or in their houses altogether. If you were old enough to still be out on the porch around ten, you'd see Mr. Charlie come out of the apartment above his store dressed in one of his pinstriped suits, looking as slick as he wanted to be. He'd get into his waxed white Cadillac, and head out to the Arch Social Club on Pennsylvania Avenue. He would return hours later with a woman, whom he'd drive home early the next morning before he opened the store.

He never messed with any of the women around our way. "Y'all trouble enough as it is," he told this one girl's mother who lived up the street from me. Then one day, I walked into his store with my Aunt Josephine, who had left the South and the man that she was living with.

"White folks is building up all over the place down there," I overheard Aunt Josephine telling my mother. "Resorts, country clubs, golf courses. People can't pay the taxes on their land no more, and they losing their homes left and right. Remember the Freys, Warrens, and the Cunninghams? Well, all of them is now working at the country club that was built on their property. Dutton lost his land to a golf course. Land been in his family since I don't know when. Now he workin' as a grounds keeper on it. He's so depressed. All he does is work and then come home to our little apartment and drink. And since he can't run them white folks off his land, he's been tryin' to run me, and you know what Momma said about lettin' a man run us."

"Yeah. Don't!" my mother laughed, which she hardly ever did before Aunt Josephine came.

I liked the sound of my mother's laughter when she was with Aunt Josephine. It made me feel as though she could fantasize about her life being more than just a house that never stayed clean, a husband that was going to work himself into an early grave, and two hardheaded daughters who were hell-bent on worrying her to death. So I would eavesdrop on their conversations just to hear my mother tee-hee or ha-ha.

Aunt Josephine sighed. "That's it for me, Lorna. I'm through with 'em. I'm not gonna so much as even look at a man. Hell, I might even go out and get myself a woman."

"Yeah right," my mother said. Then, "But if you do, for God's sake don't bring her back here around my girls."

"Ah, you know I'm just talkin'," Aunt Josephine said.

"You never just talk about anything. But you know what Momma told us about runnin' with women."

"Yeah. Don't!" Aunt Josephine said.

That sent my mother and aunt into gales of laughter. I didn't get the joke, didn't understand the difference between "lettin' a man run you" and "runnin' with women." But apparently Aunt Josephine was just talking because the minute she saw Mr. Charlie eyeing her, she started slinging her southern hips and eyeing him with her smoky gray eyes.

That day she was wearing a white silk blouse with red buttons that barely kept her "boobs," as she called them, from popping out. She had on a tight red lace skirt with a scalloped hem that stopped just above her knees. A long scar was slanted across her right knee. She'd fallen on a piece of glass while she and my mother were running home from two white boys when she was nine. My mother kept running even though she knew that Aunt Josephine was hurt and lying on the ground.

"Your momma was never a fighter," Aunt Josephine told me. "Neither was I 'til that day. Jimmy and Henry Peterson. Them boys chased us home every time they saw us, and we ran like scared rabbits. And when I fell, my life flashed before my eyes."

"Why?" I asked, from the edge of her bed, where I hung onto her every word. "'Cause you knew they was gonna beat you up?"

"No, Love. Because I tore my brand new stockings, and I got a big gash in my knee. Momma cleaned white folks' houses for a livin', so she didn't have no money to be buyin' things she just bought. And she didn't have no money to be taking me to the doctor's to have my knee sewed up 'cause I was clumsy. Lord, I was so scared of what Momma would do to me that I started shaking. Jimmy and Henry started laughing and that made me mad as I don't know what. I jumped up from the ground and whipped them white boys like their momma should have a long time ago. And I took their money and brought me a new pair of stockings and some bandages."

She caressed her knee as if the cut were still fresh and bleeding. "That's why I never cover this scar. It reminds me not to run from anything or anybody."

I came to love that scar and everything about Aunt Josephine because everything about her came with a story that told me about her and my mother. Like my mother felt so guilty about leaving Aunt Josephine and was so afraid of being put in a position to do it again that two weeks after the incident she moved to Baltimore to live with their Aunt Delores. Until that day, I'd never known how my mother came to be in Baltimore while the rest of her family was down in Mullins, South Carolina. The only thing my mother ever said about her life in Mullins was, "I ain't never going back." But she did once. For Grandma's funeral. We drove down the morning of the funeral and drove back up while they were lowering her into the ground.

Anyway, The Fish Store wasn't that big. It was shaped like a rectangle with barely room enough for the glass counter that held candy, cookies, and gum, the seafood bin where lake trout, catfish, crabs, oysters, and shrimp chilled on a bed of ice, the soda freezer, the deli counter, and the cigarette machine. But even in that little space, Aunt Josephine managed to walk teasingly around Mr. Charlie's store in her short, short dress and 2½ inch red heels, pretending to be uncertain about what she wanted. ClackClack!... ClackClack!... ClackClack! Mr. Charlie didn't miss a beat.

Neither did I.

"It's kinda hot today," Aunt Josephine said in a slow voice as she stopped in front of the freezer full of sodas. "I think I'll get something cool to drink." She opened the door and wrapped her long fingers around a tall bottle of Coca-Cola. "Oh," she said then sucked her teeth in disappointment. "It's warm."

Mr. Charlie grinned a kind of "gotcha" grin as he bopped coolly out from behind the counter. He patted me on the head and gave me a pack of Now-And-Laters, trying to get me to leave so that he could put his moves on Aunt Josephine. But nothing was gonna get me out of that store.

Mr. Charlie opened the freezer door, and just as he bent down, Aunt Josephine shifted her weight from one red heel to the other. That's when Mr. Charlie saw Aunt Josephine's scared knee and that's when he lost his cool. Beads of sweat started forming on his forehead, his eyes widened, and his lips started quivering. He thought that that scar was beautiful enough to kiss. It took everything in his power not to press his thick lips on it right then and there.

He whispered, "Lord, give me strength," as he turned away from Aunt Josephine's knee.

Mr. Charlie then reached way, way in the back of the freezer and pulled out an ice-cold Coca-Cola. He twisted off the cap and waited for the "PSSST!" to escape before presenting the soda to her as if it were a bouquet of fine wine from his private stock.

Aunt Josephine took the bottle, tilted her head back, closed her eyes, and put her lips over the mouth of the bottle. She drank slowly, and Mr. Charlie and I stood stark still, totally captivated by the sensual movement of the muscles in Aunt Josephine's throat as she swallowed. I'd never seen a throat move like that. One time at dinner I copied the way Aunt Josephine drank and my mother gave her the evil eye then slapped me in the back of my head. "If I ever see you drinking like that again, I'm gonna knock your head off your shoulders."

Aunt Josephine drank half the bottle before pulling it away with an

"Ahhhhh!" She then smiled at Mr. Charlie to let him know that that Coca-Cola had soothed more than her dry throat. And the minute we stepped on the pavement, Aunt Josephine asked me, "He got any women friends that be hangin' 'round in that store of his?"

I said, "Uh-uh."

"Ummm," Aunt Josephine said, and drank the rest of the Coke.

The next thing I knew Mr. Charlie was calling me into his store to give me free penny candy and all the soda I could drink. I'd sit up on the counter happily eating candy and letting him grill me about Aunt Josephine. But I only told Mr. Charlie what Aunt Josephine told me to tell him--No, she ain't married, and she ain't got no boyfriend. Yeah, she's been lookin' for a good man to settle down with. She's twenty-eight. But she was really thirty.

It wasn't long before Mr. Charlie was pulling up in front of our house in his Cadillac with *"She's Not Just Another Woman"* by The 8th Day blaring from his 8-track. He courted Aunt Josephine the entire summer with Coca-Colas, music, and dancing. I didn't mind them seeing each other, but whenever they'd go out, Mr. Charlie closed his store early and opened up late in the afternoon. So me and the rest of the neighborhood kids had to go to either the basement store or the alley store and their penny candy cost a nickel.

"I don't know what you see in that funny-lookin' man," my mother said to Aunt Josephine.

"I see a man that I didn't think I'd meet until I'd died and gone to heaven," Aunt Josephine said. "A man that won't run around on me, won't try to run me, won't try to put me in my grave before my time. Humph! And if you still don't understand, I see a man that makes love like a steam engine, and all I want to do is tie my legs up like a bow around his caboose. Wooo! Wooo!"

My mother laughed really hard at that. From the crack in my parents' partially closed bedroom door I saw her fall back on the bed, and she didn't look like Mrs. Calvin Mimms or Mama. She looked like Lorna

Blume, plain old Lorna Blume.

Seeing Aunt Josephine with Mr. Charlie made me wish that I were around when my father was courting my mother. My mother told me once that the minute she saw my father, she knew that he was the one for her. And my father told me that he used to walk from West Baltimore to East Baltimore every night just to see my mother. My mother has never said how she knew, and my father has never said why he walked. I'd like to know the answer to both questions.

By the end of August, Mr. Charlie had put a big old diamond engagement ring on Aunt Josephine's finger. Three months later, I was standing at the altar next to my mother, who was the maid of honor, watching my father escort Aunt Josephine down the aisle. I'd always thought that Aunt Josephine was pretty but when I saw her come down the aisle in that elegant, white satin dress, wearing her mother's pearls around her long neck, cradling that sweet smelling bouquet of roses in her lovely arms and smiling like the November sun, I thought that she was the most beautiful woman in the world. And I hoped that someday I would be as beautiful on my wedding day.

The morning of the wedding my mother had rushed out of Aunt Josephine's room to get something borrowed. I was supposed to be sitting on the couch so that I wouldn't get my dress dirty, but I was bored so I went up to talk to Aunt Josephine.

She was standing in front of the mirror in her white stockings and lace bra, humming one of Pearl Knight's songs. When Aunt Josephine saw me in the doorway, she said, "Hey, Love, come help me put on my garter."

She sat down on the bed and I kneeled and pushed the lace, sky blue garter up her calf. You could still see the scar on her knee through her stockings. When I reached it, I blurted out, "Can I marry you too, Aunt Josephine?"

She laughed. "No, Love."

"Why?"

Aunt Josephine ran down a bunch of excuses as she pulled the garter over her knee and up the middle of her thigh. "For one thing I'm your aunt, and relatives ain't supposed to marry. For another thing, you're too young to get married, especially to an old woman like me. And," she said as though it wasn't really all that important but she'd better tell me anyway, "women ain't supposed to run with other women."

"Why not?" I asked.

"Because the Bible says so!" my mother said, her angry voice startling me. "Now get your behind downstairs and sit down on the couch like I told you!"

My mother was a very religious woman, but she kept her relationship with God private. She didn't go to church, bless her food before eating, or recite scriptures that she'd memorized from the Bible. What my mother did was read a chapter of the Bible every night, get down on her knees and pray not only for her salvation but her family's as well, and whenever she felt that her husband or daughters were straying too far away from God's word, my mother would say, "Because the Bible says so!"

So when my mother ordered me downstairs, I knew that she was actually saying that I would end up in hell if I ran with Aunt Josephine or any other woman, and I most certainly didn't want to go to hell. So, while sitting on the living room sofa, I decided that if I couldn't marry Aunt Josephine, then I wanted to marry a man like my father and Mr. Charlie.

And that was who the man in the piece represented. He was walking up the stairs because my father walked all that way to see my mother, and he was bringing his woman something cool to drink because Uncle Charlie had given Aunt Josephine a bottle of Coke for her dry throat and life.

I hadn't sculpted anything this intimate in so long that I thought I'd forgotten about the man I wanted and the woman in me. But *A Glass of Cool Water* helped me to see that I was more woman than I ever thought I wanted to be, because only a woman would fantasize about allowing her heart to be gobbled up by a glass of plain old tap water. And that was what I wanted. I wanted to be standing at the top of the stairs in my man's shirt, dripping with love and lust simply because he was bringing me something cool to drink.

Absolutely, positively, without a doubt, this was what I wanted.

3

It rained heavily, almost nonstop for the next two days, but I didn't mind because rain was the only thing that I'd come to enjoy and, to a certain extent, anticipate at AAI.

America's Art Institute is one of the most prestigious art schools in the country. Located in downtown Baltimore on Saint Paul Street, it consisted of four white four-story buildings--Administration, Whitney Library, Studio Hall, and Independence Gallery. A natural stone slate sidewalk that felt like a royal carpet under my feet marked off the campus from the rest of the buildings on the block. On top of Administration was a belfry that most people dismissed as a loud, annoying gong instead of the sweet toll that I heard. In front of Whitney Library was a bronze sculpture of Jefferson Whitney, the founder of AAI, and the great sculptor that I aspired to be.

Before I enrolled, every chance I got I went down to that school and sat in the leather chairs and ran the palms of my hands over the mahogany tables that adorned the lobbies. I admired the busts and oil paintings of old, white money that echoed through the hallways, and I appraised the pieces on display in the gallery. But most of the time I stood inside of Studio Hall, peering through the small windows in the doors of the studios. They were full of large storage bins of clay and terra-cotta, had walls covered in wood blade and wire-end modeling tools, state of the art kilns, bookcases crammed with the most respected art books, and ten foot workbenches. Rows of fluorescent lights were mounted to the ceiling, and their rays mix well with the natural sunlight that poured through the shadeless windows. As I watched the art students, I dreamed of the day that I would be on the other side of the door.

The rain added a slick rhythm to the dynamic, assiduous aspirations of the art students there. All of whom were compelled by some unexplainable, indescribable something that kept us in a perpetual, passionate almost neurotic daze. We interpreted life and feelings as we experienced them or wished we could experience them with colorful pieces of lead, chalk, paint, paper, wood, glass, ice, steel, iron, stone, clay, or anything else we could get our strange, wondering, and wanting hands and minds wrapped around.

Thursday morning. The downpour lured me from under those black iron stairs and over to the radiator in front of the window, where I sat for hours with my clay-covered hands wrapped around my eighth or ninth cup of black coffee. Outside, people were moving, trying to stay dry out in the rain. I couldn't really see them, though. Canopies from buildings, umbrellas, newspapers, briefcases and tinted car windows covered their faces. All I saw were hints of people, who looked as though they had been painted in watercolors.

Around eleven o'clock, Dr. Zimmerman's gray Crown Victoria backed into a parking space across the street. He jumped out, took a quick drag on a Camel Light cigarette, then flicked it to the ground. He poured the rest of his coffee down his throat and started to throw the empty paper cup on the ground, but he tossed it on the floor behind the driver's seat instead. He then grabbed an umbrella from the back seat and struggled to open it as he hastened around to the trunk.

After cursing and whacking the umbrella on the ground a few times, the canopy popped open and spread over his head like a big black tent. That's when he unlocked the trunk and pulled out a brown, medium-sized, cardboard box. He held the box tightly in one arm, wedging it against his chest and chin, then tramped quickly, but cautiously, across the street, and ran inside Studio Hall.

I drank the rest of my coffee, put the cup in the sink then went under the stairs to cover the *Glass of Cool Water* piece. I had barely slipped a dark green plastic bag over it when I heard the squeak of Dr.

Zimmerman's wet leather wingtip shoes on the marble floor out in the hallway. Simultaneously, he rapidly but politely knocked on the door and opened it. In all the years I'd spent at AAI, I'd never thought twice about Dr. Zimmerman barging into my studio. In fact, I welcomed his company and his evaluation of whatever piece I was working on. I enthusiastically accepted his advice on how to make my good sculpture great, and smiled when he returned to see the masterpiece I'd gone on to sculpt. But today when he walked in uninvited, I sucked my teeth loud enough for the "Sth!" to echo down the hallway.

The sound grazed Dr. Zimmerman's cheek, and he turned back and looked out into the hallway to see if he were hearing things. Dr. Zimmerman shook his head, as if to shrug off the possibility that I would greet him in such a manner, implying that he had descended upon me in my personal space when in fact all he did was enter a room that I was allowed to use rent-free because of him.

He stepped in and closed the door. Before then, he hadn't noticed that the lights were off. Standing in the dark, Dr. Zimmerman looked around the studio. He couldn't see me under the stairs.

"Tonya?" Dr. Zimmerman called hesitantly.

I stepped out and met the intruder with an icy, motionless frown.

Startled and puzzled by my grim look, Dr. Zimmerman asked, "Is everything all right, Tonya?"

I stared at him and thought, Where were you two weeks ago with your cardboard box and concern? If you had been here then, I wouldn't have had time to remember what I've been trying to forget.

"Tonya, are you okay?"

I tried to stay angry so that I could make him the reason why I'd been under the stairs standing, stooping, bending, and circling all day and half the night for the past two weeks; blame him for my nibbling on stale, plain bagels and drinking black coffee because I was afraid to stop working, go home, and sit down and eat a decent meal with Nikki.

But the worry in Dr. Zimmerman's voice softened me enough to step back and see the short, thin, pink-skinned man with the dull brown eyes and full, bushy beard and sideburns but no mustache. The fifty-five-year-old man who was just beginning to lose his brown hair, a fact he tried to cover up by combing the thinning strands to the back of his head, which only highlighted his growing baldness. The suit, tie, and wing-tipped shoes man who gnawed on his fingernails when he couldn't puff on a Camel Light cigarette. The man who had been like a second father to me and had nothing to do with what I couldn't forget.

"I'm fine, Dr. Zimmerman," I said finally, then walked over to my workbench and started picking up some modeling tools.

Dr. Zimmerman switched on the lights. A twinkle then flash flood of light engulfed my studio. The bright, white light hurt my face as well as my eyes.

The room filled with the smell of rain and cigarettes as Dr. Zimmerman placed the brown cardboard box on my desk. "Been doing some spring cleaning, I see," he said.

I forced a smile and nodded.

Dr. Zimmerman went over to the shelf where my *Presidents of War* series sat and he quickly but meticulously examined my busts of Lincoln, Wilson, Roosevelt, Truman, and the other presidents. I held my breath while he reviewed my work, and hoped that he didn't find anything horribly wrong with it.

Gnawing on his thumbnail, he said, "I think this is some of your best work." Dr. Zimmerman spit a piece of his thumbnail onto the cement floor. "This goes on exhibit when?"

"Next summer at the Walters Art Gallery."

"And you have the...?"

"The *Dear North, Dear South* exhibit next month at the Baltimore Museum of Art."

"Right. I'm going to hate missing that one," he said, then proceeded to help me move and rearrange the tools and supplies on my workbench.

Dr. Zimmerman put some supplies in a neat pile on the floor under the iron stairs next to my table and stool. "What's this?" he asked, getting ready to lift the green plastic bag off the sculpture.

"Nothing," I said, rushing over and pulling the bag tightly around the base of the piece.

Giving me a curious stare, Dr. Zimmerman asked again, "Are you sure everything's okay?"

"Yeah. Sure. I'm fine." I walked away from the sculpture. My panic had already brought more attention to it than I wanted, so I figured the best thing to do was act like it was nothing.

Dr. Zimmerman looked down at the green bag covering the sculpture then followed me across the room to my workbench. His mind was still under the stairs, but everything else was focused on his reason for coming in the first place.

"Tonya, do you remember hearing about an eight-year-old girl named Hazel Cherrylane who disappeared over in Pigtown some years ago?" Dr. Zimmerman asked.

I thought back and found my memory of her, which was a little yellow around the edges, faded in the middle, and torn at the end. The only reason that I remembered her at all was because she had disappeared around the same time that black children in Atlanta were being kidnapped and murdered.

"Yeah, I remember a little something about it," I said, taking a seat on a stool. "She was white, right?"

Dr. Zimmerman nodded. "The last time her parents saw her, she was playing out in front of their home."

"Okay, yeah. And it was snowing and some people said that they saw her get into an old Ford pickup," I added.

"Actually, it was in the middle of June and the witnesses said they saw her get into a blue van."

I didn't remember it like that, but I didn't argue.

Dr. Zimmerman said, "A week ago a passerby found a box containing the skeletal remains of a small child."

"Is it her?" I asked.

"Unfortunately, that's what it looks like," said Dr. Zimmerman, moving toward the door.

"Oh," I said, sadly. "That's terrible."

The wooden baseball bat that my mother insisted my father give me had fallen down from its place behind the door and started rolling across the floor. "If she's going to be working downtown all hours of the day and night, she needs some kind of protection," my mother said to him. "Anybody from off the street can walk right on in there. And besides, you know how weird some of them artists are that go to that school."

Dr. Zimmerman stopped the bat with his foot, picked it up, and then propped it against my desk. Afterwards, he grabbed the box and put it on my workbench.

"Yes, it is terrible," Dr. Zimmerman said. "But we can't dwell on that now." He came and stood directly in front of me so that I could no longer see the cardboard box. "We have to move on to more constructive ways of expressing our sorrow for the tragic death of this young girl. Now the box was found not too far from Hazel Cherrylane's house and right in back of the house belonging to the man suspected of kidnapping her. But of course that's not exactly a positive ID."

"What about dental records?" I asked.

"There are none," said Dr. Zimmerman. "But we do know that she was missing her two top, front teeth. They've already taken a blood sample from Mr. Cherrylane for a DNA test, but the results won't be back for a few weeks. That's why I'm here. I need you to help them make a positive ID."

"Me?" I asked, frowning.

Dr. Zimmerman grabbed a stool and sat down in front of me. "You know my colleague, Dr. George Sutherland, the anthropologist?"

"Yes. The one at the Smithsonian, who also does forensic sculpting."

"That's him. Well, he's away in Egypt working on a project, and he asked me to do him a favor, but I'm leaving for Kuwait in about a week, and I need you to help me with Dr. Sutherland's favor."

"And what is that?" I asked.

Dr. Zimmerman was trying to explain the situation to me in a round about way. Then he said, "I need you to put her face on for us."

"What?" I asked, starting to stand, as it all started to hit me. Cardboard box. Skeletal remains. Skeletal remains in cardboard box. Skeletal remains in cardboard box on workbench. Hazel Cherrylane's skeletal remains ...

Dr. Zimmerman could feel that realization rising in me. I was afraid of dead people, afraid of dead things period. I had been since I was twenty, when I'd driven over to see Aunt Josephine and saw this guy lying on the ground just a few houses down from Uncle Charlie's store. He'd been shot three times in the face, and he was lying on the ground, right there on the sidewalk. The cops had roped the block off with yellow tape that had the words POLICE LINE DO NOT CROSS written in black letters. The whole neighborhood, including me, was standing around trying to get a glimpse of what used to be his face. I wondered, as I stood on my tiptoes and stretched my neck, what were we really trying to see? And why did we want to see it? Why did I run into Uncle Charlie's apartment so that I could get a better view?

The cops were standing right by his body talking as if they didn't have a dead man at their feet. I wondered how they could stand so close to death when it could just reach out and grab them? I can't describe how I was feeling, except that my stomach kept getting these horrible, horrible pangs. I mean, this person was there but not there. Gone but not gone.

It took the city morgue three hours to come and cart off the body, and then the fire department came and washed away what was left of the boy's life and death. All you saw was red flowing down the gutter. It was awful, but I continued to watch that too. The next day, all that was left of the day before was the yellow crime tape waving on the poles the cops had tied it to. It was as if no one had died there at all. But I didn't walk on that side of the street for years. And even when I go to Uncle Charlie's store today, I still, despite myself, stare at the spot.

I never wanted to see or be near anything like that again.

"Tonya, there's nothing to it," Dr. Zimmerman said. "It's just like any other sculpture."

"Not any that I've sculpted," I said, and got up from the stool. "Can't you get somebody else to do this?" I asked, trying to find something to do with my hands to keep my mind off the box on my workbench.

"I came to the only person that I know is professional enough and talented enough to do this for me."

"I can't, Dr. Zimmerman. I can't touch a dead body."

"Not the body. Just the head."

"Just the head!" I screamed.

Dr. Zimmerman chewed on his fingernails. "Tonya, you're over-reacting."

"That's easy for you to say."

"And just as easy for you to sculpt." Dr. Zimmerman sighed. "Tell you what. I'll leave this here and if you really feel that you absolutely cannot do it, bring it by my house so that I can make other arrangements."

4

Two days after Dr. Zimmerman brought Hazel Cherrylane to my studio I was still afraid to look at her, let alone touch her. I spent three days staring at the box, poking and kneading clay. Soon my mind began to wander, and instead of being in AAI, I was back inside the shower room at Northwestern High School.

I was standing there confused and sweating from the heat as all the girls around me began asking one another "Did you see that?" I was horrified that Nikki and all my friends could hear the throbbing that was going on between my legs and feel the excited pounding of my heart. And I braced myself for the name-calling, insults and rejection; waited in fear for Nikki to plead with me to deny the rumors about me being *funny* that were beginning to fog up the shower room; waited for Nikki's face to drop in disillusionment as she backed away from me, as if what I was feeling for Meyoki were contagious.

But instead, Nikki jabbed me in my ribs with her elbow and said, "She winked at me."

You? I thought, relaxing in spite of the sharp pain her pointy elbow caused to shoot through my side. She was winking at you. Of course! Of course she was winking at you. I mean, you're the one with the clear, smooth yellow complexion, the firm grapefruit sized breasts, the round behind, the scar-free long legs, the silky shoulder length hair. Of course! You're the one whose sweat smells like Jasmine. You're the one with the strut that makes your hips roll in a sort of snap your fingers, shake it but don't break it groove that keeps you dancing even when you're standing still. You're the one who always has just the right shoes, panty hoses, jewelry, and fingernail polish to go with every outfit. Of course she was winking at you. Every girl in school winks at you. We just cover it up by rolling our eyes when we get caught.

Everybody started teasing and laughing at Nikki, asking her when was she going to let Meyoki turn her out, not knowing that Meyoki had turned me out, up, down, around, and sideways without laying a finger on me. Nikki sucked her teeth in disgust, although I couldn't tell if the "sth" was meant for Meyoki or for our friends.

So now the scuttlebutt around Northwestern was that Meyoki had a thing for Nikki. And I believed it until I found a note in my locker at the end of the school day. *Meet me at The Fish Store at seven o'clock.*

All the way there, I kept telling myself that I wasn't going. That I shouldn't go. I walked slowly at first, hoping that she would be gone by the time I got there, even though that wasn't where I was going. But then the thought of her leaving had me sprinting down the street. Meyoki was sitting on the steps when I turned the corner panting more from panic than from the short run. She rose quickly when she saw me, and I stopped in my tracks at the sight of her. Our eyes locked, and it was as if we didn't know how deep a void we had in our lives until our empty souls suddenly began filling up with each other.

We didn't do or say anything. Just stood there waiting for the braver one to make the first move. And I don't know how long we would have stood there if my Aunt Josephine hadn't called out, "Hey, Love."

She was standing in the doorway of the store, a step above Meyoki. She had on a chocolate-colored wrap dress with matching high heels, looking as lovely as ever.

"Hi, Aunt Josephine," I said, wanting to go up and kiss her on the cheek as I always did, but I still couldn't move.

Aunt Josephine took a curious note of my sudden paralysis. I wondered if she noticed the sweet way Meyoki was looking at me and the soft way that I was looking at her. Aunt Josephine walked toward me, taking long, slow steps, swaying her hips and clicking her heels on the cement.

"So, you're the friend she's been waiting for," Aunt Josephine said, giving me a tight hug. "If I'da known that, I would have called your momma to see what was keeping you."

"I had to wash the dishes." I lied to Meyoki more so than Aunt Josephine.

"Well, I kept her company," Aunt Josephine smiled. "So, what do you two girls have planned for the weekend?"

The weekend? Meyoki and I didn't know what we were going to do in the next minute, and Aunt Josephine was asking us about our plans for the weekend!

Meyoki and I looked at each other and hunched our shoulders.

Just then, Uncle Charlie struggled to the door, "What you got in here, Josephine?"

He was carrying Aunt Josephine's flowered suitcase, which meant that she was heading down to Virginia. Aunt Josephine hated the city. "It's too loud and fast, and always got some mess going on," she said. "Plus, y'all's white people pretend to be something they ain't. At least the white folks down there don't claim to be nothin' but themselves."

Uncle Charlie owned a house in Harrisonburg. It was a big wooden, white house with four bedrooms, a large kitchen, and a big front porch. The windows were tall and wide with comfortable daybeds in front of them. There was a small duck pond in the front yard and a big oak tree with a tire for a swing. Everything about the house helped you to take your time about sleeping, waking, bathing, cooking, eating, talking, and thinking. Whenever city life got to be too much for Aunt Josephine, she jumped in Uncle Charlie's Cadillac and went to Virginia. I would have loved to spend the weekend with Meyoki at that house, but I wasn't going to be the one to make the first move by saying it.

"Somebody would think you was going away for a month with what you got in this thing," Uncle Charlie said, straining to hold the suitcase up to his high waist with both hands.

When he accidentally bumped it against the door, Aunt Josephine said, "Don't you mess up my suitcase, Charlie. My momma gave me that suitcase, and--"

"And her momma's momma gave it to her," Uncle Charlie cut in. "It's been in our family since 1863, when my great-great-great-grandmomma Biddy left the Preston plantation. Yeah, yeah, yeah."

Meyoki stood amazed by the brief story. So did I, even though I'd heard Aunt Josephine tell it before.

Aunt Josephine waved her hand at Uncle Charlie. "Just put the bag in the car, man."

"You see how your aunt treats me," Uncle Charlie said to me. "She lucky I love her." He kissed her on the lips.

"No, you lucky you love me," Aunt Josephine said.

Meyoki and I laughed. It was the first time that we'd relaxed since I'd gotten there.

"Well, being that you two don't have any plans, why don't you come down to Virginia with me," Aunt Josephine suggested. "I've got to get out of this God forsaken city, but your uncle can't come. And that house can be pretty lonely, and I don't feel like being lonely."

Meyoki stared at me as if she knew that I was afraid to say, *Come on. It'll be fun.* So she made the first move by saying, "I'll have to ask my mother, but I'm sure she'll let me go."

I smiled happily.

"Good," Aunt Josephine said, turning to go inside the store. Over her shoulder, she added, "And I'll swing by Nikki's and pick--"

"No!" I yelled, cutting her sentence off at the knees.

Aunt Josephine turned around and gave me a piercing "what are you up to" glare, and suddenly I felt naked for some reason. I felt like a leafless tree in the middle of winter with every brown twig and branch of my body bare for all to see.

In a silly attempt to cover my exposed body, I quickly spouted, "Nikki's not home. S-she's not h-home."

Aunt Josephine looked me up and down, then took my explanation inside the store with her. When I snuck a glanced at Meyoki to see if she knew that I was lying, she winked her left eye at me, and I went up in flames again.

Meyoki lived across the tracks, which was about seven blocks away from my neighborhood. The houses on that side were bigger and nicer. Meyoki lived in a big yellow and white single family home with her parents, her older brother Leroy, and their German Shepard named PJ.

Aunt Josephine only needed to square things away with Meyoki's mother, because her father was pulling a double at Park's Sausage Plant. Mrs. Outlaw was a buxom, walnut brown woman with a small gold Cross around her neck that she played with while staring at Aunt Josephine's scar and brown heels. There was something about them that made Mrs. Outlaw reluctant to let her daughter go away with Aunt Josephine. But Meyoki took her aside, and when they returned, Mrs. Outlaw said to Aunt Josephine's left pump, "I want her back here by six o'clock Sunday night."

The next thing I knew I was in the passenger seat of Uncle Charlie's white Cadillac cruising down I-95 with my favorite aunt behind the wheel, Bessie Smith in the tape deck singing "Tain't Nobody's Business If I Do," and Meyoki Outlaw in the back seat, her mouth tapping away to the beat.

Virginia made being with Meyoki less awkward and tense. I didn't have to worry about Nikki or anyone from school seeing us together. So I was free to lounge around with Meyoki and do all the things that I'd done with Nikki there--eat chit'lins, Hoppin' John, and bread pudding, listen to the blues, dance, and watch the sunrise and sunset while sitting in one of the big wicker porch chairs or lying on one of the daybeds by a window.

Strangely enough Meyoki's sexuality never came up. It was kind of like a 'don't ask, don't tell' deal that we both agreed to without having said one word about it. But I watched for hints of it in everything she did and said. A few times Aunt Josephine noticed me ogling Meyoki, and like a kid who gets caught with her hand in the cookie jar, I pretended that I wasn't the least bit interested in the sweet dessert I held in my eyes.

I thought that I'd see Meyoki's sexuality at night when the stereo was cold and quiet, and Aunt Josephine was sleeping in the master bedroom, and Meyoki was sleeping beside me in the same twin bed that I'd slept in with Nikki. I loved sleeping with Nikki. It was the only time that I could feel without interruption the close friendship we shared. Being in bed with Meyoki was different, though. My heart didn't gallop when I was in bed with Nikki. My hands didn't sweat and my stomach didn't flip-flop. And when I was in bed with Nikki I slept. I couldn't sleep a wink lying next to Meyoki. Her legs, her arms, her feet--Oh! They just kept me up all night.

Luckily I'd packed a bag of clay and some modeling tools for the trip. I spent Friday and Saturday night in the basement sculpting my thoughts about Meyoki, but I still wasn't sure what I was trying to tell myself about her. The closest I got to understand it at all was on Saturday afternoon when Aunt Josephine went out to the store. Meyoki and I ran into Aunt Josephine's bedroom and like ten-year-old girls we played dress up, trying on Aunt Josephine's silk and satin nightgowns and her high-high heels. Meyoki's walk made sweet music in Aunt Josephine's heels, but my walk just sounded like somebody stomping to get attention.

"How do you do that?" I asked, frustrated by not being able to make my own music like her and Aunt Josephine.

"By walking my walk and not being afraid of where my music will lead me," Meyoki said.

"And you make that tapping in your mouth?"

"By talking my talk and not being afraid that people won't want understand where I'm coming from because they've been there and are afraid to go back," she said.

I frowned, not really understanding. Then Meyoki smiled and playfully licked her tongue out at me, and I saw that there was a little gold ball inserted through her pink tongue. I didn't know anyone who had their tongue pierced.

"Good Lord, that must have hurt!" I said.

"Difference always hurts at first," Meyoki said. "But once you learn to be true and faithful to it, it feels like heaven."

I couldn't imagine something that different feeling like anything but pure hell.

We came across a few of Aunt Josephine's negligees, and Meyoki dared me to try on a lacy, black one. My eyes darted back and forth between her and the negligee.

"You scared?" she smiled.

"I don't know what I am," I said, feeling terrified.

Meyoki didn't say anything. She just turned and sauntered out of the room--Click-Clack, TapTap. She went down to the living room and put on an Etta James record. As the house filled with Etta's voice, I rubbed my sweaty palms together as I tried to rationally assess the situation. I fingered the negligee. Then, in a quick burst of thoughtlessness, I peeled off my clothes and slid the lacy, black cloth over my body. She won't try anything, I reasoned. She knows I'm not *that* way. But I wasn't so certain of that so when Meyoki came back into the room, I snatched the comforter off Aunt Josephine's bed and draped myself in it.

"Come over here in front of the mirror," Meyoki said.

"Why?" I asked.

A dreamy-eyed smile took over her face. "Because I want to show you something."

I went, dragging the comforter with me.

Meyoki grinned. Then, very slowly, as if she were unveiling a priceless work of art, she removed the comforter and flung it onto the bed. I was too shocked and embarrassed to utter a word. The sudden coolness of the air made my skin feel extra ashy. Damn! What I wouldn't do for a bottle of lotion right now, I thought.

"You turn violet when you're embarrassed," she said amazed, reaching out to touch me.

I jerked, then took a small step away from her.

Meyoki looked down at the space between us. "What's that for?" she asked.

I shook my head. "Nothing," I said in a low voice.

Meyoki stepped into the place I'd moved from, filling the gap. She took my hands and then positioned my right arm so that it was on my head and my left was resting on top of my right. Then without a word Meyoki put her hands on my waist. I sucked in a quick breath and held it. Her hands were soft and warm but they made me tremble as if they were ice-cold. She began to gently move her hands up my sides. I watched our reflections as if I was watching a movie screen. Suddenly, it wasn't me standing there. I was sitting on the bed, anxiously waiting for the drama to unfold. I was able to detach myself mentally from the event, but physically I was still there. My body was having a difficult time blocking out the deep, penetrating sensations that Meyoki's soft touch was sending through me.

My body heated and quivered as she neared the sides of my breasts. I closed my eyes, ready to protest should she temporarily lose her mind and decide to caress them. But she glided right past them, not even hesitating for a second. My breasts were of no concern of hers. Honestly, I didn't know whether I should have been relieved or insulted.

She brushed her fingertips against my armpits the way a painter strokes a nonresistant canvas with a round sable brush, applying bright reds, oranges, and yellows on a place that had been colorless.

"Open your eyes, Tonya," Meyoki whispered.

I was completely thrown off balance by her request because I could see her and the colors so clearly that I had forgotten that my eyes were closed.

"Do you feel the difference?" Meyoki asked.

Our eyes met in the mirror, and I was able to see then why my breasts disinterested her so. My breasts were not on her agenda. No. The difference was her game. The difference in her touch versus any guy's I'd been with. The difference in where she touched, how she touched, and why she touched. And she wanted me to admit that this difference, with its arousing waves, was making me weak with desire. Desire for what was the question.

The sound of Aunt Josephine calling for us over Etta James singing *"Something's Got A Hold On Me"* helped me to avoid the answer to that question for the time being. And as we rushed around putting Aunt Josephine's things away, the difference was still blazing under my arms even after I had convinced myself that there was no difference, at least not the kind she was implying. But if that was the case, why did I seem to enjoy and accept the subtle and not so subtle passes she'd been handing me? Why did my body simmer from the enticing way her eyes undressed me? Why did her attraction for me make me feel attractive and special? Why? Why? Why? I was up to my waist in why's but didn't have a single answer.

While Meyoki didn't openly discuss her sexuality, she did tell me about her dream of becoming a doctor. It was Sunday afternoon. Aunt Josephine was in the house packing, and I was pushing Meyoki on the swing.

"I want to find a cure for sickle cell, diabetes, lupus, cancer," Meyoki said while swinging so high that I thought she would loop around the branch of the oak tree.

"That's a lot of curing," I said.

"The world's very sick," she said. "It will take a while."

"What will you do in the meantime?" I asked.

"Find someone who will love me like they've never loved anybody before." Meyoki held her head back to see me, and said, "But for now I'll settle for a good friend."

"Is that why you left me that note?" I asked.

"Yes," Meyoki said. "Is that why you came?"

"...Yes," I said.

The night before Dr. Zimmerman was to leave, I drove over to his Glen Burnie apartment to tell him that there was no way that I could sculpt a corpse. Instead of making my thoughts about Meyoki go away, that skull only kept Meyoki on my mind.

He answered the door wearing a white T-shirt, black slacks, and black dress sock.

"Masaa elkheir," he said, raising his bottle of Corona to me.

"What?" I asked.

"Good evening," he laughed. "That's how you say good evening in Arabic. You're supposed to say, 'Masaa ennoor.'"

"What does that mean?"

"Same to ya," he smiled and stepped out of the way so that I could come in.

"You want a beer?" Dr. Zimmerman asked.

"Yeah. Sure," I said as I sat down on the couch.

The living room was dim because Dr. Zimmerman only had on one lamp. Books, paintings, drawings, photographs and sculptures were all over the place. "Kingdom Coming" from the soundtrack of *The Civil War* series was playing on the stereo. The doors to his balcony were open and a nice breeze blew in and rustled the pages of the books and magazine articles on Arabic history and culture that lay on the coffee table. His flight information lay on top of a book called *The Holy Qur'an: Text, Translation, and Commentary.* He would be flying out of Dulles to New York, then fly to Rome, then to Kuwait. The whole trip would take two days.

Dr. Zimmerman handed me a cold bottle of Corona. "Would you like to join me for dinner? I'm having pork chops and beer."

"Pork chops and beer?" I asked.

Dr. Zimmerman sat down on the sofa and crossed his legs. "They're illegal in Kuwait, and I'm going to be there until the end of August. So tonight I'm going to make myself so sick of this stuff that I won't miss it."

"I hear that pornography is against the law over there too," I said. "What are you gonna do about your craving for that?"

"The tape is already in the VCR. Would you like to join me for that too?" he joked.

"Noooo, I don't think so," I said and sipped my beer.

"It's a classic. *Debbie Does Dallas*," Dr. Zimmerman laughed.

"Oh, well then, of course I'll stay," I kidded.

After dinner, I stretched out across Dr. Zimmerman's couch. I'd had maybe three beers and was feeling mellow. Dr. Zimmerman had twelve, and he was leaning in the doorway of the balcony working on another. "Palmyra Schottische" was now playing on the stereo. The Spring air was cool and nice, and the moon and stars were high and bright. It was a beautiful, careless, dark blue evening.

Out of nowhere, Dr. Zimmerman said, "You're going to be great one day." His voice held a little regret in it. "Greater than I ever will be."

"I doubt that," I said and took a swig of my beer.

"Don't." He looked at me as if I were his greatest creation but also his worst nightmare. "You're twenty-eight years old and already you've reached my artistic level." Dr. Zimmerman turned his gaze outdoors again. "Do you know that now I get more recognition for being your mentor than I do for being an artist?"

I did know that, just as I knew that when he started getting credit and praise for my work, he stopped sculpting and painting his own. He was a prolific, internationally renowned sculptor and painter of American History, in particular America's wars. *America's Great Men* was the series that he was most famous for. It depicted in clay and on canvases all of the generals that commanded the Union and Confederate armies during the Civil War. That was the last thing he worked on before becoming my mentor.

I looked at Dr. Zimmerman and remembered that when I first came to AAI in 1984, I was a confused eighteen-year-old, who felt small, untalented, and out of place, especially since I was only one of maybe eight other blacks in a school with about three hundred students. And it didn't help that, whether it was true or not, I was labeled an affirmative action admittance. Each student was to be assigned a mentor, but none of the instructors wanted to be associated with me, not even the two black male instructors or the white female artist, and all three of them were rumored to be affirmative action hires.

My three-week-old life at AAI changed, though, when *the* Dr. Carroll P. Zimmerman said that of all the students admitted to AAI that year I was the most talented. But he also thought that I was the most unchallenged in the bunch, so he took me under his wing and kneaded, molded, and shaped me aesthetically as he introduced me to the great sculptors and sculptures of the world: Michelangelo's *David*, Donatello's *David*, and Myron's *The Diskobolos*. He even took me to Rome to see Rodin's *The Thinker*. I spent days admiring and studying that massive, brilliant piece, feeling overwhelmed, light-headed, weak in the knees, and creatively and sexually aroused. After I'd viewed and sketched the bronze sculpture from every possible angle, I said, "I've got to find a way to do this and nothing else for the rest of my life."

So just as a woman entrusts her heart in the hands of a man who promises her the world, I put my art career entirely in the hands of Dr. Zimmerman, and I became a well-respected and, most of all, a well *paid* working, living artist. And because of him, I was able to put Meyoki behind me.

I owed my career and my sanity to this man. So there was no way that I could tell him that I was too afraid to sculpt Hazel Cherrylane. Besides, I thought, once I really get started on it, I'll forget all about Meyoki, just like before.

5

The day after Dr. Zimmerman left for Kuwait, I went to my studio around five in the morning and stayed long enough to put my sketchbook, pencils, erasers, and pocketknife in my backpack. Then I hopped into my Jeep Wrangler and drove to Druid Hill Park. I liked going there that early in the day because the air was fresh and cool and it gave my lungs a chance to expand with the smell of green grass, flowers and trees instead of clay.

As the sunlight yawned across the city, I sat at a wooden picnic table under the pavilion by the reservoir. I looked at the fountain that sat in the center of the reservoir. I'd heard that a murdered woman was found lying naked on top of that fountain a while back. I stared out at it and the murder scene, or the facts after the murder, played like a silent film in front of me. I saw a large figure lift the woman's lifeless body over the long, black, rusty bars that surrounded the reservoir's calm, blue water. The figure then treaded down its steep, weedy, hazardous bank, swam through the dark water, and left the woman on the fountain for the pigeons to snack on. The film played again and again until I'd closed my eyes.

"I didn't come here to think about death," I said to the ghost lying on the fountain. "I came here to draw."

But I didn't draw. The thought of the bodiless head in the cardboard box sitting on the bench inside my studio chased me like a shadow. The next day I drove around in my Wrangler most of the morning trying to shake it, lose it in rush hour traffic, at the bend of a sharp corner, down an alley. But no matter how far or fast I drove that lifeless silhouette was always close behind.

I was also being chased by thoughts of Meyoki. I tried to duck and dodge those too, but they caught up to me. It had started to drizzle, and while I was sitting at a red light at Greenspring and Druid Park Drive, clear as day, I saw Nikki and me standing outside of school, waiting for the homeroom bell to ring.

It was the Monday after I'd spent the weekend in Virginia with Aunt Josephine and Meyoki, and Nikki wanted to know, "Why didn't you tell me that you were going to Virginia?"

"Because I didn't know that I was going," I said. "It was kind of a last minute thing."

"What'd you do all weekend?"

"Sculpt," I said, which wasn't a total lie.

Just then Meyoki stepped off the number 5 bus and waved at me.

"What'd you sculpt?" Nikki asked, watching Meyoki as she started in our direction.

My insides burned with fear instead of the joy that should have consumed me at the sight of my new friend. When we got home from Virginia, Meyoki and I didn't talk about the rules of this new friendship. She didn't ask if I wanted Nikki and everybody at school to know that we were friends, and I didn't tell her that I didn't want anybody to find out that I'd talked with her, walked with her, and ate with her. And the last thing I ever wanted anybody to know was that I had slept in the same bed with her.

By the way that Meyoki was walking and smiling, I knew that she thought that I was cool with people knowing about us. I mean, hell, we had a good time in Virginia. But that was Virginia. Not Baltimore. Not Northwestern High School where my best friend in the whole world went to school.

Nikki looked at me and said, "I wonder who she's smiling at?"

"You're the one she's got a thing for. So she must be smiling at you."

In the daydream, I was standing next to Nikki with my heart beating in my ears to the point where I couldn't hear anything. Ten years later, I still started sweating as if Meyoki were walking up to me right then and there. I was feeling hot enough to pass out. But just as Meyoki stopped in front of me in the daydream, I spotted a cool color blue sitting in the corner of my eye. Photographic thoughts of Meyoki tried to cover the blue, but it was so large, insistent, and vibrant that, compared to it, Meyoki seemed small and unimportant.

I turned in the direction of the blue thing that freed me from my nightmare, and found the color in the form of a tank top that was draped over a reddish-brown complexioned man. He was near the curb drinking from a black water bottle and straddling a gray, 29" ten-speed bike. And oh my goodness was he handsome! Tall and muscular, short black, curly hair, thick eyebrows, pretty-boy brown eyes, full lips. He was everything a woman would want in her bed, in her diary, in her photos, and in her dreams. I wanted him in my sketchbook, naked and reclined in a chair with his head back, muscular arms stretched out, and his powerful legs spread apart with his feet flat on the floor. I wanted his eyes and mouth closed, but an expression on his clean-shaven face that said, "Take me if you dare." And I wanted to be ready to drop my sketchbook so that I could climb right on top of that dare.

I guess he took the Oooooweeee! in my smile as the key to a locked door that he'd been trying to open, because after he saw it, he put his water bottle back on the rack and motioned for me to roll down my passenger side window.

"Are you smiling at me?" he asked, leaning in.

"Smiling at you?" I asked, as if it weren't true.

He smiled a moist, full-lipped smile that began and ended with dimples, but was separated by a gap in his teeth. That space in the middle of his smile lured me in the way a man's secret seduces a woman's ear. It was warm, playful, and innocent. I'd never been inside anything like it before, and I never wanted to leave.

"I could have sworn that I saw a pretty smile coming from you," he said.

I blushed and a nervous, unexpected laugh filled the inside of my Wrangler.

"Oh, I get it," he said. "You were laughing at me."

"No," I said, giggling like a high school girl with a silly teenage crush.

"What is it? My shorts?" He jokingly yanked at the light gray fabric that covered certain parts of his lower body and prominently displayed others.

My laughter kept me from speaking, so I just shook my head.

"Okay. You weren't smiling at me and you weren't laughing at me, but you were looking at me, right? I mean, I did see your sweet brown eyes on me, didn't I?"

"Yes," I confessed still blushing.

"Good," he said.

The light turned green and the people behind me started blowing their horns as if I were some dimwit who didn't know that in order to make my jeep go forward I'd have to take my foot off the brake and push it down on the accelerator.

"Follow me," he said.

"Follow you?" I asked. "Where?"

"I'll show you," he said and took off.

I followed as he pedaled up and down hilly Greenspring Avenue for a mile or so before turning into Cylburn Arboretum. I tailed him down a narrow tar road then had to hurriedly park my Wrangler when he disappeared inside the mouth of a trail. I grabbed my backpack and jogged to catch up with him.

I came upon two wooden signs. The first had CIRCLE TRAIL carved into it; the second had NO BIKE RIDING. It had stopped drizzling, and now it was hot and humid. But entering the trail was like stepping into a cool pond and walking until the water swallowed you whole. The trail was made of small dots of sunlight, shade, fallen leaves, wood chips, bark pieces, and soft, fertile ground. It was marked off on either side by a variety of green plants and tall trees with drapes of vines slung over their shoulders. You could smell the rich soil mixing with the scent of honeysuckle, hear and see squirrels, birds, and other small animals exploring, hunting, and feel insects sinking their teeth into your flesh.

It was a sweet, lively place, but it was also very isolated. And once you started down the trail there was no turning back. So I should have been terrified or at the very least a bit frightened. Common sense called for that. There I was alone in the woods searching for a strange man, who at any moment could have jumped out from behind an oak, sycamore, or elm tree and did unspeakable things to me. But I wasn't scared. I don't know what I was, but scared wasn't it. Anxious, maybe! Foolish, definitely. Even still, I thought that I should be smart, so I fished around inside my backpack for my pocketknife. The blade wasn't very big, but I could do some damage with it, if that's what this chase came down to. Although the closest I'd ever come to cutting a person was when I'd gotten mad at my sister, Elaine and had carved a soap sculpture of her and then chopped off her head.

I walked along the trail digging for my knife, and just when I'd felt the cool steel in my palm, his voice walked up behind me as bold as anything. "Looking for me?" he asked.

I spun around and saw him sitting on a stone bench beside a weeping cherry tree. He rose and his tall, straight body became a beautiful contrast to the bent trunk of the weeping cherry that seemed to be bowing at his feet.

"Now I'll bet that your mother doesn't know that you go around following strange men into wooded areas," he said.

"You know what? You're right," I said, and let my pocketknife slip from my hand and fall to the bottom of my backpack. There was something about him that made me feel safe. Something about him that made me feel that he would protect me, even from himself. "I'll bet that your mother doesn't know that you're in the habit of waiting for strange women in wooded areas," I countered.

"No, she doesn't, but she wouldn't be surprised because I've put my life on the line for less." He looked at me slyly. "Much less."

He bit down on his bottom lip and let his eyes fall over me in the same soft, colorful way that autumn lowers over summer. His eyes made me painfully aware of how I was dressed. My hair was tucked under an old baseball cap. I was wearing a purple tie-dye shirt, an old pair of gray shorts, and my clay-splattered, high-top Converse sneakers. I could hear Nikki saying, "You need to stop walking around here looking like who-did-it-and-ran."

I tried to spruce myself up a bit on the sly, but he caught me. Or should I say he caught my hand, and then proceeded to straighten my baseball cap on my head and brush a patch of dried clay off my cheek. I didn't know my face was dirty. God, how embarrassing!

"There," he said, looking me over again.

"Ah-hem..." I said, feeling his eyes touching parts of me that I wanted his hands to touch later. No. Maybe sooner!

"Guilty as charged," he said slightly ashamed, but only because he'd gotten caught. He walked over to his bike, pushed the kickstand up with his foot, and swung his leg over the seat. "Come on."

"Come on where?" I asked.

"For a ride."

I saw no harm or danger in taking a bike ride from this stranger, especially since he had such a pleasant place between his teeth. But I hadn't been on a bike since I fell off my 3-speed truck and broke my arm riding down this steep hill when I was eleven. I couldn't sculpt for weeks.

"The sign said no biking riding," I stalled.

He looked back toward the entrance as if he could see the sign through the trees. "It does, doesn't it." He patted the seat. "You coming?" he asked.

"I don't even know who you are," I said.

"Malcolm," he said, extending his hand. "Malcolm Holland."

I hesitated then put my hand in his and squeezed as I said, "I'm Tonya

Mimms."

He rolled my name around in his mouth as if it were a piece of bittersweet candy. "So, are you coming, Tonya Mimms?"

I adjusted the straps on my backpack, slung it over my shoulders, then hopped on the seat. The moment he started pedaling I let out a little scream and grabbed him tightly around his waist, but I couldn't hold all of him. It was almost as if everything this man was and would be couldn't fit in my arms. And if I really wanted to hold onto him, I'd have to take pieces of him and streak them through my hair like dye, dab them behind my ears like perfume, stick them in my mouth like tongue kisses, and wear them on my legs like stockings. Oh, my hands could do wonders with his body, I thought.

Some leaves crackled and twigs snapped under the rotating wheels of his bike. I was fascinated by his speed, or rather by the way his body demanded more of it, despite the fact that the bike seemed to find every dip, hole, and bump hidden on the trail. I watched in lust more than anything else as his arms performed like shock absorbers, swallowing the jarring of the rough terrain the second it reached his biceps.

But suddenly I heard the rapid ticking of the bike chain rotating backwards. Malcolm was trying to slow down. His body tightened and he was shaking his head as if he were trying to stop himself from going down a road that he'd been down before, and didn't want to go down again. But I didn't want us to stop because I hadn't been down that road, and so I wanted us to fly faster and higher than either of us believed we could.

I pressed my breasts hard against his back so that he could feel the thunder-like thumping of my heart. "Faster," I commanded.

"Faster?" he asked.

"Yeah. What's wrong? You think it's too dangerous?"

"You're more dangerous than this trail," he said, and started coasting like he had no way of stopping where he was going and no longer wanted to.

"Me?" I laughed, spreading out my arms as if I had wings. "I wouldn't hurt a fly."

"That's what they all say," he said.

My mind held onto that answer and waited for a different time to have him explain it, assuming for some odd reason that there would be such a time. But right then and there, I was having delirious, lively fun. That is until I felt a bright sting on the back of my thigh.

"Ouch!" I slapped a light green bug off my leg. "Something just bit me."

Slowing to a stop, Malcolm said, "Don't scratch. It'll only make it worse."

I was already off the bike and digging my fingernails into my skin when he'd said that.

Malcolm propped his bike against a tree. "Rubbing is better. It won't leave scars."

He touched me as if he knew that his brisk, gentle rubbing, the scent of honeysuckle mixing with the smell of fertile soil, and the sound of nature taking its course made me want to lie down on the trail and let his hands travel all over me.

"Runner's legs," he said.

"Huh?"

"You have the legs of someone who runs a lot."

I run all the time, I thought, looking at him. But not out here. I run in the woods of my mind every day, chasing thoughts or running from them. Right now I'm square on the heels of some thoughts about you, but we just met so I can't let you do...shouldn't let you do what I hope you're thinking of doing to me.

I watched the muscles in Malcolm's arms flex as he rubbed the insect bite. I liked his arms. They were easy, free-falling arms, the kind that you could die in and be totally gratified by the mere seconds you had spent on earth. As I touched them, I tried to imagine what my eyes would see, what my nose would smell, what my cheek would feel, and what the corner of my mouth would taste if I were lying in them.

"What do you want to do?" he asked.

Be with you, I thought, but said, "I don't know?"

He went over and got the plastic water bottle from his bike, and that's when I noticed that we'd come to a fork in the road. Left took us out, right took us farther in.

"If the bottle is pointing to the left when it stops spinning," Malcolm said, "then we leave so that you can go home and get ready for me to pick you up for dinner tonight."

"And if it's pointing right?"

He licked his finger and held it up to feel which way the wind was blowing then put the bottle on the ground and gave it a hard spin. It went around and around and around then stopped between the two paths, but by then I had decided that yes, I liked his eyes. They were full of deep colors, but I'd seen them before. Yes, I liked his flirting. It was charming, but I'd heard that before too. But what was new and interesting was his comment about putting his life on the line.

Now, I was basically a harmless person, and I didn't like to see anyone hurt, especially by me. So it unnerved me to hear this man imply that being with me somehow put his life in danger. But it also flattered me. I liked being thought of as someone to be leery of. Someone unpredictable. Lawless. Wild even. That was the thing that made me pretend to be looking the other way when Malcolm kicked the bottle.

6

From memory, I had sketched Malcolm Holland's face with an ebony pencil onto a page in my sketchbook. I was working on it instead of Hazel Cherrylane when Nikki came by for lunch.

She and I were as close as any two people could be. As teenagers, Nikki and I played hooky from school, smoked marijuana, and had sexual encounters with horny teenage boys, in which we'd avoided being caught by our parents or an unintended pregnancy. We listened, laughed, disagreed, and dried each other's tears when a crisis occurred. During those times we'd lie in bed together, but after Meyoki, I stopped sleeping in the same bed with Nikki because I couldn't lie to her by lying with her.

When I went to AAI, Nikki went to Howard University and earned her bachelor's then a master's degree in counseling psychology. She'd always liked trying to find out what made people tick, but she became obsessed with it after her father left. Nikki loved her father more than anybody in the world besides me. Unfortunately, he was from that generation of men who went to the store for a loaf of bread and came home three or four days later. Nikki was ten when Nicholas Roman kissed his daughter on the forehead and told her that he was going to the Basement store to get a carton of milk.

"I knew he wasn't coming back," Nikki said as she lay in bed beside me sobbing.

"How?" I asked, rubbing her back.

"He can't drink milk," Nikki cried. "He's allergic to it. Everybody in my family is allergic to it."

At age twenty-nine, Nikki was now a second-year Ph.D. student and a licensed psychologist practicing individual and family psychotherapy at an east side clinic called Positive Awakenings. She spent her days analyzing other people's problems and hang-ups and avoiding her own, insisting that she had long since gotten over her father's running off.

When Nikki came by the studio, she was dressed in a long white jacket, long white shirt, and a white miniskirt. She strutted in and kissed me on the cheek then used her thumb to wipe her berry rose lipstick off my face.

I greeted her with, "Your company left the toilet seat up last night."

"Oh, how rude," she spat in a tone that said she thought his mama taught him better than that. "You didn't fall in, did ya?"

"No. Because he left the light on. And the water running in the sink."

"Well, at least I know that he washes his hands after he pees."

"Where's Lonnie?" I asked.

"That whore?" she said, twisting her mouth. "He's in Jamaica with some slut. But I'm not supposed to know it."

"How do you know it?"

Nikki frowned and plucked a piece of lint out of my hair. "The ass hid the plane tickets in his underwear drawer." She studied the tiny lint ball on her finger then blew it into the air. "You'd think that he'd know that that would be the first place I'd look for something like that."

"Maybe he does," I said.

She grinned. "You give him too much credit. He's a cheater not a thinker."

Lonnie Chance, with his creamy light-brown skin, wavy hair, and bowed legs, was too fine of a brother to be in the arms of one woman, which was exactly why Nikki chose him as her soul mate. She was afraid of men walking out on her and leaving her alone the way her father did. So when Nikki and Lonnie got together four years ago, they came to an "understanding," which was supposed to keep their relationship simple. But somewhere along the line they complicated it by calling themselves being in a monogamous relationship. Now they argued all the time about who was the bigger whore because both of them were still creepin'.

I was in my bedroom a few weeks ago and I heard them arguing in the living room. I couldn't really hear their words, just the furious sound that knocked holes in the air whenever Lonnie threw up his hands and yelled, "Forget it!" and Nikki screamed, "No. Forget you!"

I heard Nikki stomp away. Two steps. That's how far she got before Lonnie started singing after her. *"Ain't Too Proud To Beg"* was the song he crooned. He wasn't a very good singer. Didn't even know all the words. But she stopped and turned around. And he walked up to her, dropping notes all over her feet and between her toes. Nikki picked up every note with her smile. When Lonnie finished serenading, he made love to Nikki from one end of the couch to the other. I lay in bed with my eyes closed envying the fussing, fighting, singing, and what Nikki must have been feeling as Lonnie pleased her to the point where she couldn't stand it or stand up, and then carried her limp body upstairs and down the hall to her bedroom.

"So, who were you with last night?" I asked.

"Just some dude I met, that's all. Nobody worth talking about," she said, examining my drawing of Malcolm. "He's interesting looking. Who is he?"

In my mind's eye I focused on the edges of Malcolm's strong chin as I drew and I answered, "A guy with a bike."

"Oh," she said, tilting her head. "Well, he must have made quite an impression on you."

I looked up at her briefly and asked as I turned my attention and pencil back to Malcolm's chin, "Why do you say that?"

"You're sketching the brothah," she said. "As long as I've known you I've never seen you sketch a guy before." Then, as if the thought moved her, Nikki kneeled low enough so that she could see my eyes. "Have I missed something?"

I smiled lightly. "No, you haven't missed a thing. He's picking me up tonight around eight."

"Well, then what's the brothah with the bike doing here?"

"Probably wasting my time like the others."

"Yeah, maybe, but you normally don't come to that conclusion until after you've slept with them." She stood up straight and folded her arms. "So I guess this means that you're gonna give him a chance."

"I give all of them chances. It's not my fault that they can't handle the competition."

"They could if they were competing against a person, another guy, another dick. But what can they do when they're up against history and a bag of clay?"

I told her, "Surrender. Like I do."

"Men don't surrender unless you whip them," Nikki said.

"I don't have time to be whipping anybody."

Nikki eyed the drawing. "Oh, I think you'll make time to whip this one because it certainly doesn't look to me like you're gonna do your usual?"

"My usual?" I asked, not admitting that I was wondering the same thing myself.

"Yeah, your usual. Screw him then hide out here until he stops calling the house and bugging the hell out of me after he figures out that I'm not going to tell him where your studio is."

"Is that what I do?" I asked.

"Give or take a dinner, a movie, and a couple of phone calls here and there, yeah, I'd say that that's pretty much what you do," Nikki answered.

"Well, this is just a drawing, and it doesn't mean that he's going to be any different from the rest," I sighed, and went back to drawing.

Secretly, I was hoping that he would be different.

"Come on, Tonya," Nikki sighed back. "Don't you get tired of playing with these clay men?"

"I never get tired of my work," I said.

Nikki sucked her teeth. "You know what I'm talking about."

"Yeah. The same thing you're always talking about--men. Your obsession with them is pathetic, you know that, don't you?"

"Of course I do. But when you come up in a house full of lonely, loud-talking, man-hungry women, what else are you gonna treasure? But that's not the point."

"It isn't?"

"You know better than I do that it isn't. So let's get down to it, alright?"

"All right." I lifted my pencil off the page. "I have to finish the *Presidents of War* series."

"Bull," Nikki countered. "It's done. Excuse number two, please."

"I have my exhibition at the Baltimore Museum of Art next month."

"Like you gotta do something other than show your pretty little face and smile for the people."

Nikki walked behind me and rested her chin on my shoulder. I could feel her breasts against my shoulder blades. They were like tiny pillows to me.

"Why are you trying to con me?"

Her warm, peppermint breath tickled my ear. I pushed her away with a hunch of my shoulder. "I'm not trying to con you," I said.

Laughing, Nikki took off her jacket, sat down on a stool, and crossed her long legs. "Then you're trying to con yourself. So come on," she said with a wave of her fingers. "Let's hear the next excuse, and please try to at least make this one sound halfway believable."

"I have too much going on right now," I insisted.

"Too much like what?" Nikki wanted to know.

"Too much like having to somehow get up the nerve to work on that over there," I said, pointing to the cardboard box that had been sitting in my studio unopened for a week and a half. "So you see, I don't have time for him."

"You always say that. You keep fooling around and you're gonna be a lonely, dried up, horny-ass old woman with nothin' but clay and time on your hands. Just like my mother and my aunts. Unless you cross over, like Meyoki."

I choked on nothing when Nikki said her name. Nikki liked doing that, liked throwing Meyoki's name in our conversation when I least expected it, just to see my reaction or catch me in the act of trying not to react. Inevitably, any talk about her brought up the eye winking incident. "Remember that time Meyoki winked at me?" Nikki would say, but she said it in a way that made it sound as if she didn't think Meyoki was winking at her at all. Sometimes I got the feeling that Nikki knew that the wink was meant for me, but she couldn't know that. Nobody knew that except me and Meyoki.

"You sure whipped her, now didn't you?" Nikki said.

I was beginning to be a little paranoid so I didn't take the statement as a simple comment on the fight I'd had with Meyoki. Instead I listened to the tone in Nikki's voice that made "whipped" sound erotic. Thing was, though, I hadn't had a single thought about Meyoki since I'd met Malcolm and I wanted to keep it that way.

My silence forced Nikki to change the subject. "So old Zimmerman finally broke down and gave you something to sculpt other than some dead white man," she said, standing in front of the cardboard box.

"I'll take a historical dead white man over that any day."

"Why have you stayed in this place so long sculpting this stuff instead of working on what you were passionate about before you came here?"

Humph! I thought as I remembered being passionate about capturing in clay the scenes I saw when I was growing up: black men hanging out on supermarket parking lots, talking about how it used to be while playing cards, checkers, or dominos; black women sitting on front porches gossiping and talking about how it will be while watching to make sure that little fast-tail Sally Walkers didn't disappear with slick-talking, little league players; and black kids playing hopscotch, jacks, football, basketball, or dancing around in front of fire hydrants on hot summer days, only caring about how it is right now.

"What I *was* passionate about doesn't pay the rent," I told Nikki.

"We live in one of your parents' houses. We haven't paid rent in four years."

Nikki picked up my pocketknife and slowly pried out the long silver blade, so that when it was fully extended, it made a loud clack as it locked in place. She stuck the tip of the blade into the box. "You know what, Tonya? Sometimes I think you're hiding in this school."

I watched the blade move up and down as Nikki cut open the box. "What would I be hiding from, and why on earth would I be hiding from it here?"

"You'd know that better than I would," she said, but looked at me as if she knew the answer as well if not better than I did.

As Nikki cut, I started imagining badly decomposed hands and legs popping out like a dead jack-in-the-box. Heads with maggots for eyes. A headless body. Nikki taking out an arm, a foot, and some fingers and lining them up on my workbench. These horrifying images made the thirty cups of coffee that I'd consumed over the past three days churn and bubble in my stomach, and caused my lips to pucker as my mouth began filling with sour saliva.

"I read in the paper that she was stabbed to death," Nikki said, looking down into the box.

I slammed my sketchbook closed. "Like I really wanted to know that, Nikki."

"You did," she said. "But as usual, you were just too afraid to ask."

7

"He's here." Nikki closed my bedroom door and stepped between my reflection in the mirror and me.

I was facing the dresser, standing in my lace, turquoise bikini set, taking more care than usual or probably needed to apply my eye shadow, blush, and lipstick. For close to an hour I'd been pacing around, trying not to chew off the freshly painted white tips on my fingernails while I waited for Nikki to come and tell me that Malcolm was in the living room.

"I'm so nervous," I told her.

"I know. Doesn't it feel great?" she asked.

I drew in a deep breath then exhaled. "It's just a date, right?" I asked Nikki.

"Right," Nikki said as she turned me around by my shoulders and guided me over to my bed. She handed my panty hose to me. "I hate to say this, but this is the first time that one of your sketches didn't do somebody justice."

I put on my panty hose and Nikki helped me into my slip.

"What if he doesn't like me?" I asked, sitting down on the bed.

"What if he already loves you?"

"We just met this morning, Nikki."

Nikki kissed me and said, "Love can't tell time and it's not very good with directions either."

I walked down the hall patting my hair and hoping that it would erase from his mind the sight of that ugly baseball cap I was wearing when we met. I smoothed away invisible wrinkles on the black halter cocktail dress that I'd brought just for him, and I prayed that it would make him forget about that purple shirt and shorts. And I stopped to wipe imaginary scuff marks off the black 2½ inch sling pumps I'd also brought because I wanted him to forget that he ever saw me in those dingy high-top Converse sneakers. I couldn't remember ever worrying about how my hair looked, if my dress didn't fit right, if my shoes were tacky, if my makeup was all wrong. I couldn't remember ever wanting to look perfect for a man.

When I finally stepped into the living room, I saw that Nikki was right about my sketch not doing Malcolm justice. He was wearing a black linen rayon suit that made him look like the fearless, handsome knight in shining armor that my mother said I'd find one day if I didn't spread my legs for the first man who showed a little interest in me. But Malcolm showed more than an interest. He showed a need for something that he didn't know he needed until he laid eyes on my bare dark brown shoulders. He said nothing, but he didn't have to. His eyes said everything that his mouth would have said if he could have closed it and opened it again like a cool man who didn't show his feelings so easily. But since he was a nervous man trying to be a cool man, his eyes told me that I looked gorgeous. No man's eyes had ever said that to me before. I guess that's why I believed Malcolm's eyes.

"It was nice meeting you, Nikki," he said as we headed out the door. "I promise to have her back at a decent hour."

"You do and I'll have your head," Nikki said.

Malcolm held opened the passenger side door to his black Mustang and said, "I have to apologize in advance."

"Apologize for what?" I asked.

"Well, see, I didn't know that I'd be taking a beautiful woman out to dinner tonight, and well, I have some business I need to take care of."

"It's not illegal, is it?" I asked.

"No. Nothing like that. It's...ah, you'll see. But I promise that it won't interfere with our evening."

Malcolm took the scenic route through the city to get from northwest Baltimore to the East Side. As we rode down North Avenue, I thought about my father, young, streetwise, and full of energy, walking from the

West Side to the East Side to see my mother. I looked out the window and wondered if it was love or sex that made him wear out the soles of his shoes. That was a long walk. It had to be love. I turned to Malcolm and wondered, unfairly maybe, if he would walk that far for me. And if so, would it be for love or sex?

The Silver Palace was a cozy restaurant with small, square, marble tables that had white candles burning in crystal holders and quiet jazz music playing in the background. Its walls were lined with paintings depicting black men and women dancing, gazing into each other's eyes, sharing a drink, whispering into each other's ears, holding hands across a table, walking in the night with her head on her man's shoulder. It was a place where people came to fall in love, renew their love, celebrate and flaunt their love. So when Malcolm escorted me into the Silver Palace on his arm, I decided that if he were to walk that far for me, it would most definitely be for love. But I'd have to wait for Malcolm to conclude his business with Floyd Henderson before I'd know for certain.

As it turned out, Malcolm was an accountant. He worked for Field and Simon, one of the few black accounting firms in Baltimore, but he also moonlighted by working with small black businesses. Floyd owned the Silver Palace and Malcolm had just completed his tax returns and needed him to sign the forms. It took a little while because Floyd was upset about owing the state sixty-seven dollars. He objected to the amount by writing a check and then attaching it to the form with exactly sixty-seven staples.

Malcolm said, "If I send this form in like this, they'll audit him for sure. Then he'll really have something to be pissed about."

Business out of the way, Malcolm called the waiter over to take our order. Malcolm ordered Chicken and Shrimp Creole, and I asked for the Soft Shell Crab Ashley. Afterwards, Malcolm leaned his elbows on the table and stared at me. Thinking that he was staring because of a defect in my appearance, I adjusted my clothes. When he didn't stop staring, I figured that my clothes weren't the problem. Maybe it's my hair, I thought.

So as discreetly as I could, I reached up and patted my head to flatten any wild, black strands that may have been waving to him.

"There isn't anything wrong with the way you look," Malcolm said.

I put my nervous hands in my lap. "Then why are you staring?

"Because I'm trying to figure out how you got me here."

"Excuse me, but you picked me up from my house and drove us here. That's how you got here."

"No. I was sitting on my bike, minding my own business, enjoying my day off, when you came along looking like you needed somebody to tell you that it ain't that bad."

"And you just had to be that body?" I asked, surprised that I didn't feel the pang that normally hits the center of my stomach whenever someone got that close to my thoughts about Meyoki.

His wide nostrils flared as he smiled, and the space between his teeth seemed to spread wider, seemingly to make room for me. I sat there listening to Ray Charles sing *"I Didn't Know What Time It Was"* and feeling as though I were falling into that gap. When I noticed Malcolm grinning, I lowered my head and blushed.

"Do you know that your cheeks turn dark purple when you blush?" Malcolm asked.

Now, he was really too close, and I didn't want him to know it either. I threw my hands up and covered them.

"Don't do that," he said, gently pulling my hands away from my face and staring at me again.

I wanted to cover my entire face. It was betraying me. I wasn't used to feeling this vulnerable, and I wasn't used to a guy seeing how vulnerable I was at all.

"Tell me about your first love," Malcolm said.

Now my hands were beginning to turn on me. They were becoming clammy. Geez, do I have a loyal bone in my body? I wondered.

"My first love?" I asked, hoping that my hands didn't break out into a full-fledged sweat.

I was surprised by his request. I'd never been asked anything like that before, and I never thought about truthfully answering if a man were interested enough and man enough to ask me about my first love. But I couldn't help wondering what he would do with that kind of information, so I said, "I would think that you'd be more interested in finding out about my current love."

"I would be if that were who I was competing with, but I'm not."

"You're not?"

"Nope." He released my hands. "See, I have this theory. I believe that a woman is always on the lookout for her first love because he's the one who first made her all warm and crazy inside, made her cheeks turn purple," Malcolm said. "Your first love is the one who kept you from paying attention in class because you were daydreaming about him or writing his name over and over in your notebook. He was the first guy to ever kiss you in a way that you hadn't been kissed before. He kept you up at night thinking about doing things that you know your parents didn't raise you to think about or do. He's the one that you lied to your girlfriends about how much you really liked him. He's the one who made you laugh and cry from your heart. He's the one that you still talk about with your girlfriends, and you always end up wondering what if...Your first love is the one that you measure every other guy against."

"So what you're saying is women never get over their first love?" I asked.

"Never. You go on with your life, but you never quite forget him," he said and took my hands again. "You tell me about him, and I can tell you if I'm just wasting my time."

I thought about each and every guy I'd ever been with since I'd lost my virginity to Basil Courtland when I was fifteen, but I couldn't name one who made me feel like that. And it wasn't as if I hadn't been looking and waiting for him. It was just that sculpting was my first love, and unfortunately my love for it didn't leave me much time, space, or energy to worry about such trivial things as love and commitment when it came to men. Sex, on the other hand, was a totally different story. It was a pleasing and much needed stress reliever, but the minute another project demanded my time, I lost interest in the guy lying between my legs, especially if he'd failed to fulfill me.

So I told Malcolm, "Let me show you my first love. Then you can decide if you're wasting your time."

Outside the Silver Palace, Malcolm unlocked the passenger side door to his Mustang but I didn't get in.

"It would be better if I drove," I told him. "That way there won't be any confusion as to how we got where we're going."

Malcolm looked at his car then at me. "Can you drive a stick?"

"My Aunt Josephine taught me to drive when I was twelve," I said, prying the keys out of his hands.

Malcolm didn't get into the car until I'd gotten behind the steering wheel and had started the engine.

"Buckle up," I said to Malcolm as I put on my seat belt.

Malcolm looked around as if he didn't know where the seat belt was. In fact, he fidgeted around as if he'd never been in the passenger seat of his car before. He didn't know where to put his feet, what to do with his hands, or how to sit. He kept looking around like a nervous teenager who was afraid that his homeboys would walk up and catch him letting a girl run him.

So that's why he was reluctant to hand over his keys, I thought. This will be the first time that he's ever let a woman drive him. I smiled at his discomfort, happy that I would be his first. I'd never been a man's first before.

I stayed in first gear while driving out of the city so that Malcolm could get used to me being behind the wheel of his car. When I got on southbound 295, I shifted into second and he took a deep breath that made him sit straight up. He wouldn't look at me because he didn't want to believe that he had let a woman drive his car and that he didn't even have the guts to ask this woman where she was driving him to.

I forced him to look at me by asking, "You ever open this thing up?" I thought his head was going to spin completely around. "What do you know about opening something up?"

Again, I didn't answer with my mouth. I eased up on the gas, pressed down on the clutch, shifted into third gear, and floored it. Malcolm's head fell back against the headrest and he gripped the sides of his seat. Sixty-five. Seventy. Seventy-five. Eighty! God! Fourth gear. This was the second time I felt like I was flying with this man.

Eighty-five. Road signs became green and white blurs as I whizzed by them. I'd never driven that fast in my life, but I wasn't going to slow down now that I had him.

Ninety. Woooooo! Would I do a hundred? About to go to fifth gear.

Malcolm wondered the same thing as he lean over to look at the speedometer. "Watch it now," he said, pointing up the road. "Cops usually sit up here."

I broke it down to sixty-five. Sure enough there was a state trooper sitting on the shoulder. Malcolm and I smiled at each other. When I passed the speed trap, I shifted into third, fourth gear, dug my heels in the carpet, and soared down that two-lane highway. Malcolm wasn't supposed to like my driving him, but he did. He became my copilot, watching out for cops and holding his hand out the window to play with the wind. Malcolm turned on the radio as I approached ninety-five. Stevie Wonder was singing *"Love Light In Flight."* It sure as hell was!

We got to Rock Creek Park in D.C. in less than forty minutes. I led him in the dark over to a sculpture of Abraham Lincoln. It was the first piece that I'd been commissioned to do when I started working with Dr. Zimmerman. The piece was called *Freedom*. It was born out of a controversy over a statue in Lincoln Park that depicted a male slave kneeling at Lincoln's feet. *Freedom* consisted of Abraham Lincoln and three shackled slaves who were reaching for a key that Lincoln was holding close to his chest in a manner that openly displayed his reluctance to free the slaves.

"Your first love was Abraham Lincoln?" Malcolm joked.

"No, silly," I said then pointed to the plaque with my name on it.

"You're an artist," he said. "And a damn good one."

Malcolm stepped away from the sculpture. He wasn't prepared for this. It was like Nikki said. What can a man do when he's up against a bag of clay and history? Every man I'd ever had ran. But who could blame them? I'd abandon them for weeks at a time without so much as a phone call. And since I didn't disclose the location of my studio to the man in my bed, he had no way of contacting me. So a month or two later when I called his house because I needed a break from sculpting, some other woman was usually in the background asking, "Who's that?" And I always thought that I was too much of an artist and not enough of a woman to worry myself with his answer. Tonight, though, I felt more like a woman who needed this man to be man enough to handle being second in my life.

Malcolm was so quiet that I thought he'd left so I turned around. He was standing there staring at me. He could see in my eyes what life would be like with me. There was no doubt that my art would come first. The question was, could he deal with that? Or were we out here just wasting time?

Suddenly, a handsome laugh opened Malcolm's mouth and made him appear playful and boyish. He climbed up onto the marble base and looked Lincoln in the face. Then he turned to the slaves and touched them as though he hadn't felt history before.

"So you've never been in love," Malcolm said, looking down at me.

"What are you talking about?" I asked. "I just--"

Malcolm jumped down and landed in front of me. He laughed as if he'd uncovered a dark secret of mine that I'd tried to hide behind the wheel of his car. But now he could see that I was never actually in control of that speed and power.

"You've never been in love," he said, looking into my eyes.

I started backing away from him as I began feeling less and less like a woman and more like a twelve year-old girl going through puberty. Mystified by the lumps and hairs growing in strange places, frightened by the stream of blood flowing out of me, and confused by the way a boy's hand made me hot where I hadn't been hot before.

I kept backing up until my back was against the marble platform. With nowhere else for me to go, I braced myself for a kiss I thought Malcolm was sure to give. I could hear the blood galloping through my veins. I was sweating and shaking. I'd never felt so raw and alive with wanting and anticipation.

But instead, he stripped his car keys from my fingers and said, "I'll drive back."

Malcolm didn't fly up the highway the way I did. He drove under the speed limit. He kept looking at me as if he were savoring a rare and amazing innocence that I possessed. An innocence that would be gone once we got to where he was taking us. An hour later, he pulled into Cylburn Arboretum.

"The sign says it's closed," I informed him.

"You pay too much attention to signs," he said, parking the car.

He got a dark blue blanket out of the trunk then opened my door.

"I don't think we'll be needing that," I said, hoping that he didn't think I was going to sleep with him out here, and on the first date at that.

"I have something to show you," he said.

"I've seen it before," I said.

He laughed. "I seriously doubt that." He handed the blanket to me. "I need you to carry this and close your eyes."

I took the blanket. "How am I supposed to see where I'm going?"

"I'll see for you. Trust me."

"I don't know you well enough to trust you."

He put a hand over my eyes and put his arm tenderly and protectively around my waist. I liked the way that felt.

"Do you want to trust me?" he asked.

I didn't answer. I sighed and started walking, thinking I want to do more than that.

He guided me along. I felt my feet on gravel then grass. I couldn't help wondering how many other women he'd brought out here. We walked up a hill near a honey suckle patch. I could smell it in the air and it got me thinking. Is this where he seduced his first love? Or is this where his first love seduced him?

When we reached the top, Malcolm made me promise to keep my eyes closed while he spread out the blanket then he helped me down onto it.

"So why did you bring me out here?" I asked after I was settled.

"I wanted to show you a light show," he said.

"A light show?" I lifted my eyelids and saw hundreds of tiny blinking green lights rising up from the grass.

"Lighting bugs?" I asked.

"Yeah. Aren't they pretty?"

"They're beautiful."

Malcolm caught one in his hand. "I grew up on the East Side," he said. "On a small alley street called Spring Avenue. But we called it Concrete Alley because not one blade of grass or one branch of a tree could be found on that block. If it wasn't for the curb, there wouldn't have been any way of telling when the sidewalk ended and the street began because both were made of cement. There were twelve red-brick row houses on our block, and all of them had black steel steps that led to wooden doors, and the backyards were slabs of cracked concrete with rusty, iron clothes line poles rooted in them.

"There weren't any lighting bugs around our way, so my father used to bring me out here all the time when I was little. Said he didn't want me to grow up never having seen fireflies wake up. I was amazed by them then as I am now. I wanted to catch some lighting bugs and put them in a jar, but my father said that locking something or someone up in a jar would take the fire out of any light."

I touched the bug crawling around in his palm and it flew away. Then

I caressed Malcolm's hand, stroking each finger as if I had sculpted them myself. Malcolm moved closer to me and warmed my neck with his sweet breath before he put his mouth on it. Gently, he sucked my skin, and I imagined that I was being pulled into the gap between his smile. It felt so wonderful inside that I had to tilt my head to the side and close my eyes.

Soon Malcolm's mouth was on my earlobe. "Tonya, he said in a whisper. "I know we just met, but can I have you?"

I knew that I could, would, and had to let him have me. The panty-dampening kiss he gave me, and the gentle, manly way he asked for me rather than assumed or tried to take me made it impossible for me not to surrender myself to Malcolm Holland long before he parted my dark thighs on the top of that hill.

His body wore the May moonlight as if it were a fine tailored suit. I could see the circles, curves, and straight lines that made his muscular body look as though it had been carved out of wild black cherry wood. He didn't have sex with me. He made love to me gently and teasingly, purposely abandoning certain parts of my body, leaving question marks in those excited areas, and then returning with definite answers to my prayers. I stretched my arms out past the blanket and grabbed a hold of the earth.

Mmmmm! Is this what first love feels like? What time is it?

"You caress as if you've known how to thrill a woman in this way all your life," I said to Malcolm as we lay snuggled together on the blanket at the top of that grassy hill.

My face was buried in the field of black hairs on his warm chest, my leg was draped over his thighs, my arm wrapped around his waist. The night was dark but bright with white stars. The fireflies were gone. I wondered where they went. We were all alone. The only two people in the world it seemed. I was the happiest I'd ever been.

Malcolm ran his fingers through my hair. "I wouldn't say all of my life. Maybe half."

"I've never done anything like this before. So out in the open. Where anybody can see," I said.

"Neither have I," he said.

"I find that impossible to believe," I told him.

"Really? Then tell me what you do believe," he said.

I believe that you've brought every woman that you've ever slept with to this very spot and seduced them. That's what I thought, but I said, "Tell me about your first love."

Malcolm sighed. "My first love was a twenty-eight-year-old woman who was trying to get over her first love. I met her when I was eighteen. The summer before I went to college. I used to jog around the reservoir in Druid Hill Park every morning. So did she. One morning I got up the nerve to talk to her, and she liked what I said so she took me home with her."

"What did she look like?" I asked, wondering if she looked anything like me, hoping that if I wasn't prettier than she, I was at least more interesting.

"She was dark-skinned, short and slim. Very pretty."

She sounded a little like me. "What happened?" I asked.

"Her first love came back in the form of a taller, older, richer man."

Malcolm took my hand and started kissing my fingers.

Is that who I'm up against? I wondered. I mean, if he were to see his first love jogging around the reservoir one morning, would he leave me? Somehow I got the feeling that the answer would be no. She may have been his first love, but she wasn't the woman that he'd put his life on the line for. That woman was his second or maybe even his third love. And despite his theory, she's the one that he was hoping would come back. The one I have to worry about.

"Tell me about the man in your life," Malcolm said.

"Don't you think you should have asked about him before you brought me here?" I said.

"He didn't matter then," Malcolm said. "And to be honest, I don't think he really matters now."

"Well, then why ask?"

"Because I need to know if I have any other competition besides your art."

"If there were someone else, I would be here, but not like this." I sat up to look in his eyes. "Now what about you. Are there any women in your life?"

"Nope," he said. "I'm as free as the day is long."

"What about single?"

Malcolm held up his left hand and wiggled his fingers. "That too."

"Just because you aren't wearing a wedding ring doesn't necessarily mean that you aren't living with or dating someone."

His wide, flat nostrils flared with laughter. "True. But I'm not living with anyone or trying to date anyone except you. Trust me."

I parked my car on Greenmount Avenue. Even though this wasn't the best neighborhood for me to take a long, leisurely stroll, I slowly walked down the street and around the corner to North Avenue. I headed to the middle of the block and stopped in front of a large, newly renovated red brick building that had the words "Positive Awakenings" chiseled above the entrance. I mounted the steps, held open the door and let several people go in ahead of me. Then I held it open while a group of people exited. When there was no more traffic, I sighed, then reluctantly went inside.

There was something about this place that gave me the creeps. That was why I hardly ever visited Nikki at her office. But this morning when I'd gotten home from my date with Malcolm, Nikki had left a note demanding that I come down and see her.

There were signs posted on the blue concrete walls that had red arrows printed on them. Positive Awakenings was straight ahead. I walked down the dimly lit hallway that led to the lobby. Nikki's receptionist, Kim, a tall, heavy-set girl, was sitting behind a glass window with her back to me talking on the phone. From the way she was shaking her head, I knew that she was on a personal call. I tapped on the glass and she turned around then smiled and put her hand over the receiver.

"Hey, Tonya," Kim said.

"How ya doing, Kim?"

"Alright. Nikki's in with a patient." Kim looked at the clock on the wall behind her. "She should be done in a few minutes, though. Why don't you have a seat and I'll buzz her and tell her that you're here."

"Thanks," I said then scanned the green room for a chair.

There were five other people sitting in the shabby waiting area, staring blankly at a small black and white television. I spotted an empty chair and sat down. A red-boned woman with blond hair and a nose ring was sitting on the other side of the room staring at me. I spoke but she didn't speak back.

I heard a rowdy crowd coming down the hall. There had to be at least fifteen or twenty people, men and women, lining up next door. Most of them had on scraggly clothing, their hair wasn't combed, and some looked like they hadn't taken a bath in months. None of them stood up straight. They were all slouched over, kind of staggering on their feet as if they were half-asleep. Some were too frail to stand period, so they slumped to the floor and slid along the side of the wall as the line moved forward. I knew why they were there way before I heard a skinny light-skinned guy say, "Man, this methadone shit ain't hittin' on a corner."

A loud thumping sound that vibrated the back of my chair distracted me. The blond-haired woman with the nose ring had moved her chair next to mine.

"What you runnin' from?" the woman asked in a brisk voice.

I looked around the room to see if she was talking to me.

"Yeah. You," she said.

I pointed to my chest. "Me?"

"Yeah," she said in a nasty tone. "What you runnin' from?"

I had no idea what she was talking about. "What makes you think I'm running from anything?"

She leaned in and sniffed the air around me. "You smell like you runnin' from somethin'."

I didn't want to say what she smelled like, so I just got up and moved to another seat.

She walked to the center of the waiting room. "You think I'm just a crackhead, but I know what I'm talkin' 'bout. I see people runnin' every day. Some of us been runnin' so hard and long that we done forGOT what it is we runnin' from. We think we runnin' from one thing when we really runnin' from somethin' else. Them people out there," she said, pointing to the crowd in front of the methadone center, "think they runnin' from drugs, when they really runnin' from a daddy that left 'em, or a momma that beat 'em, or a uncle that felt 'em up when nobody was lookin'."

She came and kneeled down in front of me.

"What are you doing?" I whispered, peeking around to see if anyone was paying attention.

Every eye in the place was on us. She was making a scene, a spectacle of herself and of me. Having people look at me as if I were crazy, just like her. I wanted to ask them all why were they looking at me when she was the one performing. Tell them that I'd never seen this woman before in my life and didn't know why she was acting the fool.

I got angry. "Get up," I said through clenched teeth.

She put her dark, rough palms on my knees. "You know why I'm here?"

I didn't care. I just wanted this crazy woman away from me, and the eyes of the people in the waiting room off me.

"I'm here 'cause I been runnin' from myself." Suddenly, her gaze went from my face to the empty space beside us and she hung her head. "Runnin' from who my people don't want me to be."

She was quiet for a second, and I wondered who it was that her people didn't approve of and why did she have to turn to drugs in order to escape.

Then, as if someone had breathed new life into her, she angrily jumped to her feet. "You know what, though. One day last month I got tired! And I just stopped movin' right where I was standin'. And it seemed like the stillness and rest helped me to think and I started askin' myself questions like, how come I don't see nobody bendin' over backwards livin' their lives to suit me? And how come ain't none of my people all strung out tryin' to live for me?"

She looked off into space again, and just as suddenly as she'd come over to me, she was back on the other side of the room, sitting down as if she'd never spoken a word to me. The on-lookers went back to staring blankly at the small television. The drama was over for them. There was nothing left to gawk at or gossip about. But it wasn't over for me. I couldn't help feeling as if I'd been set up somehow. Nikki knew that I hated this place, but she insisted that I come. I thought it was strange, and then to get there and have this woman come up and start talking this nonsense made me really suspicious about Nikki's motives. So by the time Kim called me, I was more than a little ticked off.

Nikki's office was a small closed in room with no windows. There was an old brown desk that wobbled because of the uneven floor tiles, and a tall, army-green file cabinet. Other than the squeaky office chair behind Nikki's desk, the only place for people to sit down was on the long, gray, leather couch. It was Nikki's favorite thing in the office. She'd purchased it herself so that her patients would have something that felt like home to lie on while they were spilling their guts. I avoided that couch.

"I hate coming here," I said as I marched in.

Nikki closed the door behind her. "Why?"

"Too many crazy people," I said, pacing in a small circle.

Nikki pulled her office chair around to the front of her desk. I thought that she was getting it for me, but she used it to rest her feet as she sat on top of the desk, leaving me with no where to sit.

"Some of them are indeed crazy," Nikki said. "But most just think they're crazy because their ideas and feelings differ from what is considered the norm. What's funny is, the norm sends more people over the edge than anything else. I've seen perfectly 'normal' people go insane trying to be normal. Why don't you just sit down on the couch?"

Now walking back and forth, I said, "Yeah, well, all I know is you must be out of your mind being down here dealing with these loons. And I don't want to sit down on the couch."

"Being out of your mind at times can be good for the soul," Nikki said. "And the couch won't bite, so just sit down and calm your nerves."

"Is that why you made me come down here, to get me on your couch?"

"No," Nikki denied, sounding like a guy who had invited his girlfriend over for that very reason. "I asked you to come down so that you can tell me what time love came a knockin'."

I stopped pacing long enough to realize that the only motive Nikki had for asking me there was so that she could find out how my date with Malcolm went. Just like any other normal friend would.

So timidly I sat down on the couch. It was still warm from her last patient. But it was also soft and comfortable. I could see how someone could relax to the point where all of her secrets came pouring out. As I stretched out on the couch, I thought about Malcolm and pretended that I was still on top of that hill lying in his arms. "What makes you think love came a knockin' at all?" I asked.

"For one thing, you were out all night," Nikki said.

"I've been out all night before," I said.

"Not with a guy."

"That doesn't prove anything."

"You slept with him on the first date?"

"Doesn't mean a thing," I said.

"If it didn't mean a thing, you wouldn't have done it. Besides, I've seen that look in your eyes before."

"Now I know that you don't know what you're talking about because I've never felt this way about a guy before," I said, closing my eyes.

"I know," Nikki said.

And it was the surety in her voice that snatched my eyelids up like window shades and made me turn to look in her face so that I could see if what my brain said that she was implying was written there. I couldn't see anything, but that didn't stop me from having a weird feeling in my stomach and making my chest tighten.

I sat up. "What are you talking about, Nikki?"

I asked the question, but I was terrified of her answer.

Nikki peered at me for several long, disturbing seconds before asking, "Is that a passion mark?"

My hands shot up to my neck. "Where?" I asked, getting up from the couch and going over to the mirror on the back of the door.

Nikki was right. I had a round, purple mark on the spot where Malcolm kept sucking on my neck. Imagine that. A passion mark.

"Admit it," Nikki said. "He's got you."

I leaned against the wall in defeat. "All right. He's got me. But what do I do now?"

"Go a little bit crazy," Nikki said, as if it were the most normal thing in the world to do.

If there was any doubt that Malcolm Holland was after my heart on that hill in Cylburn, it was erased two days later when he seduced me again. The strange thing was that he didn't do it with flowers, money, jewelry, or an expensive dinner. He knew that those things would get him into my bed again but not my heart, and that's where he wanted to be. So Malcolm found out everything he could find out about my art by our second date.

We spent that lovely May afternoon roaming around Baltimore looking at some of my work. Malcolm told me things about my work and myself that I didn't even know or believe. He didn't always get everything right. I mean, there's only so much you can learn about art in two days, but he cared enough to put himself out there.

One of our stops was The Great Blacks in Wax Museum on North Avenue. Malcolm had read an article about the curator's interest in my doing a piece for *The Slavery Era* exhibit, but I was too busy with Dr. Zimmerman's thoughts.

"You regret not having the time to work on this project?" Malcolm asked me.

I hadn't really thought about it until just then when I was standing with Malcolm inside a replica of a slave ship looking at the wax life-sized figure of a black woman. Her hands were tied at the wrists and her feet at the ankles. The rope that bound her hands was placed on a high hook so that her bound feet dangled above the floor of the ship. Her back was arched and her stomach sucked in, so much so that you could count the bones of her rib cage. Her queenly black skin had been sliced open by the lashes of a whip.

It was the most powerful exhibit I'd ever seen, and I regretted not having the time to work on such an extraordinary piece of history. As I stood there wondering how a person could have survived such a brutal beating, I felt a chilly feeling of shame cut through me like a sharp blade, because before now I hadn't even bothered to make the time to come and see the exhibit.

"So how long does it take you to do a sculpture?" Malcolm asked.

"It depends," I said.

"On what?" he asked.

"On how deeply I get involved with the subject."

He looked me in the eyes, and asked, "Do you think that you could get deeply involved with me?" Backing off a bit, not wanting to rush things, he said, "I mean, enough to sculpt me?"

"Possibly."

He grabbed me by the hand and started leading me out.

"Where are we going now?" I asked.

"To your studio," he said.

I stopped and pulled my hand out of his. "Oh, no we're not."

"Why?"

"Because it's my studio."

"So?" he asked.

"So, my studio is off limits to men like you."

He smirked. "Men like me? What do you mean, men like me?"

"Men that I'm dating," I said.

He smiled and grabbed my hand again.

"I can't take you there," I said, as we stepped outside, knowing that I would have taken him anywhere to be with him.

"Well, let me take you," he said.

"No man has ever been there before," I confessed.

He gave me a sly grin. "I won't tell if you won't."

"It's all the way downtown," I stalled.

"The car is right here," he said, as he unlocked the passenger side door.

"There's no place to park this time of day."

"It's a sunny day. Let's walk."

"It's too far," I protested.

"I'll carry you if you get tired." He leaned his lips toward me. "I have a strong back."

"I don't doubt that," I said, ducking his kiss and getting into the car.

Malcolm drove down North Avenue.

"It's my space," I said.

"I don't take up much room," he said, getting ready to turn down the wrong street.

"The next left," I told him. Then, "It's my space."

"I'll leave when you want me to."

"It's right here," I said. "But you can't come in."

Malcolm parked the car. "But I brought this bag of clay."

Oooh! Now see, he's not playing fair, I thought. "I have plenty of clay," I said.

Malcolm opened my door. "The guy at the store said it was the best."

I inspected the clay as I walked up the marble steps of AAI. "Yeah, it is, but..."

But we were already standing at my studio door, and Malcolm was confessing that he'd known where it was all along. He'd read an article someone had written about Dr. Zimmerman and me, but he said he didn't want to intrude by just showing up at the school. Again, no man had ever gone to that much trouble for me.

When I opened the door, Malcolm didn't rush or barge in. He took his time, moving quietly, gently, as if he were entering me through that small opening that I didn't even go in. That I didn't even touch unless I was bathing. An opening that I truly saw for the first time when I looked

in his eyes as he walked around, feeling and touching, as if amazed by
what he saw and felt inside.

"Let me see you sculpt," Malcolm said.

I looked at him as if he'd just asked me to strip for him. The only man
I'd ever sculpted in front of was Dr. Zimmerman.

"Anything," he said and sat down on a stool. "What are you working
on now?"

I looked over at the box on my desk. I hadn't laid a finger on Hazel
Cherrylane, and even though I wasn't sure if I was doing the right thing by
letting Malcolm in, I felt right having him there and didn't want him to
leave. So I wasn't about to scare him off by pulling out a skull. But
Malcolm wasn't the least bit frightened. In fact, he was intrigued with the
whole thing and wanted to help me get over my fears. So the next day he
went to a medical supply store and brought a fake human skull for me to
practice on.

We stayed together for five days and four nights. I sculpted while he
watched. Malcolm drove us home so that we could shower and change.
We ate breakfast at one of his client's restaurant, then he drove me back
to the studio, where he left me for a few hours while he checked in at his
office. By noon he was back with lunch, and he didn't leave again until six
when he went out to get dinner. We sat on the radiator in front of the
window feeding each other and talking. Conversation flowed between us
like a steady, calm stream. We talked about everything and, at times,
absolutely nothing. And we did something as simple and wonderful as
laughing.

He told me about an artificial Christmas tree his father had brought
and refused to get rid of.

"That sickly thing," Malcolm said. "It was the only fake tree I'd ever
seen that shed its needles."

We laughed. Freely, loudly, honestly, hysterically. I had never, ever
laughed liked that with a man.

It was around three Tuesday morning, and the moon was full and bright. Malcolm was up in the loft asleep and I was putting the finishing touches on the skull, which I was able to put Malcolm's handsome face on. I didn't hear Malcolm come down. I just felt him wrap his arms around me from behind. First he massaged my neck, then my shoulders, then my hands and fingers. His touch made me feel wonderful and hot. Finally he turned me around, then he took me right there at my workbench. Ummm!

At the crack of dawn I kissed the only man that I'd ever spent the morning after with in my studio.

"Why'd you stay here like this?" I asked. "What do you want?"

"Just to show you that I know that for years you've been choosing between something that has meant the world to you since you could feel it and breathe it and men who just don't or can't understand that." Malcolm took my face in his hands. "But I do, and I don't want you to choose. I want you to let me be a part of it."

"So you're saying that you'll stay here every time I have a project?" I asked.

"No," he laughed. "I do have a life, you know. Bills to pay, food to buy."

I hit him playfully in the chest.

"I'm showing you," Malcolm said, "that I will wait until you have time for me. Now, if you take too long, I will come and get you. But not very often and not for very long."

9

Malcolm asked me to come to his "place" for dinner. Not his house or home. But his "place." Like he was talking about some secret hideaway that he didn't allow just any old woman to step inside.

His place was long and open. There weren't any little side rooms to sneak into, no corners to duck around, any cracks or crevices to slide into. Standing in the living room, I could look straight through, to the dining room and then straight on through to the kitchen and out to the backyard. Every light in the house was on and all of the curtains, windows, and doors were open. The walls and floors were cluttered with trophies, ribbons, and medals he'd won for high school and college wrestling.

I arrived shortly after eight and he was still straightening up as he listened to a baseball game on the radio and watched a basketball game on the small color television that sat on the coffee table. When he thought I wasn't looking, he rushed over to the coffee table, grabbed a brown paper bag from the floor, and began sweeping metal objects into it. After he'd cleared the table, he squeezed the bag closed, then put it down on the other side of the room beside his bike.

Instead of asking what he was hiding in that brown paper bag, I said, "Your electric bill must be through the roof."

"At times," he said, and escorted me into the dining room.

There was a white, lace cloth on the table, candles in the center, fine white china, and long-stemmed wineglasses. He pulled out my chair so that I could sit down. Before serving dinner, he lit the two long blue and white candles, and turned out most of the lights. He then went into the kitchen and brought out a small, steaming hot pan of sweet bread pudding. I smiled as he hurried back into the kitchen and returned carrying a glass pitcher filled with milk, which he poured into the wineglasses.

He sat down and raised his glass of milk. "This toast is to Nikki, who was nice enough to tell me, after a lengthy interrogation, that her best friend's favorite dish is bread pudding."

"To Nikki," I said, tapping my glass of milk against his. After taking a sip, I asked, "What else did Nikki tell you about me?"

He cut a large piece of bread pudding and put it on my plate. "That you eat a lot," he laughed.

"You think you're pretty smart, don't you?"

"That depends. Are you impressed?"

"Very," I admitted.

"Well then, yes. I think I'm pretty smart."

"Well, Mister Smarty Pants," I said, taking a forkful of bread pudding, "answer this. Why didn't you tell me that you were an athlete?"

"Because I wasn't. I was a guy who was trying to tell my father that I wasn't a wimp just because I wanted to be an accountant."

"Did he hear you?" I asked.

"As much as any man who works fourteen hour shifts repairing water mains can hear a son who doesn't want to follow in his father's steel toe work boots."

"Parents always want you to be like them," I said. "But they swear that they want you to be your own person while doing everything in their power to prevent it."

"Tell me about your father," Malcolm asked.

I laughed to myself because the last guy who'd asked me about my father was climbing into my bedroom window.

"My father was raised in the projects, Lafayette Courts. They used to be over on Orleans and Fayette Street. His whole family lived there-- grandmother, aunts, uncles, and cousins. He said it was nice but he hated living there. Said it reminded him of a twelve-story cage. He stayed away from home as much as possible. That's why he knows this city like the back of his hand. He would roam around dreaming of blowing up the projects and moving his family into one of the big houses in Upper Park Heights, Bolton Hill, or Roland Park where his grandmother, mother, and aunts used to work as maids. When he was twenty-five, he scraped up enough money to buy this old run down house on Dukeland Street. He fixed it up and converted it into a two-story apartment, then rented it out to some relatives. He kept buying old houses and renovating them until he got his whole family out of the projects. Now he owns over sixty properties.

"Those properties keep him from seeing the practicality in what I do. My father's a very practical man. When somebody signs a rental or lease agreement, he can immediately see that he has helped someone put a roof over his head and has given him a place to call home. He can't see the roof in my work and how it shelters and gives others and me a home. He'd much rather see me sitting behind a desk in his office like Elaine."

"Elaine?" Malcolm asked.

"My sister."

"I didn't know you had a sister." Malcolm's face lit up with envy. "Are you two close?"

"Not as close as my mother would like," I said. "We had a combative childhood that didn't make us enemies, but it didn't exactly make us friends either. We never hang out together, rarely, if ever, phone or visit to see how the other is doing. Basically, we really only socialize at family gatherings."

Malcolm was a little let down by that. "If I had a brother or sister, we would be close," he said. "I'd make sure of it."

"My mother tried to make sure that Elaine and I were best friends, but things happened."

"Things like what?"

"Like Elaine and me having a crush on the same boy so we started arguing and fighting about any and everything. My mother couldn't stand that so she sat us down and gave us a lecture on the importance of family.

You see, she went through too much to get hers and she isn't going to let anyone disrupt it the way that she let the Peterson boys come between her and her sister. So she forbade Elaine or me from ever seeing the boy.

"Then one day Elaine brought home this girlfriend that she was all excited about. But when the girlfriend came down in our basement and saw me sculpting, she spent her entire visit on the basement stairs watching and asking me questions, joking with me. And we found out that we liked each other and wanted to be friends. Well, Elaine didn't want us to be friends, so she and I started fighting again. My mother told us that if this girl was going to be in our lives, she had to be friends with the both of us. That lasted a week or two. Elaine gave up and found a new best friend, and Nikki and I went on to live happily ever after. Elaine has never gotten over or forgiven me for taking Nikki from her."

That whole crazy time froze me in thought for a few moments. Then, deciding that there was nothing more to say on the subject, I said, "So, tell me about your mother."

Malcolm's sturdy, masculine face suddenly turned light and boyish. "The best way for me to describe my mother is to tell you about a dinner date we had last month."

"Okay," I said.

"I'd taken her to a fancy restaurant down at the Inner Harbor. She was dressed in one of her finer cocktail dresses, red with a choker collar. We were discussing the need for affirmative action, and she was arguing her point so well that a couple at the table next to us leaned in and agreed with her. But halfway through her argument, I stopped hearing her and just stared at her, unable to take my eyes off her."

"Why?"

"Because she had a drop of French dressing on her chin." He pointed to his. "There she was, dining in a fancy restaurant, dressed to kill, laying down her point so heavy that no one could lift it, and she had a tear shaped drop of French dressing on her chin." He laughed.

"Well, why didn't you tell her it was there or wipe it off for her?"

Out from the space between his smile came, "Because that was the first time that I'd ever seen my mother with a hair out of place, so to speak. And I liked seeing her that free. She was beautiful." Malcolm walked over to me. "That's how you look when you're sculpting. Free and beautiful." He got up from the table, took my hand, grabbed my plate of bread pudding, and led me upstairs.

Um. Um. Um. He had a king size bed with a pretty, solid oak headboard, a soft but firm mattress with a goose down topper, and two overstuffed, feather pillows that were drenched in his delicious scent.

Malcolm was a poet in that bed, but not one committed to or satisfied with rhythmically releasing or listening to words that expressed sexual pleasure. For him words lacked the force and spontaneity needed to express seduction, sexual stimulation, and ecstasy because they were too easily manipulated, misunderstood, denied, or forgotten. For him, action was the only way to voice sexual excitement and pleasure. Action was unpredictable and harmonious. He believed that action spoke what words could not describe, and showed things ears refused to hear. It unmasked lies, and let you in on secrets. But most of all, sexual action gave Malcolm the power to set the record straight on any matter concerning his manhood. So that's why he was a poet devoted to sexual action. And that's also why he never let me get on top.

But I, on the other hand, enjoyed nothing more than hearing and speaking words that conveyed sexual pleasure. It was the only time that I actually listened to the tongue because for me words were living proof that lovemaking was not only occurring but had meaning. Words gave voice to a wink, nod, frown, grimace, or smile that may have otherwise gone unnoticed. Words spoke of the reasons behind a sweet but kinky sexual act. Words spoke of things that sexual action could only hint at.

"Did you have this bed when you were with her?" I asked as he lay spent and sprawled out on the mattress while I sat at the foot of the bed sketching the oak headboard with a charcoal pencil.

We'd been in bed since the night before when he'd carried me up during dinner. He made love to me and fed me bread pudding, then he fed me bread pudding and made love to me.

"With who?" Malcolm asked with his eyes closed.

"The woman you put your life on the line for."

"Humph," he said. "I was wondering how long it would be before you asked me about her." His eyes were now open, and he was gazing pensively at the ceiling. "I didn't even have this house when we were together," he finally said. "I moved here after we broke up."

"Who was she?"

He laughed somewhat, then said, "She was...is Zona. Zona Fleet. A year and a half ago we were living together."

I kept my eyes fixed on the page and continued sketching. "What happened?"

"I don't know."

"What do you mean you don't know?"

"Exactly that."

I could hear the wrinkling of his brow in his voice.

"I went to work one day, and when I came home, there was a letter on the bed. 'Malcolm, I need you to leave. I hope you understand.' I didn't but I left anyway."

"Did you love her?"

"We were engaged," he said, already fed up with what he thought were silly questions.

"Yes, but did you love her?"

"With everything in me," he said frankly.

I put down the pencil. "Then why did you leave without finding out what happened?"

After reflecting quietly, he said, "Anger. Pride." Now he was almost brooding. "And it was over so at the time I didn't see any point in finding out what went wrong."

"What about now?" My words were outstretched.

Malcolm reached over and gathered them and me up in his arms and said, "Now, I'm with you."

We kissed and the sound of raindrops suddenly dancing through the trees caused us look out the window. The May sun was blazing in the sky, still the rain was pouring down fast and hard.

"The devil's beating his wife," Malcolm said.

"What?" I asked.

"The devil's beating his wife. My mother used to say that every time it rained when the sun was shining. But my father said that it was God showing the white man who was really boss."

"You're a mama's boy, aren't you?"

Malcolm smiled then gazed intensely at the rainy, sunny day. "What do you look for in a man, Tonya?"

"I don't know."

"Come on. There's got to be something that you want a man to be. Something that you expect or hope your man to be."

"Off the top of my head, I guess I'd look for my man to be his own man," I said. "Good or bad, I'd want him to be the man he truly is."

"What if the man he truly is isn't the man he's supposed to be?"

I turned to Malcolm and said, "The only man that you're not supposed to be is the one that you can't live with."

Malcolm pondered my answer and something else that made him scratch his head. After weighing the pros and cons of what he was about to say and do, he kneeled down beside the bed. "The first thing you have to do is promise not to laugh."

"Laugh at what?"

"What I'm gonna show you."

"Okay. I promise."

He cut his eyes at me. "I've never shown anyone this before, so don't make me regret it."

"I won't. What is it?"

Malcolm pulled a couple of shoeboxes from underneath the bed. "I'm trusting you," he said, taking the lid off one, which was filled with

HotWheels and MatchBox cars.

I started smiling.

Embarrassed and disappointed, he said, "Now, you promised that you wouldn't laugh." He shoved the boxes back under the bed.

"I'm not laughing," I said, retrieving them. "I'm just happy to see proof of your boyhood."

"Well, my father won't, so please don't mention it when you meet him." His mind wandered back to when he was a boy. "My mother and I used to smuggle the cars in the house because my father didn't want me to have them. 'Nine-year-old men don't play with toy cars,' he said. We hid them under my bed, my mother and I." Malcolm picked up a purple and white Oldsmobile racecar. "She used to play lookout for me. I'd be up in my room having a ball, and then she would come to the bottom of the steps and yell, 'Malcolm, your poppa's home.' And I'd put the cars away, and then go do something manly, like take out the trash."

"Or hide them in brown paper bags," I said, remembering the night before when he'd swept them off the coffee table into a bag. "Why did you hide them from me?"

"Thirty-year-old men don't play with toy cars."

"What about twenty-eight-year-old women?"

I put on Malcolm's shirt, grabbed a handful of cars then ran out to the hallway. Malcolm put on his pants and did the same. He kneeled at one end of the hallway and I at the other, and we played like children, rolling cars back and forth, making revving, skidding, and crashing sounds. We built ramps and bridges out of books and magazines, and had cars flying through the air.

After about an hour, Malcolm went down to the kitchen. I was sitting on the top step with my elbows on my knees and spinning the wheels of a jeep when I saw him at the bottom of the stairs with a heavy, tall, crystal glass in his hand. I saw on his face the same "I gotcha" smile that Uncle Charlie fastened on Aunt Josephine all those years ago. And as Malcolm climbed the stairs, I saw my father, handsome, swift, and streetwise, rolling through the streets of Baltimore like a big, black Cadillac as he made his way to my mother.

When Malcolm reached me, I rose, unable to believe my eyes, afraid that I was sculpting or dreaming this whole scene. It couldn't be real. *He* couldn't be real. I looked down at his large shirt hanging off my body, and I looked down at my bare feet on the stairs. Then I looked at his hand. The glass he held was filled with water so cold that a liquid frost coated the outside of it and ran down Malcolm's fingers and dripped on my toes as he presented the glass to me. I took the glass and brought it to my lips.

I'd been in love with Malcolm I think since the day we met, but I couldn't believe it until I was standing at the top of the stairs in my man's shirt, drinking a sweet glass of plain old tap water. As I sipped I wrestled with the thought of telling him this, but decided against it. I needed to keep my love for him a secret for now. I wanted time to feel my love for him by myself, if that makes any sense. I wanted my love for him to sit alone in a corner with its knees pulled up to its breasts and just listen to the late night calls he made just to hear my voice; enjoy the long drives and rides on his bike we took to nowhere and back; really smell the flowers he sent just because; savor the two a.m. breakfasts; hold him as he shivered in my arms after our lovemaking; and treasure the needs and secrets he shared with me.

Yeah, Malcolm had gotten me, I thought as I quenched my thirst. But I'd gotten him too.

10

Being in love with Malcolm Holland changed everything about me. I had more leg and hip to my walk, more rhythm and height to my talk. Most importantly, being in love with Malcolm changed my art in ways I'd never thought possible. I was no longer afraid to capture in clay what I'd seen between Nikki and Lonnie because I thought I'd never have it. So I sculpted young couples arguing, laughing, kissing, and making love.

Every day it seemed I had something new and wonderful to tell myself about my love for Malcolm. And all the sculptures said the same thing--he was the one and only I'd been waiting for.

On the last Wednesday of May, I used my new walk to go with Malcolm to meet a client of his, down on Pennsylvania Avenue. Or "The Avenue" as it was more commonly known back in the sixties before integration camouflaged a crock-pot full of assorted half-baked nuts and passed it off as "The Great American Melting Pot."

My father told me that The Avenue was the strip as far as black folks in Baltimore were concerned, although not everyone possessed the stamina and heart required to hang out there on a regular basis. It was a rough and dangerous place, but even with the drug dealers, the murders, the pimps and the prostitutes who called The Avenue home, it still pulsated with prestige and excitement. His eyes glittered with the memory of shiny Cadillacs and Thunderbirds lining the street, and he raved about the stylishly dressed black men and women cluttering the sidewalks, all out to celebrate having made it through another frustrating, degrading, agonizing, oppressive work week with their souls still intact.

He said that inside the popular Sphinx Club sweat dripped from dancing brows as the smooth voice of Otis Redding wrestled with smoke drifting up from cigarettes burning between fingers and lips, or left unattended and dying in tiny tin ash trays. Women, my mother included, were draped in sequined mini dresses, sitting proudly and seductively at the tables inside Club Casino, accepting glasses of Johnnie Walker Red and Seagram's Gin from handsome gentlemen, who coolly tiptoed over to them with their hats slightly cocked to one side for the purposes of shading half of their faces as well as their intentions.

The Regent theater was where the sounds of the crisp, buttery crunch of popcorn gave way to the shotgun blasts, love scenes, and fistfights in the latest Sidney Poitier, Clint Eastwood, and John Wayne movies. The walls of the Royal Theater used to vibrate with shouts and applause as big stars such as James Brown, Ray Charles, and Ethel Ennis performed their latest hit songs.

Now most of that was gone.

It was the great migration to the recently desegregated downtown department stores, restaurants, movie houses and the strip clubs on the infamous Baltimore Street, better known as "The Block" that brought a sad end to The Avenue's heyday, leaving its dreary nights to the pro-black, the apathetic and the too-old-for-change people who remained. And as I strolled down the street, I found it almost impossible to believe that this crime ridden, fallout shelter used to be "the joint" back in the day.

Malcolm's client owned a used appliance store that had old stoves, refrigerators, washing machines, and dryers sitting outside on the sidewalk. Malcolm said that he would be a while, so I decided to do a little sightseeing. I walked up the street and saw a book in the display window of a bookstore called "Knowledge." The title of the book was *The Blacker the Berry: The History of Black Art*, and its front cover had a photograph of a sculpture that depicted a young African man kneeling down on the ground in front of a human skull. His head was slightly tilted and his mouth was open as if he were talking to the skull, which appeared to be looking dead in his eyes as it listened and talked back to him.

The piece reminded me of Hazel Cherrylane's skull. Dr. Zimmerman had sent me a postcard from Kuwait, telling me about his visit to the oil fields, and of course asking if I'd started reconstructing Hazel's face. I felt like I was letting him down because, in spite of the practice skull I'd done, I still couldn't bring myself to sculpt her.

The store had several ceiling high bookcases brimming with novels, short story collections, nonfiction, poetry, and children's books, the majority of which were written by, for, and about blacks. I was making my way up the aisle, looking for the art section, when I heard this voice float over and tap me on the ear. It was a woman's voice. Contralto but soft, like a flute. Full of allurement and confidence, very strong and somewhat magnetic, and it gave me no choice except to follow her words.

The woman was standing behind a glass counter, ringing up sales, and talking to a man, who, along with the fifteen or so customers standing in line, was blocking my view of her.

He was a tall, flat and square, red-skinned man with glasses and sandy-brown dreadlocks. He was loud and animated, moving his hands every time he spoke. "Look, my Sistah, Malcolm X said, 'By any means necessary.'"

"That's true, my Brothah," she said in a joking manner. "But Malcolm also said that we need education if we plan on going anywhere in this world. So you see, he wasn't just referring to the use of violence. I think he wanted us to educate ourselves and use our brains more so than our fists or guns."

Some of the customers nodded in agreement.

The dreadlock man sucked his teeth. "There you go jumping on that education bit again. You think education is the key to everything."

"No, but I do believe that it will open more doors for us."

Rubbing his beard as if he had one up on her, he said, "Well, try telling that to Yusef Hawkins or Eleanor Bumpurs. What doors is all this education opening for them in Heaven?" He waved his hands across the sky.

The few customers he had on his side agreed with mumbles, but she hushed them with, "Their deaths are very educational in that they have opened black eyes that have been closed for a long time."

The dreadlock man sucked his teeth again. "Sistah, it's time for a revolution and not no intellectual one."

"But without intellect we're all muscles and no brains, and reacting without first analyzing and intelligently preparing for the situation will definitely lead to our self-destruction."

"That's the bourgie in you talkin'," he said in disgust.

They went on like that for a few more minutes. I felt myself drowning in the sweet sound of her confident voice. The line grew shorter and shorter, and soon he was the only person preventing me from seeing the woman whose provocative voice held me spellbound.

"Will you please move your Black Power, dreadlock ass out of the way," I mumbled to myself.

Finally, he drifted to his left, and that's when I got my first glimpse of perfection. She was darker than blue-black and had thick, silky, brown hair that was permed and cut into a short bob. She had full lips, high cheekbones and tea-colored eyes that seemed to be laughing even though she wasn't smiling at the moment. She covered her slim, shapely body in a yellow and white pants suit.

She was absolutely gorgeous.

"Excuse me, Sistah," I heard someone say. "Can I help you with anything?"

It took me a second to realize that I was the "Sistah" the male voice was referring to. The crowd had thinned out, and I was left naked, openly glaring at this sensual woman, who was now curiously staring at me. I quickly turned from her and peered into the face of the dreadlock man. I frowned as I struggled to recall what he'd just said.

"Can I help you with anything?" he repeated.

"Ah, no. I was just looking."

He smiled and then walked away. By now the store was virtually empty. There were only three other customers besides myself, and two of them were at the counter with their purchases. I kept sneaking glances at the sales woman, but stopped after we'd locked eyes four times. I felt stupid just standing there, so I grabbed a book and went up to the counter.

"Will this be all?" she asked, politely.

She was so enthralling that I found myself just staring at her again, speechless.

She smiled as her dark brown eyes scanned my body. We gazed at each other, transfixed by a silence that spoke only to us.

"Satin," the dreadlock man called, disrupting the quiet. She turned and answered.

"I'm gonna run up the street and get a sandwich. You want anything?"

"No thanks," she said.

"All right. I'll be right back," he said, and hurried out the door.

Satin rung up my purchase, tore off a receipt, then put it in the bag with the book. "Thank you," she said.

I smiled then turned to leave. I heard Satin come from behind the counter. Clack! Clack! Clack! Clack! She was wearing a pair of yellow, 3" high-heels, and the sweet, wonderful sound of her walk in them paralyzed me. I watched Satin's feet as she clacked past me over to the display window. Her gait was assured and sensual. When Satin saw me standing there, she flashed a smile that caused my heart to pound like someone beating a drum. I lowered my head, ashamed and frightened that she could hear how excited I was getting just by being around her.

Sensing that I would welcome her forwardness, Satin placed her hand under my chin and lifted my face. Her thumb traced and retraced a soft circle on my chin. It made me dizzy, embarrassed, and somewhat suspicious of her intentions and my own. She seemed to sense these things on my skin somehow, and so she removed her hand with an understanding smile. I hadn't felt such a connection with a woman since....

Interrupting our unspoken conversation, Satin said, "You have one of the loveliest dark-skinned faces I have ever seen." She smiled brightly.

"Don't deprive me of the pleasure of looking at it by keeping it lowered to the ground, Tonya Mimms."

She knows my name, I thought. But I didn't stick around long enough to find out how or why. I just ran out of the store thinking--Malcolm's probably looking for me.

I couldn't get Satin out of my mind. I saw her in my sleep, and had an aching need to touch her silky, tar-black skin. I reached out, but she smiled and then vanished at the tip of my grasp. I heard her voice in the deepest silence, and my body trembled from its softness. I barely knew her name and yet I admired her, had hardly spent any time with her and yet I missed her. One night her image drove me from my bed, and I stayed up until six in the morning sketching her to keep her from disappearing. Two and a half days later, I had completed a sculpture of her.

I was sitting under the iron stairs, staring at her portrait when I heard a now familiar knock on my studio door. Malcolm. I got up from the wobbly stool, covered Satin's sculpture with a dark green plastic bag, then let him in.

Malcolm looked at my hands, which were covered in clay. "Been working on Hazel?"

"No," I said, walking over to my workbench.

I pretended that I'd been putting the finishing touches on my sculpture of a black man and woman wrapped in a blanket as they lay on the top of a grassy hill. The man in the piece was sleeping, but the woman was wide-awake looking down at her man like she'd found the meaning for her life.

Malcolm's eyes took a hold of the piece. He saw what most men saw in the eyes of a virgin after they had sweet-talked her into the back seat of a car, onto a living room couch, into the nearest bed, and had with just one thrust sent her red, liquidity girlhood dripping out of her onto the metal seat belt, between the scratchy cushions, or on the stiff cotton sheets. But Malcolm didn't wipe himself off and run like some men. He moved closer and put his hands on it.

"This must be great," Malcolm said, fingering the blanket.

"What?" I asked.

"Being able to see your thoughts. Most people can't even say or write down on a piece of paper what it is they feel or think. But you can create something that tells people right up front what you want and expect out of life. That's got to be great."

"Are you most people?" I asked him.

"Sometimes," he said.

"Well, sometimes this isn't so great. Most people don't have the patience to stand around looking at some sculpture trying to figure out how I feel about them. It's easier to move on and find someone who will tell them right off the bat to call them later or take a hike."

Malcolm said, "People like that don't have the patience because they aren't looking for you to feel anything about them. They're looking for you to have a good time."

"What about you?" I asked. "What are you looking for?"

"I'm not sure." Malcolm sat down on the stool in front of the sculpture. "But I have all the time in the world to figure it out," he said. "And while I'm doing that, shouldn't you be working on Hazel?"

How can I when ever since you brought me that glass of water I've been daydreaming about us getting married in early November while there are still warm breezes blowing and the city is being showered in yellow, brown, orange, and burgundy leaves? I thought. Just like Aunt Josephine's and Uncle Charlie's wedding.

But I said, "I'm not ready to deal with that yet."

Malcolm took my hands and held them against his chest. "You know why? Because you can't see her as a living person."

"That's because she's dead."

Malcolm walked me over to the window. "Out there, physically, biologically, yes, she is very much dead. But in this room you can make her alive mentally and spiritually."

"How?"

"Research," he said, and went over to the shelf that held my *Presidents of War* series. "I'm sure that before you attempted to sculpt any of these men you did your research. You learned as much about them as you could. Do the same with Hazel. Find out all you can about her. Make her alive in your heart and in your mind, and I'll bet you a dollar that you'll be able to sculpt her."

A dollar? He wanted me to touch a dead girl's head just to win a dollar bet. He must have been out of his mind. I must have been too because I spent the next couple of days downtown in the microfilm department of the Enoch Pratt Free Library photocopying and reading news articles that appeared in the *Baltimore Sun* paper about Hazel Cherrylane's disappearance. Her grade school picture stayed on the front page for several weeks. After a month, it was moved inside to the front page of the Maryland section for a couple of weeks then disappeared. She didn't look anything like I'd imagined a Hazel to look. She was prettier. She had curly red hair and green eyes. Her face was long and dotted with bright brown freckles. She had a long, pointy nose, thin lips, and small ears. She wasn't smiling in the photo, and she appeared posed and uncomfortable, not herself. This picture gave me the perfect physical description of Hazel, but I needed more.

So after reading, highlighting, underlining, and circling the words her family used to describe her, I went to see Mr. and Mrs. Cherrylane. Marshall Cherrylane, a short, chokehold red tractor-trailer driver, showed me a picture of Hazel wearing a pink dress. "Her favorite color," he said. In this photograph, Hazel looked totally different from the one in the paper. She looked natural and alive with laughter, innocence, and mischief fueled by curiosity. She was laughing and running as she looked down at the ground as though she were being chased by something.

"Her shadow," Mrs. Cherrylane said.

Joan Cherrylane, a thin, sickly housewife, had been sitting on the couch, silent. Not looking at her husband, the wall, or me. Just had her mournful green eyes open because she was awake and had a visitor.

"Hazel was always tryin' to run from her shadow," she said, now focusing on the picture. "I kept tellin' her that it was part of her so there was no way that she was ever gonna shake it. Told her that no matter how far you run, yourself is always three steps ahead, cheerin' you on."

Maybe she saw something in her shadow that she didn't want to be a part of her, I thought.

Staring at the photo, I asked, "Can I borrow this for a while?"

Mr. Cherrylane looked at his wife, who nodded.

Before I left Mr. Cherrylane took me up to Hazel's bedroom, which Mrs. Cherrylane cleaned and straightened once a week as though Hazel were still there making a mess. It was painted pink and had Bugs Bunny posters, toys, and stuffed animals all around, some of which had been bought recently. There was a Bugs Bunny night-light on the dresser. "Hazel is afraid of the dark," Mr. Cherrylane told me.

I went back to my studio and did several drawings of Hazel from the two photographs. I sketched her eyes, ears, mouth, and nose on separate pieces of paper so that I could get a good feel for what she looked liked. Then I sketched her face intact.

I needed all of that to make myself at ease with her. She didn't quite feel alive to me, but she no longer felt dead either. To bring her closer to life for me, I asked Malcolm to move some shelves around in my studio and help me paint one wall pink. I then took the box that held Hazel's skull off my desk and set it on my workbench beside a stuffed Bugs Bunny I'd bought. Then to the pink wall I taped a copy of the photo from the newspaper, the picture of her running, and all the drawings I'd done of her. And from then on, before leaving my studio for the day, I turned on the night-light that I'd also purchased for her.

The pictures on the pink wall, the stuffed Bugs Bunny, and the night-light helped me to see her as Hazel instead of a cold skull, but I still wasn't ready to face her. But I was ready to face someone else.

The dreadlock man smiled when I entered Knowledge.

"Hello again, Sistah," he said, making his way from behind the counter.

"Hello," I said back.

He had a heavy smile on his face that could only mean that he knew who I was too.

"Looking for anything in particular?" he asked.

I peeked around his string bean frame, searching for Satin, but she didn't seem to be in. "Where is your art section?" I asked.

My question seemed to confirm that I was indeed who Satin had told him I was. He nodded knowingly, expectantly as he said, "Right over here."

I followed him to the center of the store. He stopped and pointed. "Now if you need anything else just call." He kind of waited around smiling before leaving to assist another customer.

I searched the shelves until I found the book that had the photo of the sculpture depicting the African man talking to the skull. As I was flipping through the pages, trying to find the piece, a tantalizing fragrance filled the air around me. Jasmine, I thought as I buried my nose in the scent. Sweet, yellow Jasmine.

"The blacker the berry," a woman's voice said.

I turned, and Satin was standing beside me. I'd heard what she'd said, even knew that it was the title of the book I was holding, but the unadulterated essence of her prohibited me from responding verbally. All I could do was simply look at her with a big question mark on my face as I tried to slow down my heart rate.

"The book in your hand."

"Oh, yeah." I looked down at the first part of the title and read it aloud. "*The Blacker The Berry.*"

"The sweeter the juice. If it ain't got no soul, it ain't got no use," Satin said, completing what I didn't know was a phrase. A phrase that Satin's voice would never allow me to forget.

"When I was in here the other day, you said my name. Have we met?" I asked, though I was sure that I would have remembered meeting someone who looked like her.

"No," she said. "But I feel like we have. I've read a lot about you."

Read about me? I thought. As I asked myself why, a sly tongue started making circles around my navel. But I didn't put my hand over it. I just tried to ignore it and pretend that I didn't like it.

"And," Satin continued, "I have one of your pieces at home."

"Really?" I asked, flattered that she had purchased my work.

Satin's face eased into a smile. "Your work is absolutely wonderful. The way that you highlight the incidentals of life and make them essentials is simply incredible."

Although I already felt and knew that my work was wonderful, it was just that the word laced in her breath made me feel wonderful all over.

"You're in that book, you know."

I raised the book in my hand. "This one?"

She nodded then turned to page 54 and there I was. It was great reading about myself in the pages of a book on black art. None of the hundreds of art history books that I'd read at AAI featured black artists. It was almost as if black artists didn't exist, or worse, had nothing to contribute to the art world.

In *The Blacker The Berry*, an art history professor named Floyd Lewis had written my biography. He praised me but at the same time he criticized me for embracing white themes and culture in my work. "It's a shame," he wrote, "that such a great talent is failing to set the historical record straight."

I was used to criticism, but this was the first time that I'd read the words "a shame" in association with my work. Oddly enough the criticism reminded me of the shameful feeling that came over me when Malcolm and I were standing inside the slave ship at The Great Blacks in Wax Museum.

Seeing the discomfort on my face, Satin asked, "So I take that you didn't know that you were in that book?"

"No," I said, trying now to act as if I wasn't upset. "I was actually looking in it for this piece," I said, turning to the front cover.

"Oh, *Talking Skull*," she said, taking the book.

"You know the work?"

"Yes!" she said, passionately. She turned to a page that had a black and white picture of an attractive, light-skinned, serious-looking black woman. Her thick black hair was tied into a bun and she was wearing an elegant late 19th century style dress.

"Meta Vaux Warrick Fuller," Satin said. "She was around before, during, and well after the Harlem Renaissance. She studied with Rodin."

"Auguste Rodin?" I asked, feeling like an idiot for asking such a stupid question.

"They were friends. She studied under him for at least a year in Paris. She was an extremely talented and provocative sculptor. She was intrigued by death; it was a central theme in a number of her compositions. She executed *Talking Skull* in 1937, and it is one of her most celebrated pieces."

Satin turned to the page that had the photograph of the sculpture then handed the book back to me. "You should go to The Museum of Afro-American History in Boston some time so that you can see it in person."

"Have you seen it?" I asked.

She nodded. "Twice."

I sighed as I looked at the picture of the bronze sculpture. "Well, I'm ashamed to say that this is the first I've ever heard of her and her work."

Satin said, "Don't waste your energy being ashamed! Use it to become familiar with these marvelous artists. Yourself included."

With her gold bracelets jingling on her thin wrists and the hem of her dress floating a tad above her knees, Satin showed me several books on black art that surprisingly had my work in them. I was happy to read that not all black art critics thought that I was failing to record the black experience. Some actually said that my European influences helped me to clearly illustrate how whites viewed blacks and how blacks viewed whites.

Satin provided information about Elizabeth Catlett, Augusta Savage, Richmond Barthe, and other black artists of whose existence I was oblivious to a day ago. It was refreshing learning about them and about myself, but I paid more attention to Satin licking her rum raisin colored lips and seductively lifting her thick eyebrows when she noticed my eyes sinking into the richness of her skin.

I brought a few art books, and as she rung up my purchases, we talked about Knowledge.

"I opened the store when I moved here from New Orleans about ten years ago," Satin told me. "Alan Huss," she pointed out the dreadlock man, "and I are co-owners."

Leaning on the counter, I asked, "Was it difficult opening the store?"

"Extremely. Most of the banks we went to did not want to risk investing in a bookstore dedicated to black readers because, after all, statistics say that blacks don't read."

"How were you finally able to finance it?" I asked.

"We received funding from an agency that specializes in small business loans for minorities and my parents along with a few friends lent financial support as well." She tore off my receipt and handed it to me. "And in spite of those statistics, Knowledge is doing very well."

Gradually, as if we'd come to the end of the first chapter in a book, our dialogue ceased. Once again, we stood intrigued with each other, with me wanting to flip ahead to chapters sixteen and seventeen to find out why I was there; and Satin gently closing the cover, her brown eyes saying that I'd have to slowly reread chapter one if I wanted to even vaguely understand the various complex reasons we had been drawn to each other.

For four days straight, while Malcolm was at work and Hazel Cherrylane sat alone and faceless in my studio, I went to Knowledge and brought books on black art and artists and spent hours picking Satin's brain about the Harlem Renaissance and the '60's Black Arts Movement. But what I really went back to do was to get answers to questions that I was terrified to ask even in the darkest, deepest, most private parts of my mind.

On the fourth day that I walked into Knowledge, Satin invited me out to lunch. She and I got into her red Camaro and went to an Ethiopian restaurant on Charles Street. I sat in the passenger seat peeking at her out of the corner of my eye, thinking that there was something exciting about seeing Satin behind the wheel of that automobile with her sunglasses on, one hand confidently holding the steering wheel, the other coolly gripping the stick-shift.

The restaurant was bright and comfortable with black and African art decorating its walls. It had small tables with glass tops, a thick fog of incense pervading the air and a mixture of Ethiopian and reggae music playing. There were two floors. We asked to be seated on the second level. Since I'd never been to an Ethiopian restaurant, Satin ordered for both of us. She asked for a chicken dish for herself and for me a beef dish, the name of which ended with the word Fitfit.

As we waited for our food, we talked about black artists, novelists, poets, and playwrights. She explained that I wasn't entirely to blame for my lack of knowledge in these areas. I was extremely nervous, so I fiddled with things--the tiny salt and peppershakers, the straw in my glass of iced tea, and the pink, cloth napkin on my lap. Anything that would keep her from noticing how badly my hands were shaking.

"The society in which we live is constructed in such a way as to keep us ignorant about ourselves and our history," Satin said, watching my fingers turn the saltshaker around and around. "Knowledge is power. Knowledge is the sledgehammer that can level any wall of ignorance, regardless of its height or density. That's one of the main reasons why I struggled relentlessly to open Knowledge, because it is the key."

As she spoke I thought about the critic who accused me of failing to set the historical record straight. I had planned on inviting her to my opening but was reluctant because it didn't seem to have anything to do with what she was talking about or who she was.

But then Satin said, "Contrary to semi popular belief, your work doesn't write us out of history. It marks a certain attitude about that history, which is just as important."

My God, she is something! I thought.

Our waitress returned carrying a basket that had two warm, wet towels. I looked to Satin for guidance. She smiled and took one and started wiping her hands.

Oh! I thought and did the same.

Next the waitress sat a large metal tray on our table then filled it with a nice green salad, cabbage and carrots. She placed the beef, onions, red and green peppers on my side of the tray and the chicken smothered in a red sauce on Satin's. She then placed a basket of Ethiopian bread beside me. Again I looked at Satin, who picked up a piece of the bread and then used it to dip the food off the tray. "Dig in," she said.

"Oh, so that's why we have to wash our hands," I said.

"Yes. People literally have their hands in your plate."

This was the strangest and greatest tasting meal I'd ever eaten. Sharing a meal in this manner wasn't for the shy or nervous. Satin didn't have any problem crossing over to eat my beef dish, but as badly as I wanted to taste her chicken, I couldn't bring myself to reach over to her side of the tray with my bread.

"Um!" Satin said, scooping up a chunk of chicken between a piece of bread. "You've got to taste this."

She held it out to me. But the way that she only stretched her arm halfway across the tray made me feel as if she were offering something more than a bite of her food. Satin had a slight grin on her lips and a stillness in her eyes, a grin and stillness that made me wonder as I hesitantly leaned forward, what it was that I was really accepting from her. Whatever it was I couldn't resist it. I parted my lips. Satin, moving slowly and provocatively, placed the food in my mouth. Once my lips closed, I shut my eyes and savored the food as well as the sugary taste that the tips of Satin's fingers left on my tongue.

The chicken was delicious but a little too spicy for me. It sizzled on my tongue and my forehead and cheeks began to perspire. The heat from the well-seasoned food opened the pores on my chest and sweat ran down between my breasts. When the spices reached the back of my throat and began to burn, I grabbed my glass of water and gulped it down.

"I guess I should have warned you," Satin said.

"Yes, you should have," I said, placing my empty glass back on the table.

She was smiling now, knowing that a warning would have only made the food between her fingers more irresistible. I wanted to do the same thing to her. Give her something that she couldn't possibly resist. So I said with a knowing, wicked grin of my own, "My opening is next week. Would you like to come?"

Satin tilted her head and smiled as if to say--*You play dirty. I like that.*

11

The night of my opening I got the distinct feeling that Satin had it in her to play just as dirty as I could. The early June evening was clear, warm, but a bit breezy. The Baltimore Museum of Art was buzzing with accolades, positive energy, and insightful criticisms and interpretations, all centered around my *Dear North, Dear South* exhibit. And it was just as Dr. Zimmerman had predicted--art critics viewed this exhibit as my most important work to date. It consisted of twenty Union and Confederate soldiers writing and reading letters to and from their families while sitting outside or inside a tent, resting against a tree, lying in a trench, straddling a horse, leaning against a cannon, and standing beside a mass grave. On the walls of the museum were reprints of real letters written by and to soldiers before, during, and after the battles at Gettysburg, Antietam, Bull Run slash Manassas, and Cold Harbor.

But instead of reveling in the great responses to my work, I was biting my fingernails, drinking glass after glass of champagne, and keeping my anxious eyes on the door for Satin, who was over an hour late, and my fascinated ears fixed on my mother and Mrs. Holland.

Two nights before the exhibit, Malcolm's mother phoned and demanded to meet the woman who was responsible for her not being able to reach her son for the past three weeks. Malcolm suggested we all have dinner. I suggested that his parents come to my opening, although to tell the truth I wasn't all that eager to meet his mother. My experiences with the few guys who'd introduced me to their mothers left me believing that mothers raised their daughters, loved their sons, and hated any woman their boys got involved with, even more so if the woman was anything like them.

Malcolm was without a doubt a mama's boy, which meant that life with him could be difficult if his mother and I didn't get along. So I had to make his mother not only like me but love me, and the only way to do that was to meet her on my turf. Dinner with his parents at their favorite restaurant or at Malcolm's house would have given his mother the upper hand, but at my opening, I'd be confident and in control.

Malcolm was nervous about meeting my family, but I wasn't. In fact, I could hardly wait to show him off to them. Since moving out on my own, I could have counted on one hand the number of men I'd introduced to my parents. The truth of the matter was after high school I'd never kept a man in my bed long enough to warrant or justify his meeting my parents or my meeting his. I hadn't slept with a lot of men, but I'd slept with enough to make my parents, my mother especially, worry about my health and, uh, my...reputation if they'd met all of the men who had nudged my legs apart with their knees. My mother worked damned hard to make sure that people didn't gossip about her daughters' loose morals behind our backs or hers. And I wasn't about to have my one night or seven-to-ten nightstands tell her that all of her warnings, yells and prayers were for nothing. But because I was in love with Malcolm I didn't feel like I was letting my mother down by bringing him home, so to speak.

My mother studied Malcolm and from the twitch of her bottom lip, I guessed that she knew two things: one, that I'd slept with him, and two, that he was someone very special to me. And it was the latter that allowed her to overlook and, if not forget, at least to forgive the first.

"You know, Malcolm," my mother said, "there was a time when my daughters wouldn't have been able to date someone without my knowledge and approval."

Malcolm started to answer, but his mother said, "I know what you mean."

Clarice Holland was a reddish-brown, tall, and thick-boned woman with the same smiling dimples as Malcolm. Her voice was full and pleasant and her mannerisms were graceful and motherly. She wore an elegant, black dress that would have showed off her heavy shoulders if she hadn't covered them with a white sash. She had an overawing beauty that urged you to approach her with caution, and that would have been easy enough to do if I hadn't found this sense of danger creatively arousing instead of daunting.

"Tonya," Mrs. Holland said, "you're the first woman that my son has dated without my knowing anything about it or you."

I was all set to explain to Mrs. Holland that Malcolm and I had just met and so we saw no reason to introduce each other to our parents, but I saw that Mrs. Holland wasn't really speaking to me. She was speaking to my mother. And my mother wasn't speaking to Malcolm; she was speaking to Mrs. Holland. It was the weirdest fight I'd ever heard. Two overprotective mothers going at it with words that were underneath the words that actually came out of their mouths. My mother believed that I, her inexperienced daughter, was fresh meat for a man like Malcolm, who had obviously been around the block a few times. Mrs. Holland didn't believe that her son, who had just gotten out of but not over a bad relationship, was ready to deal with a woman like me, who had been around the world more than once.

"Your work is phenomenal," Mrs. Holland said. "But I hear that art is a very jealous mistress, so you can't possibly have much time for family." So you can't have much time for my son should he be *foolish* enough to get involved with you, Mrs. Holland did not say. But she looked it.

"Oh, I don't know," my mother said. "She has just about as much time for her family as a successful accountant who also moonlights has for his." So get off my *child's* back, my mother didn't say. Oh, but did she look it.

During this whole thing my father and Mr. Holland watched the two women with little interest. My father would never admit this but he wanted sons. He could have related to them better. He could have talked to them, hung out with them, drank beers with them. But what was he supposed to do with two girls? They cried at the drop of a hat. They broke easily. They had that monthly thing. And they had boys, lots and lots of boys buzzing around them like bees around a tree full of honey. He was certain that he'd end up in jail behind his daughters and those boys. And since he didn't know what to do with us and didn't think that it would be fair to have a jailbird for a father, he left us to my mother.

Robert Holland was a man of ease and strength, handsomely light brown with a scar over his left eyebrow, which made you notice his heavy, brown eyes. His hands were rough, strong, and dependable, his voice deep and hard, and his language straight and to the point, and his walk fearless, controlled...manly. His masculinity was not an act or affectation, and it wasn't macho. It was real, smooth, natural, in a word-- him. And it was easy to see that Malcolm was more this man's man than Malcolm was his own.

So my father and Mr. Holland were men who didn't see the point in getting involved in their wives' cat fight. They distanced themselves from it with the cold superior stance that showed they believed that men were above such foolishness, and didn't indulge in or encourage this woman's game by listening to it. Especially since by the end of the night they would be the best of friends. And they were right. After ten minutes of trying to verbally scratch each other's eyes out, Mrs. Holland happened to mention something about having a hysterectomy after Malcolm was born and my mother told her about her miscarriages. Then Mrs. Holland talked about how long she'd been waiting for Malcolm to find a nice girl to settle down with and--

"Give you some grandchildren," my mother chimed in.

Of all the things my mother wanted, she wanted nothing more than to be a grandmother, and she couldn't believe that neither of her daughters had settled down and given her this one simple request. My mother was a wonderful mother, and I knew that she would have made an even greater grandmother. She had those small, soft hands that were specifically designed for playing a game of "Patty Cake." Her full lips were just the right size for kissing away "boo-boos." Her arms had just the right tenderness for giving loving, spoiling hugs, and her soft choir voice was low enough to sing sweet lullabies.

And just like that our mothers went from defending us to complaining about us.

My mother said, "Tonya's too much like her father. Work, work, work. I'll never get any grandchildren if she doesn't find a man that can get her out of the studio every once in a while."

"Malcolm's got his head all up in a cloud full of numbers," Mrs. Holland said. "I don't know how many times I've told him that he'll never get married if he doesn't stop looking for a woman who adds up nice and neat. That when it comes to women, two plus two will never equal four. Eight or nine maybe, depending on the mood she's in, but never four. Now your Tonya might be the girl who will pull him down out of that cloud."

"Well, Malcolm's gotten her out of that studio a few times. So..."

So the two women put their heads together and had decided that if they played their children's card right, they could get a wedding and some grandchildren out of this, by next year. Mrs. Holland smiled at me as if she were sizing me up for a wedding gown, and my mother was smiling at me as if tonight meant that I was going to finally make her wish for grandchildren come true. Suddenly I began to feel pressure from my relationship with Malcolm where there had been none before. Yes, I wanted to get married and have children, but not right now.

The two mothers' smiles were crushing me. I felt like I was losing my breath. I needed air but the weight from their curved lips and the white of their teeth held me so that I couldn't move. If I didn't get out from between those smiles, I feared that I would loose consciousness and fall out on the floor.

Then, as if on cue, Nikki's voice squeezed between the smiles and rescued me. "Tonya," she said, coming up to me with Elaine in tow.

Elaine always came to my openings because she used them as a way to be with and talk to Nikki, because calling or coming to see Nikki in the house that she and Nikki would have been sharing if it weren't for me was out of the question.

"There's a woman out in the lobby for you," Nikki said. "She said her name is Satin Pierce."

I'd never been so glad to see Nikki in all my life. I exhaled and hugged her then quickly excused myself. What a relief, I thought as I looked back and saw my mother and Mrs. Holland closing in on Malcolm.

When I walked out to the lobby, I saw that the security guard was outside taking a cigarette break and that Satin was standing with her back to me admiring a painting on the wall. She was wearing an elegant, plum evening dress with matching heels and purse. I didn't let her know that I was behind her. I wanted to watch her without her watching me.

Watching Satin like that reminded me of a night I'd seen my father and mother doing something totally impractical and careless. He and my mother snuck downstairs, and while my mother giggled, my father put on *"Oh, What A Night"* by The "Mighty, Mighty" Dells. I lay down at the top of the stairs peeking through the railing as my father took my mother in his arms. And they didn't dance like they had two teen-aged daughters upstairs asleep. They danced as if they were the only two people in the world. I watched them until *"Stay In My Corner"* started playing. That's when I heard my father's deep, sleek voice nudging up against my mother's laughter like an old lover who knew that she was about to let him get over. I quietly got up and went back to bed.

As I was thinking about that and staring at Satin, I heard Aunt Josephine sing out of nowhere, "Hey, Love."

I jerked my head in the direction of her voice and there was the security guard holding the door open as Aunt Josephine came in with Uncle Charlie. Satin turned around and smiled, aware now that I must have been watching her. I swallowed hard as I tried to collect myself, but that became difficult to do after Aunt Josephine hugged and kissed me then said, "How you doing, Nikki?"

I spun around and saw Nikki standing behind me. How long she'd been there, I didn't know. I also didn't know why she was watching me watch Satin.

Nikki hugged Aunt Josephine but she kept her eyes on me as I went over and greeted Satin.

"You look familiar," Aunt Josephine said to Satin after I'd introduced them.

"I do?" Satin asked.

"Yeah. I know we've never met before, but I feel as if I know you from somewhere," Aunt Josephine said, studying her closely.

Nikki was studying me, and I wondered to myself, Why in God's name is she staring at me like I've committed a crime? First you spy on me. Now you're staring at me like I went behind your back and started a new friendship. But I didn't. I just forgot to tell you about her. What? Am I required by law to tell you about every Thelma, Dana, and Satin that I meet on the street?

The more Nikki stared the angrier I got until somehow it dawned on me that Nikki was just curious. She knew all of my friends and I knew all of hers. Nikki just wanted to know who Satin was. That's all. What else could it be?

Remembering that Aunt Josephine and Uncle Charlie still spent some Friday and Saturday nights down at the Arch Social Club, I said, "Maybe you've seen Satin on The Avenue. She has a bookstore down there."

"Who has a bookstore down where?" Malcolm asked as he came out to the lobby.

He kissed me and put his arm around my waist.

"Well, well, well," Aunt Josephine said. "Who's this?"

I'd told Malcolm all about Aunt Josephine, talking endlessly about her high heels, the clothes she wore, the scar on her knee, and the way that she called me "Love." Tonight Aunt Josephine was wearing an orange suit, with a back slit on the skirt, and orange high heels. She was as irresistible at age forty-nine as she had when she was thirty. Uncle Charlie was wearing a gray pinstriped suit. Even after twenty-one years of marriage he still was gawking at Aunt Josephine as if she'd just walked into his store.

Malcolm hardly believed that such a woman existed until he'd laid eyes on her scarred knee himself and instantly fell head over her high heels in love with her too.

"I'm Malcolm, and you must be Aunt Josephine."

"The one and only, Sweetheart."

Malcolm gave Aunt Josephine a warm hug and said, "Tonya tells me that you're a pretty feisty driver."

"*Feisty?*" she asked, noting the feminine spin.

"Yeah. Where did such a beautiful woman learn to drive like that?"

"My Uncle Chester. He was a bootlegger," Aunt Josephine said. "He supplied half of Mullins with its booze."

"Oh, so he taught you to drive when he took you on some of his runs?" Malcolm asked.

"No. My Aunt Lilly did. She was his wife and his driver," Aunt Josephine said with a smile.

Embarrassment pulled Malcolm's head to the floor.

"Now, dear," Aunt Josephine said and put her arm in his, "take your foot out of your mouth and come and tell me all about yourself while we look at Love's masterpieces."

Malcolm laughed and went with Aunt Josephine, who winked at me as they walked away. Nikki and Uncle Charlie went with them.

"Sorry I'm late," Satin said. "But I had to drive a friend to the airport."

"That's okay," I said. "I'm just glad you could make it."

I took Satin inside, and when I went to get her a glass of wine, I saw my mother and Mrs. Holland's heads together, no doubt comparing notes about what each knew about Malcolm and me. I tried to hide in the crowd, but my mother spotted me and she elbowed Mrs. Holland and the two flew after me. Just as I handed Satin her glass, they sandwiched me with those smiles again.

But before they could grill me, I said, "Ma, Mrs. Holland, I'd like you to meet Satin."

They looked at each other as if to say--*Now she knows darn well we ain't no more interested in this chile than the man on the moon.*

"She owns a bookstore on Pennsylvania Avenue," I said.

That interested them and took their minds off of weddings and grandchildren. Mrs. Holland and Satin got into a discussion about literature and the different authors she'd had at Knowledge for signings, and then my opening turned into a stroll down memory lane. My father and Mr. Holland even joined in and bragged about when they bopped down on the Avenue watching my mother and Mrs. Holland strut their stuff. Their stories and laughter about those times drew the handful of blacks that always attended my exhibits over, and they shared their stories as well. So by the time Aunt Josephine, Uncle Charlie, and Malcolm came back from viewing the exhibit, we were surrounded in laughter.

Everybody was having a good time. It was the best opening I'd ever had.

I was standing in between Aunt Josephine and Malcolm, who was talking with Satin. While talking with Aunt Josephine, I tilted my head so that I could listen in on their conversation.

"You're just about the only person that I haven't met or been told about," Malcolm said to Satin.

"Actually, you were told a little something about me. I'm the 'who' that owns a bookstore down on Pennsylvania Avenue."

Remembering the question he'd asked earlier, Malcolm realized, "You were out in the lobby. Oh, I'm sorry. I normally don't overlook people that easily."

"No need to apologize. It happens all the time," Satin said.

"I doubt that," he said with a flirtatious smile, as if admitting that he thought Satin was attractive. And I'm sure that if he were still the dog he told me he was back in his early twenties, he would have hit on her, if only to see if she would go for him.

"So are you a relative or friend?"

"A fan on her way to becoming a friend," Satin told him.

"How long have you known Tonya?"

"I've known of her since 1986, but I met her a little over a week ago."

"Oh, yeah. Where?"

"She wandered into my store."

"That must have been the day that I was up the street meeting with a client."

"Must have been," Satin said.

"Well, it looks like Tonya is new in both our lives. I just met her three weeks ago."

"Three weeks ago?" Satin asked in surprise.

But I couldn't hear anything after that because Aunt Josephine asked loudly, "Love, are you listening to me?"

"Yeah," I said. "Of course. Now what did you say?"

"I said, he's sweet. I like him. He's a little bit of a boring, male chauvinist pig, but you'll change that I'm sure."

"I'm trying," I said, watching him and Satin exchange business cards.

"Your mother's happy for you. So am I. I was beginning to worry about you."

"Worry?" I asked. "For what?"

Aunt Josephine put her arms around me. "Nothing, Love," she sighed. "I'm just happy that you finally found someone. A man, I mean."

I looked at her strangely, wondering, what else could she mean?

"Tonya," Malcolm said. "Satin says that she hasn't seen the exhibit."

"That's right. Your mother and mine cornered me before I could show it to her." I grabbed Satin by the hand. "Come on while the gettin' is good."

Satin walked through the exhibit twice. She took it all in not saying a word. Then, "Family's very important to you."

"What makes you say that?"

"Your work. You could have sculpted these soldiers in a number of settings, but you made a conscious decision to have them reading and writing letters from and to their wives, parents, daughters, or anybody who cared. Keeping the family ties even in the face of death."

I hadn't thought about it quite like that, but she was right. I'd always seen myself as doing Dr. Zimmerman's work. After all, he was the one who insisted that I do the project. But the family letters were my idea. So that made this exhibit more my own than Dr. Zimmerman's. And that made me happy and proud.

Around eleven o'clock, I walked Satin out to her car.

"I had a wonderful time," she said. "Thanks for inviting me. You've made one of my most precious fantasies come true tonight." Her eyes were bright as stars. "I can't tell you how much this means to me to be with you at your opening."

"Well, I'm just glad that you could make it," I said.

"I wouldn't have missed it for the world."

Satin smiled, got in her car, and drove off. I stood out there until her taillights disappeared around the corner. When I went back inside, I found Mrs. Holland waiting for me in the lobby.

"Can I speak with you for a moment?" she asked.

She had that mother look in her eyes. That look that said she would scratch my eyes out if I ever hurt her son. I didn't want to talk to her, didn't feel like being warned or threatened, so it was with great reluctance that I said, "Sure," and sat down on a bench.

"I don't know if Malcolm's told you this," Mrs. Holland said, standing. "He's usually pretty tight-lipped when it comes to his feelings."

"Yes, I know," I said, watching her pace.

"What I'm trying to say is, Malcolm's been through a lot. I'd hate to see him hurt again," Mrs. Holland said, staring down at me helplessly, like a mother who wanted to protect her son from the evils in the world. Staring down at me the way my mother used to when she came into my room at night and said a silent prayer over me.

I stood up, took Mrs. Holland's hand, and looked her in the eye. "I won't hurt him," I told her. "I may at times make him angry enough to smash his fist through a wall, but I'll never hurt him."

12

Satin wanted to see where I worked, where I "created" as she put it. And since she wasn't some guy that I was dating, I didn't see any reason why I couldn't take Satin to my studio. Besides I wanted to show her what I thought of her.

When I opened the door to my studio, the baseball bat fell and rolled across the floor. I quickly picked it up and leaned it against the wall. "Come on in," I said to Satin.

Satin walked through the door as if she were stepping into a dream that she'd had time and time again, a dream that she didn't think would ever come true. She looked at my desk; the shelves lined with portraits, and up at the loft. She went over and placed the palm of her hand on top of my workbench as if it were the site where the miracle of birth took place.

"It's just as I'd imagined it would be," Satin said.

Still, Satin's dream of being in my studio didn't become a reality until I lifted the green plastic bag off the sculpture I'd done of her. Satin parted her lips in surprise.

"It's like looking into a mirror," Satin said touching her face.

I think that was the first time that she'd ever seen herself through someone else's eyes and hands.

"Do you really think that I'm this beautiful?" she asked.

I looked at her and felt her intelligence, sophistication, confidence, and feistiness brightening my studio as if she were holding a piece of the sun behind her back and was waiting for just the right moment to give it to me.

"I think that you are without a doubt the most beautiful woman I have ever sculpted," I blurted out.

Satin's eyes glittered.

"I mean, you're...ah." I tried to correct my statement so that she wouldn't think that I was *funny*, but I didn't know how.

"Thank you," Satin simply said. "Is it finished?"

"No," I said, happy that she'd let me off the hook. "I need to hollow you out so that you'll dry quicker."

"How's that done?"

I spun the table around so that the portrait was facing us, then I used a wire tool to carefully slice her head in two.

Satin watched my every move. "Now what?" she asked eagerly.

"Now I take this," I said, picking up my ribbon tool, "and scoop out the clay until it's a shell. You want to give it a try?"

She hesitated.

"It's easy." I gave her the tool. "Here, let me show you."

I held Satin's hand so that she wouldn't dig out too much clay. This time she was the one peeking at me out of the corner of her eye, but I couldn't tell if she was thinking about me, or the sculpture, or what. But I was thinking about how soft her hands were and how nice her body felt against mine.

As we hollowed out the piece, Satin said, "Three weeks."

"Three weeks?" I turned to see what she was talking about and saw that her eyes were on the portrait of Malcolm.

"You've been seeing him for three weeks."

"Yes."

"I was surprised to hear that."

"Why?"

"Because you never mentioned that you were dating someone."

"It never came up," I said.

"I guess you're right. But now it has."

I stopped scooping long enough to look down at her ringed fingers. "Yes, it has. So what about you? You haven't mentioned anyone. I don't see a wedding ring, but I'm sure that you at least have a boyfriend?"

"No."

"No?" My right eyebrow shot up.

Very smoothly, she said, "No," as if the thought of having a man never entered her mind.

I grabbed her hand and we started digging again. "I find that hard to believe."

"Why? Maybe I don't want a husband or a boyfriend," she said.

"Well, I'm sure that you have someone special that you come home to."

"Yes, I do."

"What's his name?"

Satin helped me dig out two scoops of clay before saying, "Robin." Two more scoops, then, "Her name is Robin."

Her! My mind shouted. Did she say her? Naw, I must have heard her wrong. Misunderstood. I looked at Satin, and her eyes told me that I'd heard her correctly, that nothing had been misunderstood.

I tried not to frown or appear concerned but I didn't pull it off very well.

"Do you have a problem with this, Tonya?"

"No. It's just that I...I ..."

"Didn't expect me to be gay?"

My mouth opened but nothing came out except gasps of air.

"It's okay. A lot of people are shocked when I tell them."

"I'm...I'm not shocked. Surprised maybe, but not shocked." I took the tool out of her hand. "Look, we're getting to the difficult parts so you better stop here."

After she'd enlightened me about her sexuality, I thought that I'd become standoffish. I mean, after all I didn't want Satin to confuse the sisterly bond I was feeling toward her with sexual attraction. But Satin's beauty and affable personality refused to allow my reservations about her lesbianism to destroy our much desired friendship, which had planted its seed, taken root, and begun to blossom in less than an hour.

When I drove Satin back to Knowledge, she said, "I enjoyed learning how to sculpt with you very much, and I would love the opportunity to get together with you again. But I noticed your reaction when I told you that I was gay--"

I interrupted. "Oh, it doesn't really bother me."

"Okay, but I'd still like to state for the record that I'm not the kind of person who forces my lifestyle on anyone. All I want is the chance to get to know the artist that I've admired for years. But I'll understand if you choose not to carry our friendship any further."

Both she and I knew that I would choose to take our friendship just as far as it could go. Just like we both knew that I would wait until I had a perfectly natural, perfectly innocent reason to do so. And what could be more natural and innocent than calling to tell her that her sculpture was almost done. She, in turn, naturally, invited me to dinner to thank me.

Dinner. It sounded innocent enough. Nothing sexual about it at all. That's what I told myself as I made a right onto Carrousel Avenue, a two lane, dead end street. There wasn't a yellow line that divided the street, but it was somehow understood that those coming into Carrousel drove on the left-hand side of the road and those leaving drove on the right.

I drove down the middle of the street to the end of the block, stopping at the last house on the right. I double-checked the address I had written down, even though I saw Satin's car parked in the driveway. I needlessly touched up my makeup and hair in the rearview mirror. When I got out of the car, I adjusted my clothes. I worried myself silly about what to wear. I didn't want to seem as if I'd dressed up. That would give Satin the impression that I was dressing up for her. But I also didn't want to dress too casually. I settled on a white rayon tank top with a long, sleeveless olive-colored vest and full-leg drawstring pants.

Admiring the neatly trimmed lawn and hedges, I slowly walked up the curvy sidewalk that led to her split-level home. Before announcing my arrival by tapping the gold knocker against the black door, I looked at the tall weeping willow standing or rather provocatively posing in the front yard. Its long, yellow branches drooped low enough to tease the blades of grass with light, sweeping kisses from its narrow, pointed green leaves, which made the tree appear as if it were dressed for an evening out on the town. A soft wind made the weeping willow shimmy to a breezy ditty, causing its thick, black shadow to move all around the yard. I fought the urge to run back to my car for my sketchbook.

The inside of Satin's house was just like her, tall and black and laced with African and black culture and history. "Our past is our future," she said, standing in front of a seven-foot tall wooden sculpture of a woman breast feeding her baby.

Her house reminded me of Malcolm's only because it was the total opposite of his place. She kept the lights at a whisper, but the house wasn't dark or dim. It was just one big shadow that quietly showed you all that she thought you needed to know about her. The living room had an aura of mystery and truth staring you directly in the face from the dozen or so portraits of Satin and her lover, Robin, which decorated its mantel and walls.

But the house was deceiving. On the outside, it seemed open and spacious, but inside the house was very closed with doors, lots and lots of doors, and all kinds of corners, nooks and crannies to hide around or in. It was almost like a maze. And I wondered which one of the doors could take me where she didn't want anybody to go. I mean, I was inside of Satin's house, but everything about it kept me outside of her. Especially the music.

Music was in every corner of the house. 36" tall speakers were in all the rooms, even the bathroom. She had a sophisticated stereo system that included a reel-to-reel and a CD player that held 301 CDs. Her extensive music collection consisted of everything--reggae, jazz, rock, blues, rhythm and blues, gospel, zydeco, ragtime, African, Spanish, a little hip-hop, house, club, rap, go-go, classical, country.

"Country?" I asked.

Satin quickly found and put on a video that featured Ella Fitzgerald singing a country song. That was the first time I'd plucked my fingers, nodded my head, and gotten into the groove of a country tune.

The music sounded differently in her house. Or did it feel differently? I couldn't tell, but my whole body grabbed a hold of the music like it was something that I needed to hear. Like it was something I'd been waiting to hear all my life. And it sounded and felt right. Peaceful. But it was all too much for me, so I was on edge.

Satin loved to listen to Sheila E. play the percussions and Stevie Wonder play his harmonica, so she brought any album that featured them. She loved the songs *"Good Morning Heartache,"* and *"Lover Man,"* so she had the album of every singer or musician who'd ever recorded them. She liked the group TLC because she said their music expressed the importance of being and loving you.

Fingering through her albums, I found that she also had every copy of Pearl Knight's recordings, and the album covers were signed, "To my beautiful daughter--"

I looked up and around and saw photographs of Satin posing with Pearl Knight and a tall, dark-skinned man. Her father?

"Pearl Knight?" I said stunned. "Pearl Knight is your mother?"

"Yes," Satin said. "You've heard of her?"

"Heard of her," I laughed. "I've been listening to her since I was seven-years-old. My Aunt Josephine is her biggest fan. Oh, my God. She's not going to believe this." Then it struck me. "That song...'When My Man Gave Me Black...Satin'. She's singing about you. Oh, my God!"

What are the odds? I thought. To be in the house of Pearl Knight's daughter. Black Satin? To have been singing a song about this beautiful woman for years without even knowing it.

"Satin, you've got to do me a great big favor. I hate to ask, but is there any way that you can get your mother to autograph one of her albums for my aunt?"

Satin smiled. "Sure. Anything for my favorite artist."

"Thanks. Aunt Josephine is going to flip."

We went into the dining room and sat down for dinner. Satin served grilled fillet of lake trout on a bed of leeks with lemon wedges on the side and sprinkled with finely chopped parsley and slivered almonds. It was accompanied by curried rice, steamed mixed vegetables, and chocolate mousse for dessert. After our stomachs were full and satisfied, we relaxed in her living room.

One of the pictures of Satin and her lover hailed my attention just as Aretha Franklin started singing *"(You Make Me Feel Like A) Natural Woman."*

"Is this Robin?"

"Yes," Satin smiled.

"She's pretty." I sat down on the couch, but not too close. "Where is she?"

Satin noted and respected my insistence on space with a slight tilt of her head. "She's out of town on an assignment."

"An assignment?"

"Yes. She's a freelance photographer," Satin said. "She'll be in Haiti for a month and a half to two months photographing voodou altars for *Ebony Magazine*. That's why I was late to your opening. I had to drop her off at the airport."

"Well, that explains all the photographs."

"Oh, this isn't the half of it," Satin said. "And if she had it her way, she'd put me in a frame and hang me on the wall over her bed so that I couldn't be seen or touched by anyone except her."

"She sounds possessive."

"Aren't we all to some extent?"

"I don't think I am. I've never had the need or the love to hold onto anyone that tightly."

"Really?" she asked. "Not even your friend Nikki?"

"Nikki doesn't count," I said.

"Why?"

"Because she's there whether I'm holding onto her or not."

"That's interesting," Satin said, crossing her legs.

My eyes started to take a leisurely stroll up her calf, but I managed to pull them away when they tried to squeeze behind her knee.

"I get the feeling that you don't need to hold onto anybody," I said, focusing on the knowing smile that raised the corners of her mouth when I stopped caressing her legs with my eyes.

"I don't now. But when I was a teenager, I had a very low opinion of myself, and I used to hold onto anyone or anything that would give me just a taste of self-worth," Satin confessed.

"That's funny because I can't imagine you being insecure about anything."

"Oh, I used to be pitiful." Her voice dropped to a bewildered whisper, revealing in it the extreme difficulty she had believing her own impetuous actions as a despondent teenager. "The names are what stand out in my mind: blacky, jigaboo, tar baby, darky, spooky, pickaninny."

"What about Ink Spot and African booty scratcher?"

"Ink Spot, yes. But I have never heard of African booty scratcher. What in the world is an African booty scratcher?"

"Something my sister used to call me. I didn't know what an African booty scratcher was and I still don't, but I knew it was something negative because so many things around me had taught me that any and everything referencing Africa had dubious admirable qualities. So what I inevitably sculpted one day were these blue-black, big-lipped, wide nosed, monkey-looking African figures with enormous buttocks, swinging naked from a tree, and landing on the jungle floor to scratch theirs or somebody else's behind. I was totally insulted by that name, and every time Elaine called me that I'd try my best to beat the hell out of her."

"You sound like me," Satin said. "I fought constantly when I was young because someone was always calling me out my name. The sweet feeling of revenge smashing into the mouths that hurled cruel names at me made violence my only gratifying defense. But, after a while, I grew tired of physically assaulting every third person I encountered, so I learned to accept the derogatory epithets as the price one simply had to pay for having the misfortune of being a dark-skinned female."

We had so much in common. It was incredible! Finally I had met someone who understood and wasn't afraid or ashamed to talk about it. Like me, Satin said, when she heard people say, "Black is Beautiful," she looked in the mirror and wondered, if black is beautiful, why is all the black I see before me so clamorously unattractive? Niggahish? Where was this beauty? Did someone steal it? Lose it? Was it locked away in someone's dusty attic just waiting to be set free? Did some gray-haired old woman have it tucked away in her bosom? Or did it simply not exist? Like me, Satin seriously questioned the sanity of the person who'd coined that phrase, and had, on numerous occasions, plotted to hunt down the lunatic revolutionary brothah or sistah and slap the hell out of him or her for creating such an asinine, rhetorical expression.

"How did you get past all of that?" Satin asked me.

"My Aunt Josephine. When I first started sculpting, I only made animals. But when she came to stay with us, I started sculpting her. Then my parents and the people in the neighborhood, and I saw beauty in them all. What about you? How did you get past it?"

"My father," Satin said. "One night he called my mother in the middle of a concert to tell her how sad I was feeling. I must have been around ten or eleven. My mother came home the next day and sang the song she'd written about me. Even though she sang the blues, she didn't allow me to listen to it because she thought it was too sexually suggestive. Most of the songs that she let me hear were about the different places she traveled to. I learned about Harlem, Chicago, L.A., Detroit, Alabama, Atlanta through that music."

Sweet memories stretched Satin's lips into a full happy smile. She asked me to accompany her to her bedroom. I was more than a little leery, but I crossed that threshold nonetheless just as Ella Fitzgerald and Louis Armstrong were singing "*I Won't Dance.*"

Out of all the rooms in Satin's house, the bedroom was the most elegant. The color scheme of black and white tailored the room perfectly. It was in that room that I was able to feel Satin's charming, energetic personality at its peak. Its presence drew closer the farther into the room I ventured. The vibrations of its movement frightened me, but I stayed nonetheless.

Satin directed me over to her walk-in closet, which mirrored doors bounced back our reflections, as she stood close behind me. She was an erect, bold five foot ten, and when she was in her heels my head just barely came to her shoulders. I could sense that Satin wanted to touch me, but she resisted the temptation. And I remembered and resisted the thoughtful temptation of how her touch felt on my face the day we met.

Satin didn't speak a word for almost a minute, just surveyed my body in the mirror. Then she left the room and returned with a warm, wet wash cloth. Satin turned my back to the mirror then began removing my makeup, which I'd taken over an hour to put on.

"As *'When My Man Gave Me Black Satin'* played, my mother took me into the kitchen, placed a mirror in my hands, and made me look at myself," Satin quietly explained as she wiped the cloth across my face. "Then she whispered--and I remember this word for word--'Never look down on yourself. There are too many people in the world willing to do that for you. You are a black *and* beautiful girl child. Don't ever let anybody tell you different.'

"After my mother showed me that beautiful black child smiling happy and dark at me, I slowly, very slowly began to feel for the first time the raw sense of self-acceptance, self-love, self-worth, self-respect, and self-reliance that was independent of anyone's affirmation of me."

Satin turned me around and touched the back of her hand to the side of my face. The smoothness of that touch pushed my eyes away from her frank gaze and over to a small mahogany curio beside her dresser. I didn't notice it when I first came in the room. There was a sculpture on the middle shelf that depicted a nude, young, black girl sitting in an oak tree with a flock of owls. Her mouth was open in a full-throated laugh and you could see a tiny round ball sitting on her tongue. *Midnight Flight* was the name of the piece. Meyoki was the model. I'd sculpted it during that weekend we'd spent at Aunt Josephine's, and it was the first piece that I'd sold at the flea market.

I was ready to sell my soul to the highest bidder in order to get into AAI. Either they never heard about my suspension or they didn't care. Whatever the case, I got in and decided that the best way to get my life back on track was to concentrate on my artwork and nothing else. My parents only had enough money to pay my tuition, so to get money for books and supplies, Miss. Miller arranged for me to rent a space at a flea market one Saturday. I guess you can say that that was my first one woman show. I sold all of the personal thoughts I believed would interfere with my goal of becoming a great artist. I made three hundred dollars.

My stomach muscles tightened as I asked myself, What is it doing here in Satin's bedroom? I walked over and stared at it, but I wouldn't touch it. "Where'd you get this?" I asked, trying to ignore the barrage of sharp pangs in my stomach.

Satin was now behind me. "I brought it at a yard sale about five years ago. Evidently the woman selling it didn't know that you would be a famous artist and that this, being one of your earlier works, would be worth twenty times more than she sold it for."

I couldn't open my mouth, and if I wasn't still standing, I would have sworn that my heart had stopped. I never thought that I'd ever lay eyes on that piece again, and now here it was in Satin's bedroom of all places.

"When I came across this piece sitting on a table next to an old waffle iron, I didn't know that it was the work of my favorite artist. It wasn't until I'd gotten it home and was looking for a place to put it that I looked on the bottom and found your name carved into the base. And you know what I said to myself," Satin laughed. "What are the odds?"

Yeah, I thought. What are the odds?

"Who is she?" Satin asked.

"Nobody," I said.

"She can't be a nobody. Her body is too intricate, her eyes are too intimate, and her laugh is too spontaneous for a nobody. Look at the ring in her tongue. It's a little off center. You had to have known her or spent some time admiring her."

"No, I didn't know her. She was just a crazy thought I had running around in my head," I said.

13

Malcolm and I had been fooling around, wrestling on his bed. Me wrestling! How free this man made me feel. Being with him was like running in an open field of daffodils, violets, and daisies up to my knees. And he was like a big oak tree standing in the middle that I kept circling with laughter so deep it split my sides.

Malcolm had put me in some kind of hold, and I couldn't get loose, so I started nibbling on his ear. He liked that. He loosened his grip and closed his eyes. I could have gotten away then, but why? And while I tasted his earlobe, he told me that he'd always wanted an earring, but he was too much of his father's son to go through with it. I told him that I didn't think that having an earring made him less of a man. Just like I didn't see that playing with toy cars made him less of a man.

Fifteen minutes later, I had threaded a needle with black thread, lit a match, held the tip of the needle over the small blue flame, then dipped it in the bottle of alcohol. I soaked a cotton ball with alcohol, cleaned Malcolm's left earlobe, then held an ice cube against it until it was numb. I thought about Meyoki's pierced ears, navel, and tongue as I prepared to stick the needle through Malcolm's flesh. I leaned over, took aim, and just as the needle neared Malcolm's earlobe, he hunched his shoulder so that I could no longer see it.

"Look," I sighed, agitated, "why don't we just go to the mall and get it done with the gun? It'll be faster and less painful."

"No!" Malcolm said, squirming on the toilet seat like a two-year-old boy in a barber's chair. "When my father sees this, I want to at least be able to tell him that I did it like a man. Just talk to me while you're doing it."

"Talk to you? About what?"

"Ummm. I don't know," he said. "Tell me how your dinner with...uh, what did you say her name was again?"

The needle slipped out of my fingers. I could have kicked myself for such a suspicious response to an innocent request. I didn't tell Malcolm too much about Satin because a friendship with Satin was definitely something that his manhood could not and would not stand still for. Satin was as attractive as Malcolm, as tall as him, as well built as him, as well dressed as him, and as well educated as him. And so his manhood would run itself ragged trying to find something that would prove to me and itself that a friendship like hers wasn't needed when I had a real man in my life.

But that wasn't the only reason I was on edge. Satin having that sculpture of Meyoki made me uneasy. I felt as if Meyoki waited for me to believe that I had left her when I walked out of the shower room at Northwestern, and then BAM! There she was. But why am I worried, I thought. It's not as if Satin and Meyoki will ever see each other. So Satin will never know who she really has in her bedroom.

I retrieved the needle from the floor and washed it off with hot water. "Her name is Satin," I said, trying not to sound guilty of having committed the crime of having dinner with a lesbian.

My hands were getting sweaty. I wiped them on the sides of my jeans. I began feeling like a suspect being grilled by the police. Sweat from my armpits ran down my sides.

Malcolm asked, "Did you have a nice time at dinner last night?"

Focusing on the time before we went up to her bedroom helped me to answer. "Yes. I had a great time. We found out that we have a lot in common."

"Like what?"

"Black sistah stuff," I said, re-threading the needle. "You wouldn't understand."

"Oh, that means y'all sat around doggin' out brothas. 'Black men ain't nothin' but dogs. Black men ain't no good. Black men ain't nothin' but liars.'"

We both started laughing. "No," I said, and I thought for a moment. "Actually, I don't think we talked about men at all."

"Well, then what did you talk about?" he asked, as if black men were the only things black women ever had on their minds.

"I told you. Black sistah stuff," I said, and pushed the needle through his flesh.

Malcolm didn't even notice. He was too busy trying to figure out how two women could be together all evening and not say one word about men. And more to the point, he wasn't sure if he felt comfortable with two women being friends who could pull that off.

I tied a tiny knot in the thread and was putting some Vaseline on his earlobe when someone rang the bell. Malcolm ran down to answer the door and when he didn't come right back up, I went to the top of the stairs. There was a woman in his living room.

Anger inhaled a deep breath then sighed when I walked down and spotted my enemy standing haughtily over by the couch. It was Zona. Canary-yellow, lean and delicately built, Zona Fleet. She was cloaked in an orange skirt suit with lace trim on the neckline of the jacket, sleeves and hem of the skirt. Her hair was cut in a short bob style and dyed blond. Zona's gray eyes were penetrating, fearless, daring against her high yellow skin.

Malcolm said quickly, "Tonya, Zona. Zona, Tonya."

We didn't say a word. We just stared at each other the way we women stare at one another when we feel threatened. That echoless, sneering, frozen scowl that replays the warnings of mothers, sisters, aunts, grandmothers, and girlfriends.

My eyes: *You have to watch women.*

Zona's eyes: *They're the sneakiest things alive.*

My eyes: *They always want what don't belong to them.*

Zona's eyes: *Can't leave them alone with your man for even a half a second.*

My eyes: *Women are devious...*

Zona's eyes, hard and direct: *Bi--*

"Let me walk you to your car," Malcolm said and pulled Zona by her arm.

When they went outside, I overheard Zona telling Malcolm, "I'm not surprised to see her. I came here expecting to find some 'thing' in your bed."

The thing was, I wasn't surprised to see her either. I'd been expecting her since the day Malcolm and I met.

"How did she find out where you live?" I asked, after Malcolm came back inside.

"I don't know. I didn't ask?"

"What does she want?"

"To talk."

"About what?"

"Why she asked me to leave."

"What makes her think you care?"

"Because she knows that I would."

I didn't know my anger could or would be so violent. So before I could even think about stopping myself, I had kicked over the coffee table. The television hit the floor with a smash and the picture tube exploded.

Malcolm watched a tiny puff of smoke come out of the television as it died. He closed his eyes. "Tonya--"

"Why?" I yelled, cutting him off. "Why do you care?"

"I don't know."

"Oh, don't give me that crap!"

"It's not crap."

I stepped around the overturned table and broken television.

"Tonya, wait. Don't leave!"

"I'm telling you right now, Malcolm. I may have shared your heart with her, but I'll be damned if I'm gonna share your bed with her."

Malcolm and I argued a lot about Zona, only he didn't find out about our arguments for a good two weeks. If Malcolm didn't call me, I'd draw a picture that swore that he'd been with Zona. If I called and he didn't answer the phone, I'd sculpt him in his bed screwing Zona. If he dropped me off early from a date, I'd do a sketch that swore he was going to see Zona. If I didn't see him for a day, I'd draw a picture that swore that he'd been with Zona. Basically, if the man wasn't sitting up in my face twenty-four-seven, I'd draw or sculpt something that swore that he was with Zona.

When Malcolm finally saw these drawing and sculptures, he got extremely angry.

"This isn't fair, Tonya. You're having one sided arguments with me behind my back."

"I'm not doing anything behind your back. You, on the other hand..."

"Tonya, I'm not sleeping with Zona."

"So you say."

"That's right. I do say. So why don't you believe me?"

"Well, it's kind of hard when she's calling your house every day, coming to your house every other day."

"I'm just trying to work through this, Tonya."

"Work through what, Malcolm?" I asked, although I knew perfectly well what.

This was about Malcolm's manhood. He needed to know what it was he, as Robert Holland's man, hadn't done to make his woman ask him to leave. Did he fail her in bed? Did he fall short in helping her financially? Did he fail to protect her the way a man should? Did he fail to make her feel safe? But of course a real man couldn't admit this. A real man could only repeat, "I'm just trying to work through this, Tonya."

And as a woman, I said, "So am I, Malcolm"

After that argument, I did a sculpture of a man standing in front of his woman blocking her view of what was behind him by kissing her. His eyes were closed, but his woman's eyes were open, looking down at his right hand, which he had up the skirt of a woman leaning breasts forward against his back. I called that piece *Cheater*.

Lonnie was back, and he had Nikki humming as he made love to her. I lay in bed listening, trying to visualize the smile that he'd put on Nikki's lips, and thinking how amazing it was that she treasured everything there was too easily to loathe about being a woman. Her period she treated as if it were a sacred, purifying celebration, her mood swings she felt were her God-given right, and her dependence on loving this man and all men she treated as a delirious and delicious morning, afternoon, and evening delight.

Nikki had two orgasms that made a scream come from her throat that sounded like the fierce, sassy sound of a note that Miles Davis might blast from his trumpet and the sweet, funky feel of a chord that Maceo might blow from his horn. Around two-thirty I listened as Nikki went into the bathroom. I heard Nikki brush her teeth and fill the bathtub with water. I didn't go in until she'd lit her scented candles and was relaxing in the tub. Between the scented candles and the red raspberry bubble bath, Nikki had the bathroom smelling as pretty as she always looked after making love, especially to Lonnie. I hated to break her peace, but I needed her advice about Malcolm.

"A woman just like Zona took my father," Nikki said.

She had her eyes closed and was very still. The flame from the candle made her face dance.

"Maybe I should just let him go," I said.

"Why? You love and deserve him just as much as she does."

"I liked it better when I didn't love him. My life was easier."

"Your life was dead before you fell in love with him," Nikki said.

"Yeah, but I didn't feel dead," I told her. "Now I feel like I'm about to die and it hurts." I sighed and stood up. "I need to get away so that I can think."

"That's not a good idea," Nikki said. "Too much time and space makes a man long for what he used to have."

"The way I see it, he's longing for it right in front of my face, and I can't bear to watch it any longer. Satin is going away to a festival this weekend, and I think I'll go with her."

Nikki hadn't opened her eyes once during the entire conversation, but now they were stretched wide with what looked like jealousy and curiosity. In the beginning, she paid little attention to my friendship with Satin because since we'd been friends neither one of us had any other girlfriends. And it wasn't until Nikki saw Satin hugging me that she began asking when and how Satin and I met; demanding to know like her life and mine depended on the day, date, and time that Satin and I first looked into each other's eyes and smiled like we'd just discovered the moon inside each other.

About a week after the night I'd had dinner at Satin's house, Pearl sent Satin an autographed copy of her album and she and I took it to Aunt Josephine, who was elated.

"I knew you looked familiar," Aunt Josephine said, staring at the signature. "Tell me something. Why did your mother stop singing?"

"She thought her family needed her to," Satin said.

Some way or other Aunt Josephine, Uncle Charlie, Satin, and I ended up at the New Haven Lounge listening to Big Jesse Yawn sing the blues. I was sitting in a booth next to Satin sketching the band and Aunt Josephine and Uncle Charlie were dancing. Big Jesse had a booming voice that was meant to sing the blues. And when he sang, he made you feel as if you hadn't lived until you had sung at least twenty or so blues songs of your own. I'd been listening to the blues practically all my life, but I couldn't get past the hurt and sadness to really enjoy the music and find the good in it.

I told this to Satin as I sketched, and she said, "Something good always comes out of the blues that makes life worth dancing to the rhythm of it."

I said, "If I had a choice, I would sidestep the blues and just take the rhythm."

"The blues doesn't work that way because life doesn't work that way. And what is blues but life set to life's rhythm."

I was thinking about that when Big Jesse started singing *"Chains of Love."* Satin rested her head on my shoulder and brought my pencil to a halt. I'm sure she had to know what her head on my shoulder would do to me. She had to know that I was straining against everything in me to keep from leaning over and filling my nostrils with the clean smell of her hair, or reaching up and stroking her face.

I wondered why she was doing this to me. Anybody else's head wouldn't have created a stir, but hers made my breathing so heavy that I held my breath so that she wouldn't hear it. I didn't want her to hear how frantically she was making my heart pound, so I willed it to stop beating. I didn't want Aunt Josephine or anyone else there to see how much I was enjoying the feel of Satin's head upon my shoulder, so I stared at the white man playing the bass. I couldn't hear a single note. But I didn't want him to stop because I didn't want Satin to lift her head. By the end of the set, I was leaning so close to Satin that Uncle Charlie joked, "Don't fall off the stool into her lap, now." Everyone laughed at his joke except Aunt Josephine.

Anyway, Satin drove me home. Just when she'd hugged me good night, Nikki and Lonnie pulled up in the car behind us. I jerked away the second I saw Lonnie's car. I was praying that Nikki wouldn't notice us, but of course she would. I wanted to be anywhere but there at that moment.

Satin found my nervousness humorous. "You look pretty when you're nervous," she said.

"I'm not nervous."

"Yes, you are," she said. Then as if the thought just occurred to her, Satin said in surprise, "You don't want them to know that I'm gay."

"What? I don't care if they know that you're gay. It doesn't matter to me." What matters is if they think that I am.

"Well, that's good because they know."

"Who knows?"

"Your Aunt Josephine." Satin looked in her rearview mirror. "And Nikki."

"How? Did you tell them?"

"No. You did."

"I haven't said anything to them about it."

"Tonya, you say something about it every time we're together."

Satin looked down at my lap, where my fingers were wrestling with one another. I put my hand firmly on the latch and opened the door. "That doesn't mean they know."

"If you say so," Satin said.

She laughed as Lonnie drove off and we got out of the car. Nikki remembered her from the opening. They did a little small talk before Satin got in her car and drove away. Nikki folded her arms and looked at me.

"What?"

"You know what," she said.

"No I don't. What?"

"Uh-uh," she said going into the house. "I'm not gonna be your conscience. And I'm not taking the heat for you this time either."

"The heat?" I asked following her inside. "What are you talking? When did you take the heat for me?"

Nikki wouldn't answer me. She just looked at me the way she was looking at me from the bathtub.

"Don't use Malcolm as an excuse," Nikki said, sitting up. Her firm breasts seemed to float on the red bubbles.

"As an excuse?" I asked, puzzled. "What are you talking about now?" I was getting frustrated with her accusations that she never followed up with explanations or evidence.

"I'm talking about you going away with Satin. If you want to go, go. But don't use him as an excuse and don't blame him for what happens while you're gone."

"Why would I need an excuse to go away with Satin?" I asked. "And whatever's going to happen will happen whether I'm here or in South Carolina."

"That much I believe is true," Nikki said as a yellow flame flickered in her eyes.

14

Friday morning. Satin and I loaded our luggage in the trunk of her car and drove ten hours to Turner, South Carolina, ending our journey at a resort called HOME. The place was owned and operated by an elderly black couple named Abe and Summer Johnson.

When we drove up, Abe grabbed his cane and hobbled down the steps of the one time "big house" of the Peter's estate. The huge, wood building was painted white and had black shutters on all the windows. The front porch was screened-in and lined with several dining tables. Inside there was a bar, a lounge area with an old floor model black and white television, a recreation room with pool and ping pong tables, pinball machines, and a jukebox. Plants of all kinds were placed throughout the mansion by Summer, whose hobby was gardening.

"Hey, gal," Abe said, as he hung his cane on his wrist and held open his arms, which Satin comfortably fell into.

Abe was seventy-four years old. He exhibited his long existence on this earth with bushes of gray hairs that grew out of his nose and ears, a rash of dark age spots that blemished his brown skin, a sunken chest, and a potbelly that sat in his lap like a contented grandchild.

"Hello, Mr. Abe," Satin said, kissing him on the cheek.

"'Mr. Abe,'" he repeated, pushing her away. Then he looked at me, shaking his cane. "This gal has been coming down here for close to five years and she still calls me 'Mr. Abe.'"

"And I'm thirty-six years old and you still call me *gal*," Satin laughed.

"Well, compared to this here old man," Abe said rubbing his stomach, "you are just a gal. Where's Robin?"

"She's in Haiti working," Satin said.

"Oh," Abe said, his thick salt and pepper eyebrows arching at me.

"So who's this?"

"This is a very good friend of mine named Tonya Mimms."

A smile caused the wrinkles on Abe's face to come together. "Nice to meet you."

"It's nice to meet you too, sir."

"So are you ready for the festival?" Abe asked me.

"Yes, sir," I said quietly.

"From what I hear it's going to be a good one. There'll be African drums, dancing, and food. You name it and it will be here. But Satin, you know I don't go for all that African stuff. I don't know one thing 'bout no Africa and Africa don't know nothin' 'bout me. But the place is packed with black people wantin' to discover their African roots." Abe shook his head. "African roots. Let me tell you somethin'. One of them black-wanna-be-African men showed me a picture of some African boy stickin' his head in a female cow or bull or somethin's private part, and I asked the guy why the child had his head in there. And do you know what he told me? He said that the boy stuck his head up there to stimulate the thing so that it would give more milk." Abe puckered his lips and turned his head to the sky. "Have you ever heard of such a thing? Now if that's what being in touch with your African roots is all about, I don't want no parts of it."

Satin laughed. "Mr. Abe, there's more to Africa than that."

"I wouldn't know. I told you I don't know nothin' 'bout no Africa."

"Well, maybe you'll learn something this weekend."

"Maybe," Abe said, walking away, his footfalls stomping doubt. "Come on and let me get y'all out this heat and show you to your cabin. I know y'all got to be tired."

Cabin number 12 with a beautiful view of Truth River was where old Abe escorted us. It was a beige, medium size room with twin beds, thank God, covered in green sheets. The bathroom was cramped with a shower stall, small sink, and of course a toilet. None of the rooms had televisions or phones, but more for my benefit than Satin's, Abe said, we were welcome to use the one in the front office of the "big house."

As Abe was telling Satin about some white developers who were pressuring him to sell the resort, Summer entered the cabin.

Summer was two years younger than Abe. On her rust-colored, frail face she wore a pair of thick bifocals, which constantly slid down her narrow nose. Her voice, coming from heavy, strong lips, was light as the air, and she kept her long gray hair plaited in one braid and tied on the end with a red ribbon.

"Satin! I'm so glad to see you, dear," Summer said, rushing over to her as fast as her old legs would carry her.

"It's nice seeing you again too, Mrs. Summer."

"Let me look at you," Summer said. She studied Satin then smiled. "Such a beautiful chile." She hugged Satin again. "I knew you'd be comin' down here. The minute I saw they was having some African festival, I told Abe, Satin'll be here. Didn't I Abe?"

"Sure did," he said.

I guess feeling a presence other than Robin's caused Summer to look around the room and settle her bifocals on me. "And who do we have here?"

"A good friend of Satin's named Tonya," Abe said before Satin had a chance to.

"Oh." She looked me over then asked, "Is this your first time down South?"

"No, ma'am."

"You got any people down here?"

"Not living."

"Oh." She turned to Satin. "Where's Robin?"

"She's in Haiti working," Abe answered again.

"Oh," Summer said, looking to make sure that we were in a cabin that had two beds.

Satin promised me a weekend of new experiences, knowledge, and spiritual uplift. Friday night we just relaxed and sat around talking with Abe and Summer on the front porch. When it was time for bed, I was hesitant about turning off the light because I was positive that once darkness covered the room, Satin would be in my bed. But strangely enough, after taking a long shower, Satin turned on the small radio she'd brought with her, climbed into bed, said good night, turned off the light, and minutes later was sound asleep. I sat up half the night using the moonlight to sketch my feeling about this, because once again, I didn't know if I should have been relieved or insulted.

Saturday morning Satin and I went for a six mile sightseeing walk around the hilly, tree covered grounds of the resort, and then we rented a paddle boat and floated for an hour on a small pond. Around three we went over to a large sandy brown building which was used for a ballroom. Inside were vendors selling African art, food, books, and music.

Satin spent the majority of her time talking with Carlos, the owner of a stall called Underground. His stall contained books by people with long African names, which I could not pronounce, and bootleg recordings of lectures, by militant black men, that blared from a tiny speaker attached to the red, wood structure.

Around seven, Saturday evening, all thirty guests boarded a medium size ship that was docked in the Truth River. Abe and Summer sat at the head table in the dining room of the ship as a black man dressed in beautiful African attire served them samples from the buffet table such as tofu, curried goat, curried chicken, brown stew fish, a variety of vegetables, rice, and sweet potato pudding.

"Miss. Summer," the chef said, "I know you wanted to cook us some chit'lins." The boat rocked with laughter. "But we had to sneak something healthy in here sometime this weekend."

After dinner we were all asked to go out onto the deck. The sun had set by then and a full moon was lighting up that wonderful night. Carlos walked out and asked us to form a circle and join hands.

"I'll be right back," Satin said, placing my hand into the hand of a big-boned, light-skinned woman.

Carlos began to speak in a very powerful voice. "It was on these waters that our ancestors were stolen from their homeland and brought to 'the land of the free' to live out the rest of their lives as slaves. It was in these waters that hundreds of Africans baptized themselves for life rather than be brought to 'the land of the plenty' to have nothing. It was in these waters that millions of Africans were murdered by cowards on their horrifying voyage to 'the land of the brave.' And it is on these waters tonight that we honor those who have lived and died for a freedom we have yet to receive."

He then released the hand of the person whom he was standing next to and called, "Sistah Satin."

My eyes lit up as Satin entered the circle. Her head was wrapped in a snow-white headdress, a cowry shell necklace adorned her long neck, her breasts were also covered in a white cloth, and tied around her waist was a kind of white skirt. Her bare feet slapped against the steel floor of the ship, calling attention to the cowry shell bracelets around her ankles. She was beautiful.

Once she was inside, Carlos said, "Let the circle remain unbroken." We rejoined hands, and then the drumming started. Loud, powerful, heart pumping drumming. Then the light-skinned woman holding my hand began to sing. Her voice, which seemed to be coming from the water, bellowed out a song in the spiritual language of the Zulus. I couldn't understand a word of what she was saying, but I was able to detect the song's messages of unity, hope, life, and freedom. Her strong and inspirational voice floated through the night, across the Atlantic, and straight home to Africa.

Through that song I could see embroidered in the dark waters we were sailing on the countless numbers of atrocities our ancestors and I, us, we had been subjected to by the hands of the white minority who ruled this world. In her voice I heard the everlasting cries of African men, women, children, and breathed the last breath of every dead, every dying person of color, and saw their rich blood washing up on the shores of this planet.

I listened and engrossed myself in the music and watched how Satin energetically displayed our pain and joy in her dance steps. She took a step forward then jerked her body back. Took two steps and jerked her body back twice. She then stood in place, and at the command of the drums rhythmically pressed the palms of her hands toward the sky, arching her back as her hands lowered, straightening it as her hands pushed upward again. She moved around hypnotically in that circle, jerking and pressing, straightening and arching, following the drums, anticipating freedom.

Satin twirled in a circle exceedingly faster until all that was left in our center was a colorful blur. Suddenly, she froze and then leaped. I saw her fly and land on the other side in front of a man, but it felt as if she had leaped inside me, and all I could feel were her heavy footsteps chanting inside my soul. My heart pounded with a homesickness I hadn't felt before as the beat of the drums entered my mind and transported me to that far away place, the place where my ancestors were born. The place people wanted me to be ashamed of.

A handsome, blue-black-skinned brothah, who seemed to be as tall as Kilimanjaro, entered the circle and raised Satin to the height of the moon. The drums, the spiritual, and their bodies all became one. Satin and the brother with the beautiful blue-black skin danced, shoulder to shoulder, head to head, breast to breast, pelvis to pelvis. They were two dancing, shiny black diamonds. How could anyone hate something so beautiful? I wondered.

I stood there, squeezing the hand of the singing sistah, able to see, able to hear, able to feel, and yes, I was even able to smell why I should be proud of who I am. And when the drums stopped, and the woman ceased to sing, and Satin and the brothah fell to the floor, I still felt good. I still felt special. I looked at Satin, and wondered if she had any idea of what I'd just experienced, and she was smiling at me. She knew.

Satin and I walked back to our cabin arm in arm and barefooted. Once inside, Satin opened a window to let in the warm dark night and turned on the radio. She removed the white headdress, but kept on the white garb and cowrie shells as she lay across the bed. With the vision of Satin's dance in my head, the high, bright moon above our cabin, the soft music inside, and her dark left thigh lying between the split in the white skirt, I thought, so help me, that Satin Pierce was the most extraordinary woman I had ever known.

I sat on my bed too wired to sleep, too filled with this insatiable need to know everything there was to know about her.

"Tell me," I begged more so than asked. "Tell me who you are."

Mahalia Jackson singing *"Sometimes I Feel Like a Motherless Child"* was coming from the radio Satin had brought with her. She let the song play halfway through before answering. "I'm a woman who takes life too seriously, who thinks too far ahead into the future and can see the consequences of my actions, but still I am helpless to prevent myself from doing things that will cause others in my life pain."

"Do you hurt people often?" I asked.

"Often enough," she said.

"How do your parents feel about who you are?" I asked.

"How do my parents feel?" Satin asked, repeating the question only so that she could think about her answer. "They feel...sad...about who I am. My mother quit singing because of who I am."

"What?"

"My father said that if she wasn't running around the world being a singer instead of at home being a mother, then I wouldn't have been looking for a mother in other women. My mother cried all the time when she stopped performing, and it hurt me deeply to hear her sobbing in the middle of the night. It took me months to realize that her weeping was her revenge, her motherly way of punishing me for disappointing and disgracing her and my father, for making her give up her career. After she discovered that crying was not going to wash away my homosexuality, she started setting me up with every black male in New Orleans. She has   .

this crazy idea that a man can fix whatever it is that's wrong with me. She still hasn't realized that I'm not broken."

"What about your father?"

"Oh, he has a better approach. He ignores the situation, as he calls it. I'm a situation. Me. His daughter. A situation. And like all situations that he can't control or change, he pretends that it doesn't exist, thinking that if he imagines long and hard enough the situation will simply fade away. Racism, ignore it and it will disappear. Mama's miscarriage, ignore it and it will disappear. Grandma's cancer, ignore it and it will disappear." She laughed again. "Unconsciously, at least I like to pretend that it wasn't a conscious effort on his part, he began ignoring me, hoping that my homosexuality would disappear.

"I thought that after I'd moved out of the house things between us would get better, but they didn't. My mother was constantly mourning the loss of grandchildren she said I was denying her. And at times my father would purposely leave the house when he knew that I was coming over. I couldn't bear seeing them in such misery over my lifestyle so I moved here."

"How do your parents feel about Robin?"

"They hate her. Not because she's a bad person. Not because she treats me badly. But because I care for Robin in a way that they say God says I shouldn't." She ended it there. "So," she sighed, "how do your parents feel about who you are?"

"My parents don't know who I am. They know who they want me to be and that keeps them happy."

"Who do they want you to be?"

"Someone smart, loving, respectful, happy, careful...normal."

"And you don't think that you're either of those things?"

"I am to a point," I said.

"Well, I've spilled my guts to you. Now it's your turn. I want to know who you are beyond that point."

"You know everything there is to know about me," I said.

"I know what I've read about you, what I've seen about you in your work. But I want to hear about you, about your desires from your tongue to my ears."

"I don't trust either of those things to accurately voice and receive me. My hands tell my story, even when I don't want to hear it."

Satin took a moment to think about that, then said, "Fair enough."

She got up and went into the bathroom and took a forty-five minute shower. Teena Marie was singing *"Out On A Limb"* when Satin came out wrapped like a piece of dark, sweet chocolate in a peach colored towel. Her body was glistening from the sprinkles of water that the terry cloth failed to absorb.

"Go over to the mirror and close your eyes," she said.

I shrugged and complied with her request. I smelled her behind me before I felt her. A nectarous, seductive fragrance always clung to her as if it were part of her skin.

"Open your eyes," she whispered.

She had draped a multi-colored silk scarf over my shoulders. My hands glided easily over the shiny, slippery material as I admired its African print.

"Do you like it?" Satin asked.

"I love it," I said, turning to hug her.

My hands rested on her bare shoulders. I held her longer than I had intended because I was letting the fine oils of her shoulders soak into my palms. Unconsciously, I began running my fingers over the upper part of her back, and I was able to really feel the satiny smoothness that justified her name. Hearing Satin release a pleasurable sigh alerted me to what I was doing. Immediately, I put my hands in park on her shoulders and would have released her if she hadn't placed her hands on top of mine. Quietness surrounded us.

Satin had an interrogating look in her eyes. They questioned why I came on this trip with her. She stroked the backs of my hands with her thumbs, and her eyes said that she knew that if she lifted her hand, my fingers would touch parts of her that would tell her exactly who I was and what I wanted.

She was taunting me and trying to coerce a confession from me. She wanted me to admit that I came there because I longed to be near her in a special way. She wanted me to say that the strokes of her thumbs were making her more desirable to me. That I wanted her touch to wander in places that I'd only allowed Malcolm's hands to venture. She wanted me to admit that I wanted very much to taste her lips upon mine. But more than anything, she wanted me to admit that I wanted her to make love to me.

My glare refused to answer her accusations.

A seriousness that I'd never seen before covered Satin's face. She looked me dead center in the eye and said, "I think you'd better get in your bed now, Tonya."

It took me a moment to get myself together and even longer to shake the unequivocal message behind her warning.

I pulled my hands out from under hers and off her shoulders. That movement seemed to take hours. I got deep under the covers.

Satin turned off the light. Her sheets rustled and her box spring squeaked as she lay down. "Tonya," Satin called in the darkness, "what do you do when your hands tell you something that you don't want to hear?"

I looked out the window at the moon, inhaled a chest full of warm night, and exhaled, "Get rid of it."

15

Except for the music, the trip back to Baltimore was quiet. Satin slept most of the way while I drove sixty miles an hour, stopping at nearly every rest area. I wasn't ready to go home because I didn't know what I'd find when I got there. For all I knew, Malcolm and Zona had run off and eloped while I was in some cabin wondering about a woman's touch.

It all made me angry, as angry as I'd felt that day I waited outside of Principal Menefee's office. Back then I was worried about losing out on getting into AAI. Now I was afraid that I had lost Malcolm. And today just like then, my loss was behind some woman.

Your life can't be right, I thought, looking at Satin sleeping in the passenger seat. If it were, you wouldn't have to give up so much in order to live it. I don't want to give up my parents, and I don't want to give up Nikki. And I especially don't want to give up my dream of someday walking down the aisle with Malcolm. So, just like I didn't let Meyoki ruin my dream of getting into AAI and becoming a great sculptor, I'm not going to let you, Satin, spoil my dream of marrying Malcolm. I just have to watch my step with you, that's all, and make sure that I don't end up somewhere that I'll have to crawl out of.

It was one o'clock in the morning when I pulled Satin's car up in front of my house. She could tell that something was bothering me, but she knew that I didn't want to talk about it. I dropped her keys in her hand and grabbed my bags out of the trunk.

Satin hugged me. "I had a great time this weekend."

"So did I," I said, shrinking from her embrace. "I'll call you."

"Be sure you do," Satin said.

Satin got into her car then glanced up at Nikki's bedroom window, where Nikki stood just watching us the way I imagined she watched her patients as they spilled their guts out all over that couch in her office. Satin pulled off, Nikki left the window, and I wrestled my bags into the house, leaving them by the couch. I dragged my exhausted body to my room. There was a blue velvet box on my pillow. I opened it and found a door key inside. My body sprang back to life. I pulled open my top dresser drawer and retrieved the black box that contained a ½ carat round diamond earring set in 14K gold. Then I ran down the steps two at a time and out the door. I jumped in my jeep and ran red lights as I sped to his house.

On his porch, I paused before putting the key into the lock. I knew that it opened more than simply the door to his place. So I had to ask myself if I was ready for what the key was really opening. Asked myself if I understood that once I put the key in the lock and turned, there would be no turning back. Asked myself if Malcolm was what I really wanted. And then I got angry with myself for even asking such stupid questions. Of course he was what I wanted.

I put the key in the lock then smiled when I heard the dead bolt release. I opened the door and was greeted by the gap in Malcolm's smile. He rose from the couch where he was sitting naked and ready for me.

"Does this mean that there's no more Zona?" I asked, still standing in the doorway.

"No," Malcolm said, walking toward me. He closed the door, locked it, and pulled me to him. "This means that there hasn't been a Zona since I fell in love with Tonya."

"And when was that? Yesterday?" I asked.

"Why do you always think the worst of me?" he asked.

"I don't. I always think the worst for me. That way I'm not disappointed."

"Well, Tonya Mimms, I hate to disappoint you, but I've been in love with you since the first day we met," he said.

I looked inside his eyes to see if they mirrored his words. They looked sincere. So did mine when I inserted the diamond earring into his earlobe, kissed it, then told Malcolm Holland, "I love you more than I ever thought I could love a man who wasn't made of clay."

I'd been working nonstop on a sculpture of Satin and the blue-black brothah she'd danced with on the boat. I'd made a mental sketch of it and was working from that to recreate the rhythm of their bodies together. Sometimes, I just let the memory play in my mind without sculpting at all. I could actually smell the river, feel the drums, hear the woman singing, and hear Satin's feet dancing on deck. She was so beautiful, so musical. So, Um!

I decided to take a break. I called Malcolm but he was out of the office, so I stopped by Knowledge to have lunch with Satin, and the place was overrun with people. Finding her proved to be a difficult task. Every two steps I found myself saying excuse me three and four times to people who were refusing to move for fear of someone else finding the book he or she was in search of. I came upon this mound of shouting people, and found Alan buried under them. I'd been wondering if Alan knew that Satin was gay, and if he did, did he think that I was *that* way. He never really said anything to me when I came by. He just sort of looked and smiled politely, almost as if he didn't trust me for some reason.

Satin emerged from a crowd and hurried to the back of the store, dragging me along by my arm.

"It's a mad house," she said. "I won't be able to get away for lunch."

"How about dinner? Malcolm will be at home working tonight, and I really want to be around somebody made of flesh and blood not clay."

"Dinner sounds fine," she said. "But it'll have to be late. I probably won't get out of here until seven, and I don't want to go out." Satin grabbed her purse from under her desk. "So why don't you cook dinner for us."

"Me?"

"You can cook, can't you?"

"You'll have to decided that when you get home," I said, snatching her keys out of the air as she softly tossed them to me.

When I walked into Satin's house, I gathered up the mail that had been pushed through the metal slot in the front door. I don't know why, but I was curious as to the kind of mail she received, like her mail was some how different than mine. Gas and electric bill, credit card bill, bank statements, a letter from her parents, four other personal letters, sales papers, and some magazines. All the normal stuff. What was I expecting? I asked myself. *Black Homosexual Digest* or something?

I went upstairs. I knew that I was invading her privacy, but I did it anyway. I don't even know what I was looking for, but I pulled on the brass handle and opened the top drawer of her dresser to find it filled with colorful, silk and satin bras and panties. I pulled out the second drawer where she had neatly placed a dozen or more negligee. There was a new photograph of Satin and Robin on the dresser. Before leaving the room, I lay down on her satin covered bed and relaxed. The fabric was cool and soft. I could have easily slipped off to sleep. But then it hit me. She and Robin probably sleep together in this bed. Hugging and kissing each other.... I was up before I finished the thought.

Satin walked in the door around nine-fifteen. She went straight into the living room and put in an Earth, Wind, and Fire CD. She hummed "Can't Hide Love" as she came into the kitchen.

"Dinner smells good," she said, going through her mail.

I placed the roast chicken, rice, hot-and-spicy collard greens, and rolls on the dining room table then finished washing some of the dishes I'd used to prepare the food. Satin stopped looking over her mail, tilted her head to the side and watched me.

"What are you staring at?"

"I'm not staring; I'm thinking," Satin said.

"About what?"

"About how nice it feels coming home to you."

"Yeah well, don't get used to it because I normally don't cook elaborate meals like this for anybody except Malcolm."

"And what does he give you in return for such a delicious service?" Satin asked.

"Something almost as filling and delicious. What are you going to give me?"

"Something far more scrumptious and satisfying than anything Malcolm could ever dream of," Satin boasted, licking her red lips.

Her sly comments were becoming less and less sly, and I used to respond to them in the same sly manner, giving the joking impression that I just might be willing to take her up on her offer. But I could see that she was starting to take me seriously. So I thought that I'd better put an end to the seductive games I'd been playing with her, because if I didn't, pretty soon, Satin wouldn't be playing anymore.

But instead of telling her that her sexual comments were inappropriate, I dropped the carving knife on the kitchen floor, and said, "I'm not even gonna ask you what you're talking about."

Satin looked at me then at the knife. "Oh, you know what I'm talking about," she said.

I ignored her. Satin left the kitchen as she started singing the words to *"Can't Hide Love."*

Robin phoned after dinner. Satin and I were in the living room watching the film *"Daughters of the Dust"* on her VCR. I got up from the couch and stood under the arch between the living room and hallway where I could eavesdrop, and I overheard Satin saying, "So you don't trust me?" There was a pause. Satin laughed hard. "We're just friends." Another pause followed by another strong laugh from Satin. "Have I given you any reason to doubt me other than the time I've spent with her?" Satin chuckled. "All right then, answer this. In the last three years have you ever tasted anyone other than you on my lips?"

Things were getting a little too personal, so I quietly crept back to the couch. As I stared at the television, I asked myself why I felt it necessary to eavesdrop on their conversation.

"What are you thinking about," Satin asked, scattering my thoughts.

"Nothing." I aimed the remote at the VCR and began rewinding the tape.

"Nothing had you looking pretty intense."

"When's Robin coming back?"

"She's not sure. Why?"

"I don't want to be the cause of any misunderstandings between you two."

"We're just friends, right?" Satin asked with a gleam in her eyes. "So why would there be any misunderstandings?"

"I don't know. I was just saying."

"You just say a lot of things without saying anything at all."

"Maybe you have to learn to read between the lines."

Satin laughed. "Line reading is a dangerous game."

"For whom?"

"The inexperienced."

"Judging from this conversation, I wouldn't say that either one of us is inexperienced."

"Well," Satin sighed, "I'm not convinced of that so why don't you just tell me what's on your mind."

That was how it always started. I'd say something sodden with ambiguity, then she'd say something equally as vague. Then I became tongue-tied as she became more direct. But that night I was having fun with the seductive game we were playing. I knew I was toying with fire, but I stuck my hand in the flame anyway. "Earlier you said that you can give me something more stimulating than anything Malcolm can. I'm curious. What can you do better with your equipment, our equipment, that Malcolm can't do with his?"

"I can demonstrate it much better than I can explain it," Satin said.

I decided that it would be best to leave that one alone. So I skipped it by asking, "Does Alan know that you're gay?"

Satin smiled. "I make it a point to let everyone close to me know that I am."

"What does Robin think about you and me?"

Still smiling, Satin said, "The same thing that Malcolm thinks about you and me."

16

A week after I'd gotten back from my trip with Satin, and Malcolm had given me a key to his place and his heart, Dr. Zimmerman sent me a postcard.

Dear Tonya,

I am having an interesting time here in Kuwait.

I rode the bus once, but will never do it again. They are extremely hot, dirty, crowded, and the camel I rode was more dependable. I have become fascinated with the women since hearing an old Arab proverb: "When a daughter is born, the threshold of the house weeps forty days."

Some of the women I've asked about this say that their thresholds only wept a day. Some say that theirs' are still weeping.

Dr. Zimmerman
P.S. I hope the Cherrylane piece is going well.

The piece wasn't going well at all, and I felt guilty for not working on it. So I pushed aside my fears and superstitions, went to my studio, and opened the box that contained Hazel Cherrylane's skull.

My stomach only jumped a little as I examined the skull. It was small but long, smooth, oval shaped, and very clean. Her eye sockets were dark, rectangular in shape and spaced far apart. Her nasal opening was wide. The area directly below her nose was protrusive. Her teeth were tiny and close together, except for her two top front teeth, which were missing.

Before I first approached Hazel Cherrylane, I grabbed all of the clay modeling tools off the wall and put them on my workbench. But damn if the skull didn't seem to turn away like a child refusing to eat every time I put a tool near it. I don't know if I was dreaming or what. I finally had to put those tools away and work with my hands. I worked on her for three days.

It was eerie touching her at first. She was cold, angry, hurt, and very, very sad. I could feel the cold on Hazel Cherrylane's ears, which were small and pointy. On her forehead, which was short and round, I felt her anger. In her eyes, which were large, I saw her pain and sadness. In her nose, which was broad and strong like mine, I felt...her. And by two o'clock Wednesday morning, I didn't know who she was, but on the full lips that my fingers sculpted next, I could feel her tell me that she wasn't who Dr. Zimmerman and the police thought she was.

This was the first time that I didn't believe what my hands were telling me. With anger reserved for close friends who'd turned on me for no reason at all, I looked down at my hands. "What are you trying to do? Ruin me?" I asked them. "This isn't who I need her to be."

So I reworked the skull. Three separate times. And she sat there quietly, stubbornly until I reluctantly accepted the fact that no matter how many times I put my hands or tools on her face, she was not going to be some little white girl named Hazel Cherrylane.

Slowly, I sat down, swallowed my breath, and looked at my aching, clay-covered hands. Then I looked at her face and asked, "Where did you come from?" Her clay eyes seemed to blink, as if she were puzzled by my question.

"Nobody wants you here. You know that, don't you? I mean, what am I supposed to do with you? You're supposed to be somebody else. How am I supposed to explain to people that you're not who they think you are?"

She stared back at me as if she couldn't care less about who people thought she was. She was who she was and there wasn't anything anyone could do to change that. I snatched Hazel's picture off the pink wall and held it to her face. "This is who you're supposed to be."

But she just sat there.

I yelled at her. "Don't you get it? People don't like it when you're not who they need you to be. And you're not going to like it either. I can promise you that."

Early Sunday morning, I was sitting on the windowsill in my studio racking my brain trying to figure out what to do about the little black girl not being Hazel Cherrylane. While I was thinking about how Dr. Zimmerman was going to react, Satin called to ask if I wanted to play a game of tennis with her. I thought it would be the perfect way to exercise my stiff muscles and get my mind off things for awhile. So I went with Satin to Druid Hill Park.

Keep your eye on the ball, I told myself as I looked down the court at Satin, who was tying up her tennis shoes. I bounced in place and gripped the handle of my tennis racket as I practiced a forehand swing.

It was about ninety degrees. Satin's dark skin glistened as the July sun beat down upon her brow. Her sweaty expression was serious, but I could tell she was enjoying herself just as much as I was. Satin pulled a green ball out of the pocket of her shorts, set her feet firmly on the clay, and prepared for her serve. In one swift motion, her head and arms looked toward the sky. The hand holding the ball dropped a second before the strings of her racket smashed against the ball and sent it humming over the net. When I saw that ball flying ninety miles an hour at me, my knees locked and I couldn't move. I held my racket out and shielded my face with my left arm. The ball hit my racket and knocked it to the ground.

"Tonya," Satin called, "what are you doing?"

"Trying to stop you from killing me," I said, picking up my racket. "Who do you think I am Althea Gibson or Zina Garrison?"

"Just swing at the ball the way I showed you," she said, coming to my side of the court.

Satin turned my body so that my right side was facing the net, then showed me, for the sixth time, how to correctly hold the racket and how to follow through on my swing so that I'd be able to hit the ball instead of having the ball hit me. It didn't help. I stumbled from one side of that court to the other; awkwardly swinging the racket at the air while Satin laughed and gracefully returned whatever balls haphazardly drifted over to her side of the court. She finally gave up on me when I sky rocketed two balls over to a nearby basketball court.

We went back to her house. While Satin was downstairs on the phone, I undressed in her bedroom. Before coming upstairs, Satin put on a Rufus and Chaka Khan CD, and the intro from *"Ain't Nobody"* filled the house.

Satin knocked on the door, and I put on one of her robes.

"You've got some nerve locking me out of my own bedroom," she said, handing me a towel and wash cloth.

Satin pulled off her shirt. That was my cue to head for the shower, but as I placed my right foot forward, a painful twinge gripped my calf. My leg stiffened in agony. "Cramp!" I screeched, hopping over to the bed. "Oooh! I've got a cramp!"

"I told you to stretch," Satin nagged.

"I don't need to hear that right now," I moaned through clenched teeth, feeling the throb worsen.

Satin shrugged her shoulders and kneeled down. She pushed the robe up to my thighs and began massaging my calf. Gradually the pain ceased and all I could feel were her soft hands on my leg, and I could hear Chaka singing.

I relaxed. Satin stopped squeezing my leg and she began taking slow strokes up and down my calf.

"Better?" she asked.

"Yeah," I sighed.

Her strokes traveled longer in distance, etching their way along the outside of my thighs, circling to the inside, and back down to my toes. The third time that her hands moved up my thighs they went under the robe, over my hips, and across my stomach. She circled my navel with one of her long fingernails. Satin, seeing no signs of objection from me, untied the robe and pushed it away from my skin. I opened my eyes and thought,

Oh shit, Tonya!

How do I stop this? I asked myself. Should I be cruel and insensitively shove her to the floor, and run from the room screaming obscenities? Or should I embarrass her with a patronizing rejection such as I like you, but not *that* way.

While thinking, I centered the rest of my attention on the ceiling fan. It had five black blades with two gold stripes painted on their edges. It rocked slightly and hummed a windy tune that mingled with Chaka's voice and grew louder as the whispers from her touch grew louder. I envisioned the fan rotating viciously on its axis, shaking loose from the bolts that fastened it to the ceiling, and then crashing down and slicing us in half. I know that that was a horrible thought, but I had hoped that it would help me to detach myself from "the difference" as I had a long time ago. But this time "the difference" was different. It was stronger and more direct, and I couldn't free myself from its hold.

Again seeing no resistance, Satin's hands journeyed up toward my breasts. And when they arrived, brushing lightly over my hard, dark nipples, I had to take a deep breath in order to downgrade some of the pleasure that they wrapped my body in. Satin stood looking down at me lustfully, and held out her hand. I hesitated. Her persistent hand hung in the air, patiently waiting for me to reach out.

The robe fell to the floor, gathering around my feet, and I was standing naked before her. How was she able to strip me naked without so much as a nod from me in protest? I wondered. I was further baffled by my diminishing need to cover myself.

"You are gorgeous," she said, carefully sounding out each word.

She touched me and I waded in the enticing waters of her foreplay, and then ran back to shore before the tide of surrender could sweep me out to her sea. I did that a few times. It was my way of proving to myself that I was in control. And since I was the one who was in control, I could stop this before it went too far, as if it hadn't already.

Satin brought her face to mine. That's when I attempted to assert my control. But I couldn't halt what was happening. I tried but I couldn't. Satin pressed her luscious lips against mine, coating them with a sweetness so addicting that I couldn't resist kissing her back. My lips had never felt a warmer, more arousing kiss, and her tongue broke down any resistance I had.

What am I doing? I asked myself. But I didn't have an answer. My mind was simultaneously cloudy and delighted. I couldn't understand why I was letting it happen. I'd always been told that this was sinful behavior. That it was freakish and disgusting. By all rights, I should have been angered and repulsed by Satin's touch, but I was neither. I was highly excited.

Everything seemed to be moving in slow motion, but at the same time, too fast for me to stop it. How far are you willing to let this go? I asked myself. I didn't have an answer for that either because it wasn't up to me. What I should have asked was how far was Satin going to take me.

I watched in amazement as Satin released her medium, firm breasts from the confines of her red sports bra, and then removed her red panties, revealing something too erotic for words. Her stomach was flat. Her long and shapely legs were absent any markings of childhood. They were smooth and tender looking. Tattooed on the lower right side of her pelvis was a weeping willow with long, drooping branches draped in dark green leaves that kissed her thick, curly, black pubic hairs, which could have easily been mistaken for the willow's shadow. Oh, yes! I thought. Black is very Beautiful!

She motioned for me to come nearer, but my feet wouldn't budge. Confusion and fear rooted me to that spot. Her light footsteps circled my body. I expected her to round me a second time, but she stopped behind me, placing her hands on my hips. I jumped and she pressed her hands firmly against my skin as if to assure me that I had nothing to be afraid of. Satin cupped my breasts and sent heat hurtling down to my crotch, setting my clitoris ablaze. I became light-headed as she repeated the act several times. I tried to dip in and out of the fiery water to reaffirm that I still had control, but even the warmth at the shallow end of her sea was too abysmal for me to resurface.

Somehow she managed to lay me down on her satin covered bed. Feeling my petrified body shaking under hers, she whispered, "I'll stop if you want me to."

I stared at her afraid and perplexed, wanting to say stop but unable to make my mouth function. Her soft hands were stirring up a vortex of emotions. I twirled inside the twister thinking that maybe if she kept her hands still, just for a moment, I'd be able to think clearly. But she wouldn't do that. Her tranquilizing hands traced my body, unleashing stronger desires that only added to my confusion. Receiving no answer from me one way or the other she continued.

Satin rinsed my body with kisses, leaving puddles of passion everywhere as she leisurely wafted her way down my frightened frame until she reached my thighs, and then she kissed deep inside them. She ran her tongue along the inside of my thighs and that made me weak, so weak that I couldn't remember how to resist even if I wanted to. Suddenly, a sensation stronger than any I'd ever felt before unmercifully clutched my clitoris. It was so intense that my eyes slammed shut and I stopped breathing for a second. I wiggled in its grasp, half trying to escape and half trying to make sure the feeling didn't stop. And then I lost control, something that I never truly had in the first place.

Warm, wet, and tender. Those were the three things that were sending my body into convulsions. My head turned from side to side on the pillow, and I was drenched in sweat as I neared my climax, a climax that I was almost too frightened to have. The sensations that were bolting through me bordered between pleasure and pain. And the stronger the feelings got, the less distinguishable their characteristics were. They joined together as one feeling, having one purpose: to give me as much pleasure as I could stand. Only thing was, I didn't know how much more of it I could handle.

My hands choked the sheets, my head pressed hard against the damp pillow, and my facial muscles tightened as a surge of untamed, ineffable pleasure settled on the very tip of my clitoris. Sultry and weakened by whatever it was she was doing, I exploded. And before I could grab it by its collar and yank it back, an uninterrupted, earsplitting moan rushed up my throat and leaped from my mouth. It was loud enough for her neighbors to hear, loud enough for my voice to crack as it escaped, loud enough for me to feel embarrassed for having screamed at the top of my lungs like that.

I know that I only had one orgasm, but it resounded through me with a booming force that made it seem as though I had three or four. It felt so wonderful that it brought tears to my eyes, and left me limp, tired, shaky, and wanting more as I lay in a puddle of sweat.

My breath was coming out in short puffs now. My heart had stopped. I opened my eyes, licked my chapped lips, and turned my sweaty face toward the mirror, and what I saw nearly blinded me. I saw her. Saw us.

Sooner than immediately I thrust myself to the head of the bed, banging my back against the brass headboard in the process. A sharp pain entered the middle of my spine, but I was so at a loss for words that I couldn't even say "ouch." Satin looked at me, but I felt so ashamed that I turned away from her. The need to cover myself returned with a vengeance. My hands were trembling so that I could hardly pick up the quilt that had been haphazardly thrown to the floor.

Satin asked, "Are you all right?"

I said nothing.

"Tonya," she called.

"I have to go," I said.

Satin shook her head understandably and rose. "I know," she said, peering down at me.

Without watching her, I watched the light from the hallway disappear as Satin closed the bedroom door behind her. Chaka screamed under the door.

When I thought that she was far enough away, I burst into tears. The reflection of myself in the mirror lying in her bed left me frightened and sick to my stomach. I leaped from the bed, throwing the comforter as hard as I could. The sheets rustled, alerting the most distant ear that I was departing from Satin's bed. I slid across the floor trying to put some space between the mattress and me, still hot and wet from the orgasm she'd given me. But the room seemed a lot smaller, and the bed followed and cornered me against a wall. From the curio, Meyoki was laughing at me, her mouth stretched wide, her teeth as big as a horse's, her pierced tongue asking if she could have a taste of me too.

Never in a million years would I have ever dreamed of letting a woman place her lips on me like that. But I did. And worse of all, I enjoyed it! So what does that make me? A dyke? A homo? A freak? That's what my mother, my father, Aunt Josephine, and Nikki would call me.

I have to pull myself together enough to get out of here, I thought. Tearfully, I searched for my clothes. I got dressed, dashed down the steps and out the door.

I ran to my studio, but the first thing I saw when I got there was the sculpture I'd made of Satin. Before I knew anything, I had the baseball bat in my hands, and I was smashing her in to pieces. I lifted the bat up over my head and then brought it down as hard as I could on top of hers. I did this repeatedly until the bat cracked in half.

I dropped what was left of the bat on the floor and stripped as I made my way over to the sink. I desperately needed to be with Malcolm, but before I could face him, I had to get Satin off me. I let the hot water faucet run until it was scalding, then I frantically scrubbed my face, neck, breasts, stomach, and thighs where Satin's lips had feasted, but I couldn't remove her lipstick. It smeared and clung to my skin like syrup. Afraid that I'd never be rid of her, I began to cry again. Finally, after using up a whole bar of soap, I realized that the red blemishes had long since been washed down the drain.

When I was putting my clothes on, I felt like I was being watched. I looked around and saw the little black girl on my workbench staring at me. Her eyes were quiet but telling, saying that everything I'd done in the past, today, and in the next few hours could not and would not change what had happened, would not change what I am. From the pink wall, Hazel's green eyes echoed her mother's words--"No matter how far you run yourself is always three steps ahead cheerin' you on."

"That may be true," I said, zipping my pants. "But I can try to change it."

I jumped in my Wrangler and headed over to Malcolm's. As I tore through the streets, I wondered why did this have to happen? I was perfectly content with my relationship with Malcolm. And for God's sake, if I were going to cheat on him, why couldn't it have been with another man? At least then I'd be able to find some natural explanation for its occurrence. Like his hands are bigger than Malcolm's, his voice is deeper than Malcolm's, or his chest is hairier than Malcolm's, or his dick is bigger than Malcolm's. Something! Anything! But I wasn't concerned with large hands, deep voices, hairy chests, or huge dicks. No. I was interested in Satin's small, soft hands, her sweet, tender voice, and her lovely firm breasts, and the lower half of her body that resembled mine on the surface but possessed a richer quality.

17

Malcolm was sitting on the couch, watching television, listening to the radio, and doing some paper work when I let myself in with the key he'd given me. I didn't say anything, just flounced down on my knees between his hairy legs, ripped off his shirt, buried my face in his chest, and started not kissing but biting his nipples as I inhaled his manly scent. I moved down to his navel. Then I did something that I'd never done to any man. I didn't want to do it then, but I needed the strong taste of Malcolm's manhood to dissolve the sugary, womanly flavor of Satin that was still singing on my lips.

I untied the string on Malcolm's shorts, pulled them down to the middle of his thighs, took him in my hand, and kissed him. To tell the truth, it wasn't all that bad.

First extremely aroused then shocked by my sudden aggressiveness, Malcolm sprang to his feet and ran to the other side of the room. "What are you doing?" he asked, pulling up his shorts, looking at me sideways.

"You don't like it?" I asked with a devilish grin.

He scratched his head. "I didn't say that."

"Then don't say anything."

I led him into the bedroom and continued.

"Tonya, wait a minute," Malcolm said, arresting my hands. "The blinds are open."

He gave me another suspicious look then went to the window and closed the blinds, which really weren't open far enough for concern, but he wanted time to gather himself, time to figure me out. "What's wrong?" he asked.

I took off my panties. "Nothing."

"Yes, there is. You never come at me like this."

"Like what?" I squatted in front of him.

"Like...this..."

The feel of my tongue on him quieted his noise. And as he stood with his hand pushing the back of my head, I kissed him, I licked him, and I sucked him down to the bone!

But that wasn't enough to get rid of Satin, so I dragged him over to the bed and begged him to make love to me. Malcolm's body felt like steel compared to Satin's soft skin. After five minutes with him on top of me, I made him stand up while I bent over. It felt good, but not good enough. I was determined that Malcolm was going to make me come stronger than Satin had. We changed positions a dozen times, but again I wasn't satisfied.

Finally, I pushed him on the bed and straddled him, and for once, Malcolm didn't resist. I bounced up and down on him like the biggest whore in the world, and that's when my clitoris began to throb. Yes! He's going to make me come. I don't need you, Satin. Malcolm is better. Malcolm is safe. Malcolm is acceptable. Malcolm is understandable. Malcolm is a man. Goddamn it, I don't need you, Satin. I don't need you!

While I was on top of Malcolm, I saw myself standing next to Nikki outside of Northwestern High School and the memory of that day came flooding back and ran like a 8mm film.

Meyoki was walking toward me smiling.

Nikki looked at me and said, "I wonder who she's smiling at?"

And knowing that Meyoki was smiling because she and I had spent a great weekend together and could now be considered friends, I said, "You're the one she's got a thing for. So she must be smiling at you." Then I turned my back on Meyoki and walked in the building.

Nikki followed saying, "Must be."

I didn't see Meyoki again until that afternoon in gym class. We were playing basketball and she was sticking me.

"What's going on, Tonya?" Meyoki asked as I grabbed a rebound.

"Leave me alone," I said, and ran down the court.

"What? You don't want people to know that we're friends or that we spent the weekend together?" Meyoki asked, slapping the ball out of my hands.

I gritted my teeth and said, "Shut up!"

After noticing that Meyoki wasn't really playing ball but was trying to talk to me, Nikki and the other girls started whispering and giving me suspicious looks. I got scared and angry at the thought of them teasing and laughing at me. I had to prove to them that I hadn't been turned out. So I punched Meyoki in the mouth. Twice! Before she could blink. Meyoki was surprised at first as she stumbled backwards from the blows, but when she regained her balance, she punched me in my stomach so hard that I fell to my knees. When I got up, Meyoki hit me in my chest, and that's when we started battling as if we were life long enemies. I kneed Meyoki, punched her, slapped her, kicked her, grabbed her by the throat and tried to choke away the feelings that I had for her, the weekend I'd spent with her, and the taunting smiles of my friends.

I kept hearing the shrill sound of our gym teacher's whistle blowing in my ear as she fought her way through the crowd that had surround us. She pulled me off Meyoki then ordered both of us down to the showers and said to meet her at the principal's office.

"Why, Tonya?" Meyoki asked my shoulder blades, as I showered with my back to her.

I turned around but said nothing.

"I didn't deserve that and you know it," she said.

I know you didn't, I thought. For months I've noticed first small then larger pieces of myself being blown away by tiny breezes, melting under the cool gaze of a cloudy day, falling away at the slightest nudge. And I ignored it, told myself that nothing had changed, that I was still the same person I'd always been. Even though I saw the truth with my own watery eyes, felt the truth throb all over and inside me, heard the truth even when I wasn't listening, and tasted the truth like a starving person, I still hit you to keep yours and everybody else's mouth shut about it.

I felt awful for the way that I had treated her, but I couldn't say anything. I lowered my head and started crying. I heard Meyoki's feet clapping as she walked on the wet tile over to me. When she was in front of me, Meyoki put her hand under my chin and lifted my face. I looked into her brown eyes, trying to find exactly what she was looking for in mine. She tapped her pierced tongue against the back of her teeth, and the rhythm drew me in. I closed my eyes and moved my mouth toward hers. And in that instant, I told myself what I'd been telling myself all along in my sketches, sculptures, and in our reflection in Aunt Josephine's mirror. I liked her. I liked her the way that I liked boys, only I liked her better than I had any boy. I liked the way she walked, talked, the way she wore her hair, the way she dressed. I liked the house she lived in, liked how smart and ambitious she was, liked how independent she was. I liked everything about her. And I liked how she made me feel the difference and how it made me weak with a desire to feel her lips pressed sweetly against mine, aching to feel that gold ball on her tongue in my mouth.

So it was with all of this swirling around in my mind that I found myself leaning, almost falling toward her saucy lips. But when I was just a breath away from kissing her, Meyoki took her hand from my chin. My head almost dropped on the floor. When I looked up, Meyoki was glaring, and her lips were wet with disgust and contempt. And I answered her glare with my own treacherous glare. My glare asked her: Don't you understand what admitting to these truths could mean for me? Don't you know that there is no way that I can ever concede that I am feeling such unnatural, sinful emotions? Don't you know that the consequences I'll have to face for allowing myself to acknowledge these desires will be detrimental to me? And if nothing else, don't you know that if it came down to it, I would hit you again to keep others from knowing that I am *funny, that* way, or whatever you want to call it?

Meyoki stood there still as a statue, and said in an awful, awful voice, "You are worse than anybody in this school."

As the horror of that day and this afternoon flooded through me, Malcolm called out my name. We'd been together for almost two months and he'd never said a word while we were making love, but today Malcolm said softly, "Tonya." The word was surrounded by all the love he felt for me; all the trust he had for me. And as he released every precious, powerful, loving drop of him inside me, he said, "Tonya," again. But this time the word was covered in all the love and trust he thought I had for him, and he collapsed into a mountain of hot, sweaty, breathing flesh on top of that lie. When I was sure that he was asleep, I left. I didn't want to be in his bed when he woke up because I was afraid that he would take one look in my eyes and see why I was there, why I needed him to make love to me.

18

I needed a place to hide.

Some nightspot where the quiet was louder than the musical screams of Chaka Khan mixed with the inharmonious sound of the baseball bat smashing my beautiful clay sculpture. I had to find a haven where the air wasn't so hot and heavy with the sweet smell of weeping willow dipped in the thirst quenching sweat from his body. I searched for a hideout that would allow me to breathe so that I could forget them both, looked frantically for a space where I wouldn't feel like a complete stranger to myself.

After hours of wandering around the city in my jeep, I went home. Not to my house. Home. To my mother.

The windows of my parents' house were fixed on me like glowing, black cat eyes that sensed that I was on the run yet again. I lowered my head to avoid their intrusive stare and then limped up the steps and unlocked the front door. The house was dark and quiet except for the rumblings of my mother and father's snores, which drowned out the screaming and the smashing. It was much cooler and lighter there. The air smelled of my father's favorite Sunday meal, fried pork chops and collard greens. My ears and nose inhaled the familiar, comforting tones and smells.

Before tackling another flight of stairs, I reached down and massaged my calf, which was beginning to stiffen. I half tiptoed and half hobbled up the stairs and down the unlit hallway, successfully making it to my old bedroom without waking my parents. Once inside, I climbed into the twin bed I'd slept in during my teen-aged years, but it now felt elbows and knees crowded. Memories from then and a few hours ago wrestled. Their scuffle kicked and shoved me to the very edge of the mattress, where I lay feeling cold, empty, and out of place.

I lay in bed watching the daylight creep in, filling the bedroom. Despite my protest the morning came. However gloomy the sky may have been, the day rose triumphantly over its gray clouds, taking away the haven I'd found in the darkness. I didn't sleep all night.

Every time I closed my eyes, I felt Satin touching me. Saw Nikki standing at the foot of Satin's bed shaking her head; saw my mother crying; and my father trying to tell her that it wasn't her fault; and I heard Malcolm's mother saying, "You promised me that you wouldn't hurt my boy." But one face, more than any other ridiculed me harshly. Malcolm's face. The love that used to glow from his eyes dissolved and a look of hatred shaded over him. Everyone else hovered around me, but he began to fade away. I was losing him because of Satin. Because of the way she made me feel, because of what she made me do.

My mother knocked on the door. "You okay?" she asked, peeking in.

"Yeah," I lied, enclosing her image inside my eyelids as I turned away from her.

I rolled out of bed and tried to get up, but my calf was still stiff and tender from the day before.

"What's wrong with your leg?" she asked when it refused to support my efforts to stand.

"Oh, I caught a cramp yesterday," I answered, trying to sound unconcerned.

"Let me see it."

"No, Mama. It's all right."

Ignoring me, she reached down and attempted to doctor my leg.

"No, Ma!" I said, pushing her away with my angry tone. I flopped back down on the bed and began massaging my own calf. I didn't mean to snap at her, but the last place I wanted her to touch me was there. She could touch me anywhere but there.

My mother acquiescently kept her distance and settled for embracing me with her eyes. Looking into her face, I noticed that the crevices of her forty-something laugh lines, which wrinkled her forehead, cupped the corners of her mouth, and stabbed at her eyes, were becoming more prominent. I could see my teenage years in those wrinkles, could see the many times that I had boldly sashayed in an hour past curfew. Could see the times that she knew, but couldn't prove, that I'd entertained horny teenage boys in my room while she and my father were at work. Could see the times when I was feeling exceptionally brave and had gone word for word with her.

"I'm sorry, Ma," I said, apologizing more so for her wrinkles than for my disrespectful tone.

"Malcolm called here looking for you last night," she said, suspecting that whatever was going on had to do with him.

I got back in bed.

Sitting down next to me, my mother said as she rubbed my back, "And so did Nikki."

I sighed heavily.

"You wanna tell me what's going on?"

Her voice was so patient, so soothing. I turned to face her and that's when the tears came. My mother cuddled me in her arms. In her arms I felt so close to myself. My old self. Not that stranger who came into my life yesterday. So maybe she isn't really here, I reasoned. The devil can't simply walk into a person's soul and make herself at home. No. She has to be invited. But didn't I knowingly encourage this wild woman's possession of me by ignoring her arrival? Can I deny being aware of her motives and feelings that very first day I dreamed her sinful dream and wished it to be my reality?

Yes, I can. I can and I will deny it. None of it is real. Not the dream and not the reality! "Tonya, baby, what's wrong?" my mother asked again.

If I told her, she would hate me. If I told her, she would torture and quilt me to death with the tears of a God-fearing woman, unable to conceive the reasons why she had been confronted with the indisputable fact that she endured eighteen hours of brutal labor giving life to a daughter who wasn't going to give her any grandchildren; a daughter whose soul was now destined to spend all eternity in the fiery mansion of hell.

My father came and stood in the doorway. What a strong looking man my father is, I thought. Even more so when he was worried about his family. He didn't touch, didn't talk. He didn't even look particularly sad or angry. And it was his distance, his silence, and his look of indifference that let me know that all I had to do was point to whatever or whoever was causing me pain, and he'd take care of it.

I wanted to run to him for protection. But I thought about the baseball bat he'd given me for protection, and how it had snapped in half, the way he would if he ever learned the truth.

So I told my mother and my father that I was just tired and stressed out from hours of sculpting, trying to meet deadlines. This got them out of the house and off to work. I made myself a cup of black coffee, went out onto the front porch and sat down on the banister. Malcolm came around twelve o'clock, but I didn't see him until he was two houses away, and by then it was too late to duck inside undetected because he was staring directly in my face from his car. I was, however, able to avoid the confrontation for a few minutes by going in the house and then only coming back out when he rung the doorbell.

"Let me tell you something," Malcolm said, yanking open the screen door, stepping inside then slamming the front door. "Don't you ever, as long as you live, call yourself hiding from me again!" He was pointing his finger in my face. I simply peered up at him, looking and feeling like a child who was being scolded by a totally pissed off father.

The vein on the side of his temple had so much blood pumping through it that I thought it just might burst. "I've been all over the damn place looking for you. Nikki didn't know where you were, and I really got worried when Satin didn't know where you were. Now, where in the hell have you been?"

"Here," I answered, stepping out of the way of his agitated finger. "I came here last night."

"What's going on, Tonya?"

"Nothing," I said.

"Don't give me that shit! You come in my house, rip my clothes off, go down on me, something you've never done before, and then you disappear for two days, and you're going to stand here and expect me to believe that nothing's going on? You better tell me something!"

"Nothing's wrong," I kept telling him, but he wasn't going for it. He wanted an explanation, but I didn't have one, at least not one that I was willing to give.

"So what, am I crazy?"

"No, Malcolm."

"Then tell me what Sunday was all about."

"Nothing. It was about nothing."

"Why are you lying?"

"I'm not lying! Now will you just leave me alone!" I started banging him in his chest. "Just leave me alone," I yelled.

Suddenly Malcolm grabbed me by my wrists, backed me into a corner and wouldn't let me out. He was yelling and carrying on in a way I'd never seen before. I was scared and too terrified to show that I was scared.

"Oh, so what you gonna do, hit me?" I asked.

"Hit you?" That made him angrier. "Hit you? No I'm not gonna hit you! And do you know why? Because my father raised a man! And you damn well better be glad that he did."

He left, slamming the front door behind him. I lay down on the couch and slept. In what seemed like minutes after I'd closed my eyes, I heard my mother calling my name.

"Oh, hi, Mama." I yawned. "You're just getting in?"

"No. I've been home for two hours."

"Two hours? What time is it?"

"A little after eight."

"Eight!"

"Yeah. I tried to wake you when I first came in, but you wouldn't budge. Is everything okay, Tonya?"

"Yeah, Mama. Everything's fine. I just needed some rest."

"Obviously." She got up from the couch. "You need to eat something. Come on in the kitchen."

I sat down at the table. "Where's Daddy?"

"At work. Where else?"

The doorbell rang. My Mama set a plate of liver and rice in front of me. "Eat," she commanded.

A few seconds later Malcolm was sitting down at the table with me making small talk with my mother until I finished eating. Then we went out onto the porch.

Before he said anything, Malcolm pressed his lips on mine. I sighed and sank to the very bottom of the kiss.

"Talk to me, Tonya," he begged.

Right at that moment, I realized just how alike Malcolm and Satin were. Always pressing for the unspoken, neither understanding that words, if you didn't say them in the right manner, or if the person that you were speaking to wasn't prepared to hear them could do more harm than good in some cases. Sometimes silence was best. In this case, silence was definitely best.

"There's nothing to talk about, Malcolm."

"Tonya, you're lying to me. You know you're lying and, more importantly, I know you're lying. And I'm telling you now, as much as I love you, I will not be with someone who lies to me."

If I tell you, will you love me the same? Will you wrap your arms around me and make passionate love to me like you did on Sunday? Will you smile at me? Will you listen to the reasons I didn't resist until it was too late?

No. If I tell you, you will hate me. Not only did I cheat on you, but I did it by sleeping with another woman.

"Malcolm, I don't know what to tell you."

"How about the truth, Tonya?"

"The truth is I love you, and I don't want to lose you, but I can't tell you what Sunday was about because I don't know myself. And that's the truth."

Malcolm sighed then stood. "All right," he said.

As he walked down the steps, I said, "I really do love you, Malcolm. You know that, don't you? Please tell me that you know that."

With his back to me, he said, "I do. I wouldn't be here if I didn't."

19

Early the next morning I went to my studio. What was left of my baseball bat rolled across the floor and rested next to the now broken portrait of Satin. I sighed then got a box and cleaned up the pieces. When I finished, I sat down in front of the little black girl. We were staring at each other when Satin knocked on the door.

"Why did you leave before talking about this?" Satin asked. "We need to talk about this, Tonya."

I rested my forehead against the pink wall, next to Hazel's picture.

"Tonya, don't do this. Don't shut me out."

"What do you want me to say, Satin? That I'm happy about what happened. If you think I am then you've got another thought to think!"

"I know you're not. That's why we need to talk."

"Talk about what?" I asked sharply.

"About how you're feeling. About where we go from here."

"I want to go back to the life I was living before I met you," I said.

"So do I," Satin said, "but we can't." She sat down on a stool. "There are a lot of wonderful things about this life, Tonya, but there are also a lot of difficult things too, and I didn't want you to have to deal with any of that if I could help it. But I couldn't."

Satin shook her head, blaming herself. And I let her because I just wasn't ready to accept responsibility for my part in this.

"I've never been unfaithful to anyone before," Satin said wearily. "But there's nothing I can say to justify what I've done because I knew from the first day you walked into my store that when the right opportunity presented itself, I would sleep with you."

When? I thought to myself as the presumptuousness of the word sent chills down my spine. When? As if Satin knew that she, like Meyoki, had come into my life bestowing love that I didn't want to feel, but nevertheless, I needed it and felt it very intensely. Love that frightened the hell out of me, but at the same time soothed and excited me. Love that was overflowing with trust and responsibility but was also extremely abstruse. But whether I understood it or not was beside the point, because right or wrong I loved Satin just as much as I loved Malcolm.

"So where do we go from here?" Satin asked.

"You're asking the wrong person," I said.

"I can't pretend that we're not here. Can you?"

Silence invaded the room. Not a quiet or still silence. This silence clamored and floated its sulky mass about the room, bumping and knocking against everything in its path. Satin knocked the silence out the window by suggesting that I see a psychiatrist. I told her that there was nothing wrong with me so I didn't need to see a shrink.

"I know that there's nothing wrong with you, but there's also nothing wrong with talking to someone who isn't so close to the situation and who can help you figure out what you're feeling and what you want to do about those feelings. Now, I know someone--"

I shook my head.

"All right then Nikki should--"

I shook my head again.

"Well, there are some black lesbian support groups--"

Shook my head again.

"You can go to one of the groups in D.C. where no one knows you," Satin said.

"No," I said.

"But Tonya, you need to talk with someone who can help you through this."

"The only person I need to help me through this is you," I said. "So just forget about the shrink and support group business because I'm not doing it."

Against her better judgement Satin dropped the subject for the time being. I agreed to meet Satin at her house for dinner later in the week so that we could talk. When she left, I sat down in front of the *Glass Of Cool Water* piece. I moved the black woman from the top of the stairs and put her on the middle step. Then I spent the next two days sculpting another black woman, whom I put at the top of the stairs. Like the black man at the bottom of the stairs, the woman held a glass of water for the confused black woman in the center.

He said that he wouldn't have stayed with me if he believed that I didn't love him. But he lied, to himself and to me. The lie he told wasn't intentional, though. At the time he honestly thought that he was telling himself the truth. I mean, what man in his right mind would stay with a woman whom he suspected didn't love him?

I didn't like the way he started looking at me--a little afraid, a little distrustful, a little insecure. I also didn't like the way he started listening to me, waiting for a lie to come out of my mouth. Or the way he refused to let me kiss him in certain places because it made him feel too soft, too vulnerable. But what I hated was the way that he began touching me, trying to hold back his feelings, trying not to let so much of me inside him and trying desperately not to let anymore of him out.

I tried to reassure him, but he said that that wasn't what he needed. When I asked what did he need, he just looked at me as if to say, If you have to ask, then to hell with it, and to hell with you.

"I need to see you," I said to him over the phone. We hadn't been together in over a week. There was silence on his end. "Malcolm..." I pleaded.

Nothing for about a minute, then, "Where are you?"

"At my studio."

"I'll be there in fifteen minutes."

Malcolm knocked on the door about eight o'clock. He looked very tired and still dressed in the dark blue suit and tie he'd worn to work. I wanted to run into his arms, but instead I reached up and stroked his handsome face.

He wanted to be outside, so he drove to Cylburn, where we walked around in silence until it was dark. I kept looking up at him, but he never looked at me. His eyes were focused straight ahead, staring at trees and plants. At anything except me. As we walked, the clouds got dark and low, and soon it was raining. We sought shelter under a large tree. As the rain poured, I asked, "Why don't you believe me?"

Not looking at me, he said, "I do."

"Show me," I said.

Malcolm put his arms around me and backed me up against the trunk of the tree as we kissed. He unzipped my pants and kneeled as he pulled them down. Then he kissed me there. Um...right there.

And I thought, See Satin. I don't need you if that's what this is all about.

Satin was in the kitchen cleaning up what was left of the dinner she'd prepared for us. It was funny how we'd automatically fallen back into the same routine, as if we hadn't been apart at all. But although our shopping and dinner plans hadn't changed, our conversations had. They were filled with discussions about the scary and the beautiful pieces that made up this sometimes ambiguous and other times thrilling situation we'd found ourselves in. One thing was for sure, though. My feelings for Satin went way beyond what Malcolm did to me the night before. I was in love with her. I was in love with her joys and fears, cares and indifferences, lies and truths, strengths and weaknesses, conceits and insecurities, idealities and imperfections. But I didn't tell her because I was afraid that it would lead to something that I wasn't ready for.

Since I'd refused to see a shrink, Satin started helping me come to terms with this whole thing by getting me to read about the experiences of other black women "in the life" as she'd put it. And I learned that no, there wasn't a *Black Homosexual Digest* but there were magazines and newspapers and books, whole books devoted to the lives and stories of black lesbians. I read Audre Lorde's *Zami: A New Spelling of My Name*, Alice Walker's *The Color Purple*, Gloria Naylor's *The Women of Brewster Place*, Rosa Guy's *Ruby* and others. I could see a lot of myself and Satin in Lorraine's and Theresa's relationship in *Brewster Place*. Lorraine was fine with her homosexuality as long nobody knew about it and treated her differently, and Theresa could give a damn who knew. But there was one major difference between Theresa and Satin--Satin would never end up at a Brewster Place because I was too ashamed of us.

Still, all of the stories got me to wondering when Satin realized that she was gay and how she reacted to the news. Did she accept it as something so natural that she just decided one day that she was going to sleep with a woman the way Audre Lorde had, or something so normal that it needed no explanation like Shug and Celie or Ruby and Daphne?

I was sitting on the couch reading the last pages of *Ruby*. Lena Horne was singing *"Deed I do"* when Satin sat down on the floor next to the table and started reading a letter from her parents. I put the book down on my lap and let my eyes traced her face and her lips catapulted me back to the day that they had caressed me so tenderly.

"What?" I heard Satin say.

"Huh?"

"What are you staring at?"

"I was staring?"

She placed the letter back in the envelope. "What were you thinking about?"

"Nothing."

"How am I supposed to help if you start keeping things from me?"

I shrugged.

"Am I going to have to play twenty questions, or are you going to tell me what that deep stare was about?"

"There's nothing to tell, but I do have a question. When did you realize that you were gay?"

She grinned and said, "When I met you."

Forgetting about Robin for a minute, I almost believed her.

"Bull," I said, laughing as I threw one of the couch's small pillows at her.

She caught the pillow and tossed it back.

"I'm serious."

"So am I," she smiled as she left the room. She returned carrying a wine cooler, and then she propped herself on the other end of the sofa. "When I was sixteen," she said after taking a sip.

"That young? How did you know? How did you find out?"

Satin's smile vanished, leaving a reticent streak in its place. "Do you have to know tonight?"

I sprang to my feet and pretended that I had a microphone in my hand. "Can you believe this folks?" I said, talking to an imaginary crowd. "Satin Pierce is dodging a topic. For the first time in her...How old are you again?" I asked, shoving my invisible microphone in her face.

"Thirty-six."

"Getting up there, aren't you?" She slapped my hand away. "For the first time in her thirty-six years on this earth, Satin Pierce is avoiding an issue."

Satin smiled brightly. "I'm not avoiding the issue. I just don't want to talk about it."

My hand dropped by my side. "Why is it when I don't want to talk about something, I'm avoiding the issue, but when you don't want to talk about something, somehow you're not avoiding the issue?"

"All right," she said.

Satin played with the bottle in her hand. She was normally so calm and straightforward, eager to divulge any information. But tonight she was avoiding not only my question but my eyes as well. She sat the bottle on the coffee table then nestled down in the couch.

"I had a girlfriend named Tara. I called her 'Terror' because she was so mischievous and she drove everybody crazy at times. We did everything together. Even lost our virginity on the same day." Satin paused for a second, rolled some thoughts around in her head then jumped back into the story. "Anyway, we were up in her bedroom one night talking and laughing about boys while doing each other's hair. I was sitting on the edge of Tara's bed and she was standing in front of me working on my bangs. That's when I really noticed how curvy her hips were and how flat her stomach was, and I had to fight this urge, this enormous impulse to circle her navel with my..." Satin paused and slowly closed her eyes as she took a deep breath. "Later that night I found myself refraining from touching her small, brown breasts as she lay asleep in bed next to me. I actually had to get out of bed to prevent myself from kissing her.

"I went out onto the porch because I couldn't breathe, but even outside I was still gasping for air. I went into the living room and turned on the stereo. Music has always kept me breathing during some of the most difficult times of my life. Suddenly the air wasn't so thick. So I put on another album. I stayed up all night long listening to music.

"I could breathe, but I still didn't know what was going on. Tara and I had been sleeping in the same bed for years, and I'd never thought about her in a sexual way. Also, I had a boyfriend at the time, whom I was having sex with quite frequently," she said, smiling lightly.

"How frequent was frequently?"

"Every day frequent," she laughed out loud.

"Every day? What are you, a nymphomaniac?"

"That's what Rob--" Seeing my smile crumble, Satin decided not to finish that statement.

During one of our shopping trips last week, Satin said that she couldn't promise me anything and at the time I didn't exactly know what she was talking about. Later, I realized that she was talking about Robin. She was talking about not giving up her relationship with Robin. She was talking about talking with Robin, spending time with Robin, kissing Robin, and making love with Robin. Somehow I hadn't counted on that.

"I couldn't understand where these feelings were coming from," Satin continued. "And I was scared. Especially when my eyes began meandering around the locker room before and after gym class while my girlfriends pranced around naked, oblivious to the fact that I was the fearful, vampiric dyke who was sent by the homosexual commander and chief to Patterson High to suck the heterosexuality from the necks of young girls and transform them into homosexual zombies."

"So one day you were okay and the next you weren't?" I asked.

A tad offended, Satin said, "I'm still okay."

"You know what I mean."

"No. What do you mean, Tonya?"

"I mean, how can you be straight on Saturday and then gay on Sunday?"

"It's easy when you constantly tell yourself on Monday, Tuesday, Wednesday, Thursday, and Friday that you just admire women instead of adore them in the way that you're only supposed to adore men. That it's just a phase that you're going through, a phase that you'll soon grow out of."

"So you're saying that you were born this way?"

"I was born the same way everyone else was born, Tonya, with a need to love. And like everyone else I needed someone to talk to about who I wanted to love me back. I was naive enough to think that I could talk to Tara. After all, we were best friends. And best friends should be able to tell each other anything."

"Not anything," I said, thinking about Nikki.

Satin evaded my eyes by looking out the window at the weeping willow dressed in the dark, still night. I'd never seen her so near to tears as I had this night. She looked like she was going to break down at any minute, but I knew she wouldn't. It was plain to see that she wasn't too thrilled with the idea of losing her composure in front of me. Her voice was shaky, but that was about it. No tears. Not even a sniffle.

Not having ever seen her in this state before made me want to take her in my arms and hold her close to me. But I remembered how wonderful her soft skin felt, and I didn't want to complicate our lives any further by acting impulsively. So I remained aloof and balled up on the other end of the couch.

"When I told Tara, she called me every derogatory name she could think of. Then she went over to my house and told my parents what was going on. For reasons that I'm still uncertain of today, she told my parents that I wrestled her down on the bed and fondled her. But it wasn't the lie that angered me. What disturbed me more than anything was that she told my parents something that I should have had the right to tell, when and if I chose to tell them. I tried to explain to them that it didn't happen the way Tara had said, but they didn't want to hear that. They wanted to hear that nothing to that effect happened--period! And I couldn't tell them that.

"I marched over to Tara's house and confronted her, and we ended up getting into a huge argument. Her parents called the police, and a female officer dragged me kicking and screaming off their porch, then stuffed me in the back seat of her patrol car, and drove me home."

"I can't imagine you losing it like that," I said.

"Well, Tara rather enjoyed witnessing me make a spectacle of myself. So I promised myself that I would never let anyone see that vulnerable side of me again. When people know what's in your heart, they tend to take advantage of you."

"I'd never do that to you," I said.

Satin smiled, although I don't think she believed me.

"Do you ever run into Tara when you go home?"

"Not anymore. Tara died a few months before you and I met." Satin reached for her wine cooler again. She didn't drink it at first, and she was quiet for so long that I didn't think she was going to continue. Finally, she took a small sip and placed the bottle between her legs.

"My mother called and told me that Tara was very sick. I flew home the next day and went straight to the hospital. Tara was lying there with tubes running in every part of her body that gave access to her insides. Her skin was a dull gray. She used to be as light as your mother is. And she'd lost so much weight that I could actually count her ribs through the sheet that covered her. Her eyes were huge because the skin around her face was wasting away. There was no life in them. There wasn't any life in that room.

"I sat down beside the bed and reached for her hand. My mother said that Tara didn't have strength enough to blink her eyelids. But when I touched her hand, Tara moved it away. She slowly focused those poppy eyes at me and whispered, 'You're the one that's supposed to be here. Not me. You're the freak. Not me.' She started crying but no tears came from her eyes and no sound from her chapped lips. But I knew she was crying, by the way her nose flared in and out. Her nose always did that when she cried.

"She didn't want me to, but I held her hand anyway as she continued to cry. I kissed her gray face, her poppy eyes, and her chapped, peeling lips. And, I told her that I have lain in that bed so many times that I've lost count, that I've watched friends of mine, gay and straight, die over and over again, one right after the other, in reality and in my dreams, and each time all I could do was kiss their gray faces, and their poppy eyes, and their chapped lips."

AIDS. Tara died of AIDS.

Nothing was said between us for a long time. Then I asked, "How old were you when you actually slept with a woman?"

"Twenty-two. During my junior year at Morgan I became friends, best friends with a girl named Faye Dupont, one of the most beautiful women I've ever known. She had tar black skin and the bottom half of her face was all nose and lips. She wore her thick black hair in a neatly fluffed afro. She had an apartment off campus and I would stay there during breaks so that I wouldn't have to go home and listen to my mother cry and watch my father staring at me, searching for his little girl. The one who wasn't a lesbian. We spent a lot of time at Faye's place, studying, debating, cooking, or just listening to music and dancing. She was a breath of fresh air for my life. Two days after graduation, Faye was preparing to return to

California and I was going back home. Faye gave me a goodbye kiss that turned into good morning." Satin smiled about the sweet memory of her first love, then asked, "When did you first realize that you were gay?"

The question made me uncomfortable. I still wasn't ready to use that word to describe myself. I don't know, somehow the word made me feel vulnerable, unsafe somehow.

"It's not a dirty word, Tonya."

"It is for me right now," I said.

Satin looked away from me for a minute. "Okay," she said when she was facing me again, "When was the first time that you realized that you were something other than straight?"

I didn't like that phrasing any better, but I answered anyway. I didn't tell Satin about the first time I saw Meyoki and thought how beautiful she was. I told her about the week after I saw Meyoki, and Nikki had spent the night at my house.

"Elaine, Nikki, and I were in my room, and Elaine asked which superhero we'd like to sleep with. Elaine was always asking stupid questions like that. Nikki said, 'The Dark Knight, of course. Batman's got an edge to him that I'd like to feel all up inside me.' Elaine said, 'Superman. They don't call him 'The Man of Steel' for nothin.' I didn't want edge or steel. I wanted graceful and wondrous curves and softness. So the whole time they were talking, I was deciding between Batgirl, Wonder Woman, and Supergirl. But neither of them could hold a candle to Eartha Kitt as Cat Woman. So in my mind, I choose Cat Woman, but I told them that Spiderman was the guy for me."

Satin laughed. "Eartha does have a little somethin'-somethin' going on, doesn't she?"

I blushed because it was the first time that I'd ever admitted to anyone that I had a crush on Eartha Kitt. It seemed a silly thing to admit but to Satin it was a monumental step toward self-acceptance.

"Look, it's late," Satin said. "Why don't you just stay here?"

"I'm not so sure that would be a good idea."

"You can stay in the guest room. I promise I won't try anything."

"I'm not worried about that," I lied. That was the first thing that entered my mind.

"Yes, you are."

"There you go again, telling me what you think I'm thinking."

"I know you, Tonya. Probably better than you know yourself."

20

Three weeks after Satin and I became more than friends and Malcolm and I got down in the pouring rain up against that tree, Robin came back from Haiti. It was on a Monday night at the end of July. It was Satin's birthday. She called and said that she wanted to see me, but she was adamant about my not coming over before nine. I was curious as to why so I arrived at her house a tad early, a half an hour early to be exact.

The murmur of their conversation spilled out onto the steps, and like quicksand, began to pull me under. My aching heart didn't know whether to give the order to retreat or stand my ground. Although I had good reason to flee, my reasons for staying outweighed my one cause to get back in my jeep and drive away.

Why should I leave? I asked myself. I have plans. It's her birthday, and I brought her a gift, an African statue. I brought all this food to prepare, and after dinner, I want us to sip a little wine and talk until the sun is sitting on her windowsill.

You see. I have plans. And besides that, I thought, I'm in love with her. So there is no reason in hell why I should even consider leaving. The only thing I should be contemplating is a plan of defense because I damn well have the right to stay.

Satin opened the door wearing an expression of extreme annoyance. Bitterness ticked inside me as I walked past Satin, like a bomb ready to explode. There were dishes sitting on the dining room table and a small statue of a Haitian woman sitting on the coffee table.

"Robin, this is Tonya," Satin said in a controlled tone.

She smiled and held out her hand. "It's nice to finally meet you."

I shook her hand and smiled cordially, but I was too pissed off to act like I wasn't, and couldn't bring myself to say anything to her.

I looked at her thinking- *You hate me for having her, don't you?* And I could tell by the squint in her eyes that she was thinking- *With a passion. But I don't have to worry about that now because I'm back.*

Satin walked Robin outside. I watched them from the living room window. Satin glanced over at me. She continued talking as if I wasn't in her house and waiting for her. Robin got into Satin's car and started to back out of the driveway, but she stopped suddenly and called to Satin. They exchanged a few words then Satin darted a worried look in my direction. Reacting to something humorous Robin said, Satin laughed, leaned into the car window, and kissed her. If you were on the outside looking in, you would have thought that it was just a case of best friends saying good-bye. But I knew better, and that inside information almost brought tears to my eyes.

"Look, Tonya, I asked you not to come over before nine for this very reason."

"Why didn't you tell me that she was back?"

"Because I wanted to see you tonight, and I can't mention her name without you getting all upset. If I had told you that she was here, you would have caught an attitude and changed your mind about coming."

"Why is she driving your car? Doesn't she have one of her own?"

"Yes." Satin walked into the kitchen and started cleaning up the remnants of their dinner. Dinner was our thing!

"Well, why is she driving yours?"

"Because I picked her up from the airport last night."

"Last night?"

Satin ignored me. She closed the door to the dishwasher, pushed the start button then turned out the kitchen light.

"Where did she sleep?"

Satin sat on the couch and just looked up at me.

"Did you--"

"Don't, Tonya," she said, folding her arms. I was starting to irritate her. It was easy to tell when I was pissing her off because she always sat or stood with her arms folded across her chest. "I don't question you about your sex life with Malcolm, and I expect the same courtesy where Robin is concerned."

"Why'd you have to kiss her in front of me?"

"Why did you come here so early?

"That's not the point."

"Yes, it is. I don't like being spied on."

"I wasn't spying."

"Tonya, I'm too old to be playing these games. If you had done like I asked, you wouldn't have been here to see me kiss her."

"Why'd you ignore me when she was here?"

"It wasn't you I was ignoring; it was that childish game you played."

"You're the one who's playing games."

"I'm not the one sneaking around your house trying to catch you with Malcolm."

"You make me sick!"

Satin sat motionless in the chair. Her listless stare showed no evidence of hearing my abusive words.

"You're full of it!" I said, trying to provoke a response. I couldn't stand it when she ignored me.

Satin shook her head. I guess it was difficult for her to believe that I was saying these things to her. Part of me couldn't believe it either, but I couldn't stop myself. So I continued by questioning the reason she was with Robin. Satin had given me the book *This Bridge Called My Back: Writings By Radical Women Of Color*, and we'd gotten into a heated discussion about some of the black lesbians who seemed to me, anyway, to be obsessed with the idea of having a white lover. I wondered if their preoccupation with white women had to do with some deep-seated self-hatred and a need to be validated. Satin denied it vehemently.

So it was with this argument in mind that I said with a smirk, "And another thing. If dark skin is so precious, like you're forever preaching, what are you doing with a light-skinned lover?"

"I never once said that light-skinned blacks' complexions weren't as precious as ours. I don't discriminate against my own people because they happen to be lighter than I am."

"Right," I said, unable to come up with anything else.

"Aunt Josephine is light-skinned and so is Nikki," Satin pointed out. "You know what I'm talking about."

"Yes, I do, and you're absolutely wrong."

"No, I'm absolutely right, my sistah," I said in a mocking tone.

"If you believe that then you don't know me very well. The only person I need to confirm my beauty or my self-worth is me. I'm with Robin because I care for her, because she's a beautiful woman inside and out."

Oh, that hurt, and she knew it would. But two could play that game.

"Well, if you care for the beautiful, high yellah bitch so much, why are you trying so goddamn hard to get me into your bed?" I asked in the meanest, most raunchy tone I could pull from my gut.

And if that last comment didn't strike a nerve, I don't know what did. Her stare was coated with hurt and disbelief as she slowly rose to her feet. She simply stood there for a second glaring at me as if she were trying to figure out a foreign language. Then, after the translation was complete, Satin grabbed her keys and left. Since she didn't have a car, I figured that she'd gone for a walk to cool off. I waited at her house until eleven, but she didn't return. She'd been angry with me before, but this was the first time that I had angered her to the point where she felt compelled to get away from me.

Days later, after we made the peace, Satin asked me to accompany her to one of her favorite nightspots. I couldn't believe that I was actually in that building. If someone had told me ten minutes earlier that I'd be sitting at a table inside a place called The Gray Mist, I would have asked what insane asylum had he or she just escaped from.

The club was on Fulton Avenue. It was owned by a friend of Satin's named Jasmine Ploy, who opened the club back in 1980 because she grew abhorrently weary of the discrimination she, as a black lesbian, encountered at the white gay clubs. I don't know if I found the fact that white homosexuals discriminated against black homosexuals ironic, hypocritical, or typical. I mean, I watched them march on Washington demanding equal rights and equal treatment, then turned around and in the same breath said, "I might sleep with someone of the same sex, but hey, at least I don't sleep with no niggers." Now was that ironic, hypocritical, or just plain typical of some racist, ignorant white people who just happened to be homosexuals?

In all fairness, Satin said that there were some white homosexuals who were not afraid to cross the color line, but most of them did so only under very discrete circumstances. Their secretiveness was reminiscent of the slave masters and mistresses who crept out to the slave quarters in search of what Satin called a piece of "Ebony Ecstasy."

"We are taboo to them," Satin said. "And that makes us all the more erotic in their little racist minds. But they can't afford to have their lily-white reputations tainted by having an open relationship with a black homosexual."

I asked Satin if she had ever slept with anyone outside of her race, and she said, "No. I refuse to be anyone's dirty little secret."

Somehow I got the feeling that that statement was directed towards me as well.

"See, Tonya, it's just a club," Satin said, waving hello to a group of women sitting at the bar.

I halfheartedly agreed as I observed the scene. In most respects The Gray Mist was just another club. The music was blaring through giant speakers that were strategically placed in every corner, pumping out the latest club jams. The overhead lights were dim so that they wouldn't interfere with the colorful disco lights whirling around the dance floor. Tables were crammed close together, making it impossible to leave your seat without disturbing the people at the neighboring tables. And of course, cigarette smoke hovered overhead, migrating down every so often to make its irritating presence known.

The Gray Mist was just another club except for one thing. It was a gay club. A black gay club! Homosexuals or homos, freaks, lesbians or lesbos, butches, dykes or bulldykes, or bulldaggers as I'd once heard my mother refer to them, were all here, sandwiched on the small dance floor, sitting at the bar drinking, talking and laughing, and stealing intimate seconds by whispering in the ear of the person next to them.

Was this the only black gay club in Baltimore? I wondered. Where did they all come from? Do I know any of them? Though I certainly hoped not! In her book, Audre Lorde talked about feeling as if she were the only black lesbian on earth. Until tonight, I felt as if Meyoki, Satin, and Robin were the only ones in Baltimore.

I was experiencing the most extreme case of culture shock that I could have ever imagined. I wasn't surprised to see two black women kiss on the lips as they greeted, or by the intimacy that surrounded their mouths as they talked, or by their laughter, hand holding, hugging, or even by their dancing across from one another. I'd seen and participated in that kind of activity before. But I was stunned to see two black women out in public engaged in an open mouth kiss, shoving tongues down each other's throats, seemingly trying to lick each other's tonsils. And, I was dazed to see two black women pressing their bodies close together as they freaked to *"I Like the Girls"* by the Fatback Band. And because of my infancy in this type of atmosphere, I couldn't help staring and thinking that I could never dance like that out in the open.

"How about a dance?" Satin suggested, after sipping her Long Island Iced Tea, confirming my suspicions that she had totally lost her cotton-pickin' mind.

Go out there and dance? With her? Go out there and admit to everyone that I'm *that* way?

I turned to the dance floor. Couples were now snapping their fingers and clapping or waving their hands in the air as their bodies swayed to

"Shackles" by R.J.'s Latest Arrival. They were all enjoying themselves, expressing openly and affectionately feelings that surprised, disconcerted, and at times disgusted me.

"I don't want to dance," I said, turning my attention back to Satin.

"Fine," she said. "I'll dance by myself."

Satin sipped her drink then clapped and danced her way to the floor when the DJ played *"House Call"* by Maxie Priest. I reared back in my chair and watched as a light-skinned woman eased her way onto the floor and began dancing with Satin, who rocked her body smoothly and very femininely. She was wearing a tight blue mini dress and a pair of sheer black stockings that had a vine of roses climbing up the sides of her long legs. She looked gorgeous.

While I was watching Satin, a woman said, "Hello, Tonya."

Even before I turned around with my mouth hanging open, I knew that Meyoki Outlaw was standing at my table. She was more beautiful than I had remembered. Her brown-sugar brown eyes sparkled, and her pretty pink tongue still adorned that musical gold ball. She now had five earrings in each ear and a gold band on every finger. I wondered if she still had the ring in her navel.

"Meyoki?" I said quietly.

"It's good to see you, Tonya," she said, holding out her hand.

I glanced at her ringed fingers for a second before shaking her hand. "It's good to see you too," I lied.

"May I sit down?" she asked.

"Yeah. Sure," I said, looking around for Satin.

She was still on the dance floor and hadn't noticed me talking with Meyoki. The DJ had slowed things down and now Satin was slow dancing with a woman to Patti Labelle's song *"We're Back Together."*

"Well, it's been a long time," Meyoki said after a sigh and an awkward smile.

"Yes, it has. So how have you been?"

"Good," she said. "And you?"

"Good," I said, and reached for my glass, which was empty.

"Oh, let me buy you another drink," she said eagerly.

"No thanks." A smile timidly crawled across my lips.

"So," Meyoki said, "do you come here often?"

And that was all she asked, but I heard, so, you're *funny* after all, huh?

"No," I denied quickly, too quickly. Meyoki knew that tone well, knew that I was denying more than just the question of how often I frequented gay bars. "What about you? D-Do you come here a lot?"

"No. This is actually the first time I've been here. I just got back in town about three months ago. I've been out in Seattle for the last few years finishing up medical school, and now I'm a resident at Liberty Medical Center."

"Oh, so you're that famous doctor you've always dreamed of becoming," I said, genuinely happy for her, but also happy to be talking about something other than the place we were in.

"I don't know how famous I am, but yes, I've captured my dream. And so have you. I hear that you're that famous sculptor you vowed to be. Looks like we both got what we wanted." Meyoki paused and gazed at me as she tapped her tongue on the back of her front teeth.

"But looks can be deceiving," I thought aloud, not intending for her to hear.

"So. How about a dance?" Meyoki said, licking her full, saucy lips.

And I don't know why, but I couldn't say no to her. I accidentally knocked over my empty glass, and then knocked over Satin's drink, but I didn't say, No. I'm afraid of what people will think if I go out there and dance with you.

Meyoki took my hand and led me through the crowd, and soon I was staring at my empty seat from a far away corner of the dance floor. The road back to our table expanded and stretched out before me like an open highway. Only there were no large, green trees huddled on the sides of the road to make the journey cool and pleasant, and give the illusion that the drive was only two hours instead of four. Nor were there any oil paintings of blue horizons, bright orange sunsets, or grassy farm scenery to pull off to the shoulder to marvel at. Nothing. Just a long, hot, tar-black road.

In actuality I was only twelve to fifteen feet away from my safe heterosexual haven, but each of those feet equaled a hundred hot desert miles. Patrice Rushen's song *"Remind Me"* was playing. Meyoki pulled me to her and placed my shaky hands around her waist as she draped her arms over my shoulders.

"Just follow my hips," Meyoki instructed, as she twisted them slowly.

I was too nervous and perplexed to follow much of anything. Feeling that we were the main attraction, I peeked at the people surrounding us.

"Poor Tonya Mimms. Still worried about what other people think," Meyoki said.

Right then I wanted to hit her because I didn't like her knowing that after all these years, I was still worried about what other people thought, what other people said, or how other people felt about me. I wished that I didn't give a damn about other people. I wished that I believed that what I thought and felt counted more than my family's and friends' approval or their sorry ass opinions. I wanted to punch Meyoki for knowing that I was still a coward.

But instead, I did the most cowardly thing of all. I pushed Meyoki away from me and started to run. But at the same time the DJ started playing *"Dance to the Drummer's Beat"* and everyone in the building it seemed rushed onto the dance floor. I pushed and shoved my way through the crowd so that I could leave this dancing den of homosexuality, but Meyoki grabbed my wrist.

"I think it's time that I show you how wrong you are about us," she said.

And suddenly I didn't care about anyone's opinion except Meyoki's, for a while anyway. Tonight may be the last time that I ever see her, and I couldn't stand it if I let her go away thinking that after ten years, I was still worse than anybody at Northwestern High School.

The night turned into an Old School dance fest as the DJ played all the old club jams from the eighties--*"Hip Hop Bee Bop," "Funkin' For Jamaica," "Let's Start A Dance," "Din-Daa-Daa," "Heartbeat," "Funky Sensation," "Dazz," "All Night Thang," "Looking for the Perfect Beat," "One Nation Under a Groove."* All the club jams that I used to freak guys down to the ground at Odell's and house parties when I was in high school.

The music was loud, hypnotic, seductive, and wild. I listened to each instrument separately and let their beats control my body. The drums were banging in my feet, the bass was strumming in my thighs, and the bongos were beating in my hips. What else was there for me to do but dance?

I watched myself dance with Meyoki in bright, white flashes, as though a strobe light was upon us. At one flash, Meyoki and I were dancing face to face with her arms on my shoulders and my hands on her waist. And in the next flash, Meyoki had her back to me and my breasts were pressed up against her shoulder blades, and her behind was gyrating against my pelvis. She held up her arms, and I ran my hands down her fingers, past her wrists, her elbows, armpits, and sides before resting my hands on her hips. Then I leaned to her ear and asked, "Do *you* feel the difference?"

Meyoki placed a hand on the back of my neck and I pulled her close to me. "Oh, most definitely," she said.

We danced dirtier than I ever thought I knew how. Without missing a beat our bodies rotated to the sound of the music. I felt happy and free. We danced until the DJ yelled, "Good night, Baltimore!"

Both Meyoki and I were hot, sweaty, and breathless. As people started leaving the dance floor, Meyoki and I stared and smiled at each other.

Meyoki reached up and wiped the sweat from my forehead. "Are you here with someone?" she asked.

Oh, my God! Satin! I thought. I tried to stay cool as I darted my eyes around the building trying to find her.

"Are you?" Meyoki said.

"Uh, s-sort of...um...yes," I mumbled.

"That's too bad," Meyoki said. "You know I've thought about you a lot over the years. I've always wondered what if..."

Should I tell her that I've thought about her too? I asked myself. Should I tell her that I've been trying to escape my feelings for her but the only place running from her has taken me is straight into Satin's arms? And after all that running, I've ended up in her arms anyway.

Meyoki and I walked back to the table where Satin was sitting, watching, waiting, and thinking, I know that face.

"Meyoki, is it?" Satin said after I'd introduced them. "And you know Tonya from..."

"High school," Meyoki said.

"That's what I thought," Satin said, handing me the napkin, from under her drink, so that I could wipe the sweat off my brow, neck and cleavage. "That's what I thought."

I walked Meyoki to her car while Satin got into hers.

"It's been really good seeing you again," Meyoki said.

"Same here," I said. Then, "Meyoki, I'm really sorry about all that stuff in high school."

"No need to apologize. We were teenagers, trying to find our way." She smiled. "Say, how's Nikki?"

"Okay," I said, wondering why she would ask about her. "She's a doctor, too. A psychologist."

"Why doesn't that surprise me?" Meyoki smiled.

With nothing else to say, I said, "Well, maybe I'll see you around."

"Maybe," Meyoki said.

Then she puckered her lips and leaned forward. Oooh! Did my heart race. I felt like I was back in the shower room at Northwestern. I'd been waiting for that kiss for ten years. And when she kissed my lips, then drove off, I held the residue of her lips in the palm of my hand. As I stood there, I thought about what Malcolm had said about first loves, and knew that Meyoki was my first love. She was the one who first made me all warm and crazy inside, made my cheeks turn violet. She kept me from paying attention in class because I was daydreaming about her or sketching her in my notebook. She kept me up at night thinking about doing things that my parents didn't raise me to think about or do. She was the one that I lied to my girlfriends about how much I really liked her. She was the one who made me laugh and cry from my heart. And tonight she had me wondering what if...

"Your first love is the one that you measure every other guy against," Malcolm had said during dinner.

And it was true. I had measured Malcolm against Meyoki, but I'd also measured Satin against her. And Satin measured up in every way. Yeah, Meyoki was my first love, but I had moved on. And Satin was who I loved now.

21

After The Gray Mist, Satin changed. As she drove us home that night, she said, "I should have known better than to get involved with a bisexual. You are a confused group of people, and you make the worse lovers. You spend your entire life running. First from your homosexuality then from your heterosexuality. When one becomes too demanding or unpredictable, you run toward the other."

"I'm not running from anything," I said.

"Don't insult my intelligence." Satin took her eyes completely off the road. "Do you think I'm blind, Tonya?" She laughed. "All this time you had me believing that had I not touched you, we wouldn't be here. When in fact, you've been here since high school. Probably before."

She was so angry, but she wouldn't really let it out. She just tried to force my hand at everything. Things between us started getting a lot more decisive as well as hazardous. Before The Gray Mist, Satin didn't press the sex issue too much, but all of a sudden she began to demand affection. She wanted us to cuddle up on the couch, hold hands, in the house of course, and kiss all the time. I wouldn't let her stick her tongue in my mouth. Her tongue made me forget myself and caused me to do things that I regretted later. There had been times when her tongue had talked me into spending the night lying next to her in her bed.

It was difficult to remain abstinent when I was that close to her. The urges that I got were so much stronger and louder than my feeble, soft-spoken no's. I'd wrestle with my desires for a time, but I'd get tired of fighting pretty damn quickly. I wanted to let myself go, and I did. My hands wandered in the dark room, exploring her luscious body and listening to her moans. Then Satin touched me and my body caved in as the heat from her kisses permeated my skin. I wanted to feel that explosion rock me again. But just as I was about to give her all of me that ever-present feeling of shame appeared at the foot of the bed and doused the flame.

The look of hurt that filmed Satin's eyes when I pulled away tore me up inside. I felt guilty for succumbing to my sexual attraction for her and for leading her on and then rejecting her at the last moment. But instead of telling her that I didn't know when or if I'd ever be able to fully commit to her in that way, I blew up and said cruel things to her.

Subconsciously I was hoping that Satin would take offense to my harsh words and angrily defend herself, thereby easing some of my guilt. Only thing was, Satin never argued with me when I was ranting, most of the time she walked out. Which was exactly what she did two nights ago, after we'd gotten into yet another argument about the absence of sex in our relationship.

I was lying on the couch listening to Patti Labelle *sing "Kiss Away The Pain"* when Satin tried to kiss me.

"Goddamn it. Will you please get off me!" I yelled. "Every time I turn around you're trying to kiss or touch me like some old pervert."

The words I used to fight off her enticing advances almost killed her. I know because after I'd said them, they almost killed me. I turned away so that I wouldn't see the sadness that forced her to grab her car keys and leave her own house. As usual, I slept on her couch and waited for her to come back the following morning. And as usual, she stopped in the hallway when she saw that I was still there. We stood staring at each other through blood shot eyes. I opened my mouth to tell her that I was sorry, but the words fizzled on their way out so that they were hardly recognizable.

Satin shook her head and turned up the volume on the stereo. That was the other thing about her. The more we argued the louder the music. It was so loud that morning that we had to shout at each other to be heard.

I followed Satin upstairs and she walked around me getting ready for work as if I wasn't there.

"I didn't mean it, Satin," I finally was able to shout over Anita Baker's *"Sometimes I Wonder Why."*

"You never mean it," she yelled back then left the house.

When she returned the next morning, I followed her upstairs. She began taking off her clothes, and I turned my back. I heard an empty laugh come from her.

"I was worried about you," I said. "Where did you spend the night?"

"You know where."

Anger rushed in me so hard and fast that it made me woozy, and I had to put my hands on my hips to steady it and myself. "Oh, you couldn't get any from me so you ran to her?"

Satin shook her head again unable to believe how insensitive I could be when I was angry.

"Did you fuck her?" I asked, amazing her further with another uncaring, insulting remark. She rolled her eyes and started out of the bedroom. I walked behind her asking, "Well, did you?"

My acrimonious question plowed through the house, rumbling inside the walls, shaking the floors, and drowning out Al Green's powerful voice.

"Leave me alone, Tonya," Satin demanded. If she were a different person, I'd say that she begged.

"I want to know." I raced in front of her, blocking the entrance to the bathroom.

Satin's arms were wrapped across her chest almost as tightly as the silk belt of her robe that was wrapped around her thin waist. Her anger was like a caged lion. It meandered about in front of the metal bars she had imprisoned it in, trying to find an exit in which to escape so that it could defend her. But she refused to open the gate, and she barricaded every possible out to ensure that not one fragment of hostility broke free.

Over the weeks I'd been slowly murdering the beautiful, zealous parts of Satin with my savage, disrespectful remarks that seemed to dig ulcers in her queenly black skin. I wished that I could take my hands and mold her back into the person she was before she met me.

Satin seemed to shrink in the corner as I assaulted her. I saw the water swirling in her eyes, and I watched as her eyelids blinked furiously, preventing from falling any of the tears that would prove that she was not the philosophical, controlled, practical woman she portrayed herself to be.

"Did you f--"

"Tonya, don't ask me questions that you don't want the answers to," she said in that nettlesome yet sensible tone of hers, still trying to perpetrate this image of the unshakable woman.

"So in other words, you--"

Satin let out a dark sigh that seemed to circle the hall twice before dissipating. "Stop this, Tonya!" Her voice was dry and calm.

I was angry because I knew that she had slept with Robin, but the fact that my brutal words couldn't destroy that unflappable attitude of hers got under my skin. "Answer the question!"

"Yes. Yes, I slept with Robin."

To cover up my true feelings I began laughing uncontrollably. I wanted to ask Satin why did she have to sleep with Robin. I wanted to tell her that I loved her. I wanted to say that I was sorry. I wanted to cry. But my laughter wouldn't allow me to say or do any of that.

Hurt, anger, guilt, confusion, and just downright meanness unearthed my next vengeful question. "Which one of you plays the man when you're in bed, huh?"

"Neither. If I wanted to sleep with a man, I wouldn't be a lesbian," she answered without the least bit of antagonism.

"You make me sick!" I hissed.

"Tonya, what do you expect from me?" she asked solemnly.

"Just what I'm getting." I moved away from the door.

"Tonya, why is it you expect me to give up everything that I have with Robin while you keep intact all of what you have with Malcolm?"

"Don't be throwin' Malcolm up in my face. You're the one who left here last night and slept with someone else."

"Robin is not 'someone else,' Tonya. She is to me what Malcolm is to you--my lover."

"Why is it you feel called upon to throw her up in my face all the damn time?"

"I don't mean to, but sometimes you need to be reminded."

"Reminded of what, Satin? That every time I refuse to sleep with you, you run to her. That every time I'm here you spend an hour on the phone with her. That sometimes I can't come to see you because she's in your bed. That sometimes you forget to wipe her lipstick off you neck. Now tell me again what I need to be reminded of!"

Satin sighed, rubbed her eyes, and said, "Look, Tonya, Robin was in my life way before you came along, and she'll probably be here long after you're gone."

"Who says that I'm going anywhere?"

"I know you, Tonya."

"You know me. You know me. I'm getting sick and tired of you acting like you have some kind of insight into my future."

"It's not just your future," she said quietly. "Tonya, this has got to stop. Either make up your mind to stay or leave, or find some way of dealing with my relationship with Robin, because I'm not going to stop seeing her no matter how many temper tantrums you throw."

22

"Tonya, where are you?" Malcolm asked.

"At the studio," I lied.

"It's seven o'clock. You were supposed to be here two hours ago."

"I know. I'm on my way."

"Dinner is cold, and I don't feel like heating it a third time," he muttered sounding not unlike a neglected housewife.

"I'm sorry, Malcolm."

"You could have called to let me know that you were going to be late."

"I didn't plan on being late." Satin came and stood in her kitchen doorway. "I was working and time just got away from me."

"Time has been just getting away from you a lot these days."

"I know. I'm sorry."

"Ain't you always," he said.

Satin sat down at the kitchen table. We were arguing again. She wanted me to spend the night. I said I couldn't. She threatened to go to Robin. I told her that she and Robin could go to hell. She smiled, shook her head and sipped on a wine cooler.

"Look, Tonya, I don't feel like arguing with you tonight so I'll see you tomorrow or whenever you can pull yourself away from your work," Malcolm said.

"Oh, so it's like that?"

"You damn straight it's like that." Malcolm slammed the phone down.

"I have to go," I said to Satin.

"You always do," she said.

The phone rang. After Satin answered it, she held the receiver to her chest and said, "I'll see you later."

"Oh, is this a private conversation?" I sat down at the table just as she had while I was talking to Malcolm. Satin simply laughed and put the phone to her ear.

"I'll be there soon," she said to Robin with a cool expression. "Whatever you want to do is fine." She paused then said as we eyed each other, "You know I do. I'll prove it when I get there."

Knowing what she planned to prove and how she planned to prove it, I said loudly, "You make me sick."

I walked in the house and there were two plates of cold food on the dining room table. The candles he'd left burning were nearly stubs and the bouquet of red-red roses seemed to have withered. I blew out the tiny flames. Guilt filtered the air, and its criticizing hands pushed and shoved me into his room, where he was stretched out on the bed watching television.

Sometimes when I looked at him, or kissed him, or felt him, or listened to him, or...um, tasted him, I could swear that that man was made especially for me. He treated me more like a woman than I did. He supported, inspired, and challenged my art. He massaged my hands and fingers because he knew that they needed it after I'd been modeling and sculpting all day. He made love to me with his entire being. He told me the truth, as best he knew it. I had him in the palm of my hand to do with as I pleased simply because he loved me with all of his heart.

So why was I fucking over him like this?

"I'm sorry, Malcolm. What can I do to make this up to you?" No answer! "It'll never happen again."

He turned off the television. "Are you sure that you were at your studio?"

Leaning back from him a little, I said, "Yes. Why?"

"Because I came by there and I didn't see your car and when I knocked, you didn't answer the door."

Thinking fast, "Maybe you came by when I went to get something to eat."

"Why would you go out to eat when you knew that you were supposed to have dinner with me?"

I started to answer, but then I got defensive. "I said that I was working."

"I know what you said. Now what you were actually doing is a different story."

"What do you think I was doing?"

"What do I think?"

"Yeah, what do you think?"

"I think you were with Satin."

I sighed heavily. "Why would I lie and say that I was working if I was really with Satin?"

"Maybe because every time we have plans you're late because you're always running around with her, and I'm sick of it."

I rose and looked down at him. "I was working. Now whether you choose to believe me or not is on you."

I walked downstairs and sat at the dining room table. I was nibbling on a cold piece of steak when Malcolm came down and kneeled beside my chair. I turned around and kissed the throbbing vein on his temple then kissed his lips. He refused to kiss me until I pulled a racecar from my purse and began rolling it slowly up and down his crotch, an action that lured his tongue out of his mouth and into mine. Soon I felt his rising need to accept my apology.

"You forgive me," I whispered.

In a voice meant to heal all wounds, he said, "Let me heat this up for you."

My father stood over the grill in his red apron flipping burgers as a charcoal scented gray cloud rose from the pit. Mr. Holland and Uncle Charlie were standing next to the grill, sipping beers and arguing about a baseball game. Malcolm, Nikki, Elaine, and I were sitting at a bench eating crabs. And my mother, Aunt Josephine, and Mrs. Holland were seated at the table next to us.

"All we need around here are some children," I heard my mother say.

"Well, it certainly doesn't look like any of our children agree with you at the moment, Lorna," Mrs. Holland said.

"I've been on Elaine's back for the last three years, trying to get her to stop all this running around and find herself a man to settle down with before it's too late," my mother said.

"Young girls these days just don't seem to hear their clocks ticking," Mrs. Holland said.

"Oh, they hear it," Aunt Josephine said. "They're just ignoring it. They think they got Timexs."

Ha-ha's, tee-hee's and yuk-yuk's were thrown around the backyard.

"I'm serious," my mother said. "I want some grandchildren while I'm young enough to enjoy them."

"You and me both," said Mrs. Holland. "I might look good for my age, but I definitely ain't getting any younger."

"Tonya, you better hurry up and walk down that aisle so Mama can get off my case," Elaine said.

I started to respond, but Satin walked into the backyard. I suddenly lost my appetite and got a headache. Satin knew that I was having the family over today, and she came on purpose because she was trying to make me choose what side of the fence I wanted to be on. But I was determined that I would choose on my time, not hers.

Satin was wearing a bright yellow shorts set with sandals and sporting a pair of shades. She went over to the grill first to say hello to the men, then hugged my mother, Aunt Josephine, and Mrs. Holland. My stomach was doing flip-flops because except for a few times when Satin was leaving my house as Malcolm was coming in, they hadn't been in the same place for an extensive amount of time since the day they met at my exhibit.

"You okay, Tonya?" Nikki asked.

"Yeah. I think I cut my finger."

I got up, ran in the house, and washed my hands. Satin came in after me. I was actually happy to see Satin because I hadn't spoken to her since we had that fight three nights ago, and I wanted to apologize to her.

"I'm sorry," I said.

"I know, but Tonya, you've got to remember that I have needs just like you."

"I know that. It's just that I hate to think of you being with her."

"How do you think I feel when I know that you're sleeping with Malcolm?" Satin asked.

"To be honest, I didn't think you cared one way or the other. I mean, you've never said anything about it."

"There's no point. When I agreed to give you time to sort out your feelings, I knew that your sexual relationship with Malcolm would be one of the things I'd have to deal with. So that's what I've been doing, and that's what you have to do."

Satin had plans with Robin. I wanted to object, but I couldn't and didn't. I just walked her out front after she'd said good-bye to everyone.

"I'll call you tomorrow," I said, stopping by Satin's car.

"Call me before six because I'm going out with Robin."

Again I wanted to object to her plans, but Satin gave me a look that warned me against it. Instead I rolled my eyes and puckered my lips, refraining from saying anything else that would cause an argument.

"You know what I'd like to do right now?" Satin asked, her voice low and hot. "Kiss that frown off your face." Her eyes blinked slowly as she ran her beautiful pink tongue across her lips.

I looked around in a panic.

Satin moved closer to me. "You said some pretty hurtful things to me the other day. You owe me more than an apology."

"What do you want?" I stupidly asked.

Satin and I were standing almost mouth to mouth. I was scared to death because I knew that she was bold enough and hungry enough to kiss me right there and not think twice about it.

"I want you." Her eyes already had me lying on her bed.

"I'm serious."

"You shouldn't play with me like that, Tonya." She lowered her eyes and circled my breasts with them. My nipples, feeling the directness of her glare, swelled.

I was vehemently commanding my face not to move toward hers, but her desires, my desires, our desires were reeling me in.

"Satin," I whispered. "Don't make me do this."

"I'm not making you do anything," she said softly. Oh, so softly. "Why do you always blame me for what you want to do?"

"But I don't wanna do this."

"Yes, you do."

My eyes were becoming somnolent. "Satin, Malcolm might see us."

"Not if you come with me now," she whispered. "Come on, Tonya." Her voice was soft yet forceful. "I know you want me."

"I can't."

"Yes, you can. I'll call Robin and tell her not to come over, and we can spend the night together."

"I can't just leave Malcolm."

"'I can't. I can't,'" Satin said, duplicating my tone down to the last breath. "I'm getting tired of hearing you say those words." Satin moved over to my ear and whispered, "Malcolm can't even begin to please you in the many ways that I can, Tonya. It's beyond his comprehension. You remember how good I made you feel, don't you, Tonya?"

"Yes," I sighed.

"You haven't had an orgasm that strong since, have you?"

I didn't want to negate or confirm her true summation of my sex life with Malcolm, because she would use that to get me to lie in her bed again. And I knew that I did not have the strength to fight her.

"You don't have to answer. I can see it in your eyes, taste it on your lips." Satin's cheek brushed against mine as she faced me again. "Spend the night with me, Tonya."

My eyes closed completely as Satin's lips neared mine. Then Malcolm called my name, and my heart hurtled up my throat, flew out of my mouth, and burst just above my head. Shaken, I quickly backed away from Satin, nearly tumbling over. Satin stood in the same spot as placid as ever. She was facing the backyard and she saw Malcolm coming, yet she didn't ease up nor did she warn me. She purposely let him see us trapped in a lover's gaze.

Malcolm paused and narrowed his brow. I'm not sure what made him turn a deaf ear to what his eyes were telling him, but he simply walked over to his car and said, "Tonya, we gotta go get some ice."

"All right. I'll be there in a second." My entire body was shaking. I was on the verge of tears.

Satin got into her car. When she shut the door, I leaned over. "That wasn't right and you know it."

She put on her sunglasses. "Malcolm is waiting for you," she said.

"Look who's playing games now."

"I wasn't playing." She put her car in gear then drove off.

23

"You want to be alone," Malcolm said, as he lay next to me.

"Why do you say that?" I said into the dark with my back to him.

"Every time I touch you, you move away."

"That doesn't mean that I want to be alone."

"Well, what does it mean?" he asked.

"That I don't want to be touched."

"Then you want to be alone."

"No. I don't want to be touched," I insisted.

I hadn't had a craving for him in weeks. No matter what he did, Malcolm didn't come close to making my body vibrate and tingle the way Satin had. I thought about that tingle often. And she knew it. Knew that I wanted her.

I had a sculpture in my studio. It was the first sculpture I had ever done of myself. I was standing at the center of the piece. Satin was to my left and she was watching me. Her brown eyes were slicing through me like a knife, severing the pieces that held me to Malcolm. Her mouth was open and when she talked to me, her voice quivered inside my heart, asking if I remembered the explosion. I said, yes. She had a hand on my lips and her fingertips told me that they were waiting. All I had to do was taste them like I did in the Ethiopian restaurant.

I was leaning toward her, ready to take one of her lean, dark fingers into my mouth and lick its sweetness. But then, out of nowhere, Malcolm appeared at my right and placed his strong fingers on my lips also, and I found that his sweetness was just as delicious and just as addicting. He was trying to lure me away from Satin and take me off to a place where she couldn't find us. He was watching me and his eyes were burning flames through every inch of me, melting away the hold that pulled me to

Satin. His mouth was open as well, and when he spoke to me, his voice howled inside my body. And those cries said they could give me more than Satin. And his fingertips begged me to just give him time to show me. I called that piece *Triangle*.

Malcolm climbed on top of me. "Tonya, we haven't made love in almost two weeks."

I pushed at his chest. He rolled over onto his back and I sat up.

"I need you, Tonya," he groaned and stroked my back.

"All right...here...come on," I said, lying down. "Take it. You need it so bad. Come on."

Malcolm got out of the bed. "That's all right," he said, snatching on his clothes. "You keep it, 'cause I don't need it that bad."

With his shoes unlaced and his shirt on backwards, Malcolm left the house. Seconds later I heard his car racing up the block.

"What's wrong?" Satin asked, as I eluded a kiss she attempted to give me when I walked in her house.

I flounced down on the couch. Satin sat next to me, and before I had a chance to object, she had her lips on mine and her hand on my breast. I untangled myself from her grip. Satin sighed heavily, making her frustration with me very apparent.

"I came here to be with you not sleep with you," I stated firmly.

"I'm tired of just keeping your company whenever you have a fight with Malcolm."

"Who says I had a fight with Malcolm?"

Satin turned up the stereo. "I'm not playing your games tonight, Tonya."

"I'm not asking you to," I yelled over B.B. King as he sang *"The Thrill Is Gone."*

"Well, I'm asking you to let me hold you tonight."

"Call Robin. That's who you usually hold when you're horny."

Satin gave me a slight smile, turned up the volume some more, then strolled off to the kitchen. After five minutes had past and she still hadn't returned, I went into the kitchen ready to explode, sure that she had done what I'd suggested. But I found Satin standing on her back porch, sipping a wine cooler and gazing up at the stars.

"I'm sorry, Satin."

"You know what, Tonya," she said, her eyes fixed on the moon. "I've finally heard something that sounds sweeter than music to me."

"What?"

"Your moans as I'm making love to you. That's what I want to hear tonight. Not your apologies."

"I need more time, Satin."

She let a tiny laugh escape. It floated up and hung onto a few stars, causing them to brighten. She drank from her bottle then turned and went back into the house. The phone rang just as I closed the back door. Satin put her hand over the receiver and asked, "How long do you plan on staying?"

"Why?"

She ignored my question and continued listening to the caller and tapping her foot to *"Been So Long"* by Anita Baker.

"That was Robin, wasn't it?" I asked when she hung up.

"Yes," Satin said. She left the kitchen and went to her bedroom. She pulled a pants suit from her closet and put it into a garment bag along with some underwear and shoes.

"Where are you going?"

"Why do you ask questions to which the answers are obvious?"

"Fuck you!"

A highly agitated look marred Satin's face. She unzipped the garment bag, went back to the closet, pulled out a large suitcase and started loading it up. After she couldn't stuff anything else in it, she tried to leave the room, but I blocked the doorway.

"All right, Satin, don't go. I'm sorry. I didn't mean that, okay?"

"No, it's not okay." Her broad shoulders sighed. "Tonya, why don't you do us both a favor and admit that your feelings for Malcolm are stronger so that we can get on with our lives?"

"Who says they're stronger?"

"Who do you sleep with?"

"That's not fair."

"Yes, it is. You leave my arms to lie in his."

"And you're leaving mine to lie in Robin's."

"True. But you have to stop and ask yourself why."

"You don't care about me that's why."

"If that's what you want to believe."

"Your running to Robin every time we have a disagreement proves that I'm right. You don't give a damn about me and you know it."

"I wish you would drop this self-pity routine."

"I wish you would drop her."

"Why? So I can sit around here waiting for you to make up your mind? I'll drop Robin when you drop Malcolm."

"You make me sick!"

"I know. You've told me that several times already." Satin made another attempt to leave.

"I don't want you to spend the night with her," I protested.

"All right." Satin softly kissed my lips. "Spend the night with me then."

"I can't." I ran my tongue along my lips then rolled her sweet taste around in my mouth.

"Make sure you lock the door on your way out," she said, as she picked up her bag.

"You make me sick!" I screamed at her back. She kept walking. "I hate you!" I yelled. The front door closed quietly.

I was too depressed about this whole situation to go home so I slept on Satin's couch. When I got home the next day, Malcolm was sitting in the living room talking to Nikki, who immediately went to her bedroom after

I said good afternoon. Malcolm followed me back to my bedroom. Since I didn't have a change of clothes, I didn't bother washing up at Satin's, so I stripped and took a shower.

"Where did you spend the night?" he asked as I was drying off.

"At the studio." I threw the towel on the bed and began putting lotion on my legs. "What time did you get here?"

"Ten o'clock last night," he answered with an angry expression. "I slept in your room, waiting for you to come home."

"I'm sorry," I said, noticing that my bed was unmade. "I didn't know."

"Why did you spend the night at the studio?"

"I just didn't feel like coming home."

"Was Satin there..." He paused then accused more than asked, "Sleeping with you?"

"What?" I asked, angrily yanking my dresser drawer open.

He regarded me in silence for several seconds, then, point-blank and as a matter-of-fact, "Is Satin gay, Tonya?"

My heart slammed against my chest then fell to the pit of my stomach.

"Well, Tonya?" he persisted.

"Well, what?" I stalled, trying to pull myself together.

"Is Satin gay?"

"H-how would I know?" I stammered, snatching out my panties.

"You're her friend, right?"

"That doesn't mean I know all there is to know about her. And for your information, Satin spent the night at a friend's house last night."

"Male or female?"

"How should I know?" I slammed the closet door. I had to get this conversation off of Satin. "Look, Malcolm, what you're upset with me about has nothing to do with Satin."

"Yes, it does. I want you to stop hanging around her so much."

"Oh, so now you're trying to tell me who my friends can be?"

Malcolm was saying something about him being suspicious about my defensive attitude in regards to my friendship with Satin when Nikki knocked on the door and told me that Satin was on the phone.

"You just left there. Tell her to call you back," he demanded.

"Are you deaf? I said that I spent the night at my studio. And in case you've forgotten, my father lives at 513 Arlington Drive," I said, and went out into the kitchen.

"I'm just calling to make sure you locked up when you left last night," Satin said.

"Yeah, I did," I said.

"Hang up the phone, Tonya," Malcolm yelled.

"Don't tell me what to do!" I said.

"Look, Tonya, I need some time away from--" Satin began when Malcolm grabbed the phone.

"Satin, Tonya and I are in the middle of something. Now you two had all night and half the morning to talk so I'd appreciate it if you would give me some time with her."

I snatched the phone back from him. "I told you that she spent the night at a friend's!"

"Look, Satin, I'll call you later."

"You can't. I'm not home. I'm in New Orleans."

"What?" my heart cried.

"I flew here last night."

"Well, when are you coming back?"

"Tonya," Malcolm yelled. "I'm leaving and I'm not coming back if you don't hang up that phone right now."

I'd never seen the vein on his temple pound as hot as it was doing now.

"I don't know when I'm coming back," Satin said.

"Well, at least give me a number where I can reach you," I begged.

"No. I need time to think."

Malcolm stormed to the door.

"Satin, look I've got to stop Malcolm from leaving. Call me, please."

"I'll call you when I get back."

Malcolm opened the door.

"No!" I screamed to both of their answers.

Satin hung up and Malcolm slammed the front door. Since I had a better chance of reaching Malcolm than I did yelling Satin's name at the dial tone, I ran outside and persuaded him to come back into the house.

Vein throbbing, arms swinging, Malcolm said, "You put everything and everybody on hold for her."

"I do not."

He kept throwing out accusations as if he did not hear or did not believe my denials.

"You lie about how much time you spend with her."

"I do not."

"And you're ready to fight whenever somebody pulls you up about her. Now, I'm sorry, Tonya, but ain't no two women that goddamn close. Not unless they .."

I looked him dead in the eye. "Not unless they what, Malcolm?"

He threw his hands up and walked to the other side of the room.

"Not unless they what, Malcolm?"

This time he turned and faced me. Right then, he changed from being Mr. Robert Holland's man to Malcolm's man, and this man was not afraid to admit to himself that not only wasn't he man enough to keep his woman from sleeping with Satin, but he wasn't man enough to get her out of Satin's bed. But that was okay because my sleeping with Satin had absolutely, positively nothing to do with his manhood. And it was with this realization that Malcolm said, "Ain't no two women that damn close. Not unless they're sleeping together."

His saying it threw me off guard because I didn't think that he had the guts, didn't think that he was man enough to take it beyond a suspicious thought and put it into real words. "That's what you think, huh? That I'm sleeping with Satin?"

"Well, you haven't been sleeping with me."

I had to make my denial sound as ridiculous and out of the question as possible. So I laughed when I said, "And that means I got to be sleeping with Satin? Why can't it mean that I'm sleeping with Nikki? Or myself, for that matter? Thanks to you I've done that once or twice."

"I'm not stupid, Tonya," he yelled. "I know when I'm being played."

"Ain't nobody playin' you."

Pointing his finger in my face and gritting his teeth, he said, "Tonya, you've been playin' me ever since that day you came to my house and sucked my dick!"

The last three words he pronounced as mean and vulgar as he could. And it hurt. It really hurt. I sat on the middle cushion of the couch while Malcolm sat on the arm at the other end, glaring at me. Nikki, who had been waiting for an appropriate moment to leave, walked downstairs and quietly closed the front door behind her.

"I want the truth, Tonya, and I want it now or it's over."

"Just like that?"

"Just like that."

I started crying. "But, Malcolm--"

"Tears ain't gonna cut it this time, baby. I want the truth."

"Malcolm, I love you."

"Well, tell me the truth."

"I don't want to lose you."

"Well, tell me the truth."

"Malcolm--"

He banged his fist on the coffee table. "Damn you, Tonya, I want the truth," he yelled. "That's all I want. I don't want none of your crocodile tears. I don't want none of your sorry ass excuses. I don't want none of your I'm sorries. I want the truth! All right, Tonya! That's all I want! If you can't give me that, then leave me the hell alone!"

So I told him the truth, then tried to explain it.

"Malcolm, I swear to you--"

Malcolm cut my sentence off while it was still forming in my throat.

Then without the least bit of humor he laughed, "Don't swear! The last thing I want to do is hear you swear anything to me."

Malcolm sat down in a chair and rubbed his chin.

"Malcolm--"

He held his hands up and shook them. "I don't want to hear it because I don't know what I'll do if I sit here and listen to you."

Malcolm got up and headed for the door. I grabbed him by the arm.

"Tonya, don't touch me, please." His voice was shaky and mean. "Because you see, right now...I'm not man enough to be this close to you."

24

I stepped out in front of a moving car today. Not on purpose. I just wasn't paying attention. My mind was on Malcolm and Satin. I hadn't heard from Satin in over a week, and Malcolm wouldn't accept any of my phone calls. I couldn't eat, couldn't sleep, and couldn't even sculpt. So I went for a walk and I made a mistake and walked off the curb. All I heard were tires screeching to a halt and then a guy was in my face yelling about how I could have gotten killed.

My eyes were fixed on his angry face. It was long, steely, black, and so cold that it sent chills through me. On second thought, the chills could have come from the fear that had me shaking and sweating hours before when I was in my bedroom thinking of ways to end my life.

Death by an overdose of birth control pills, a quick slash of my wrists with my pocketknife, leaping from the window of a tall building, or confessing my sin to my mother. I felt like Ruby in Rosa Guy's novel when Daphne broke it off with her, and Ruby decided to get back at her by going to the roof of her building and jumping off so that she could land at Daphne's feet.

All but the first choice seemed entirely too painful and, most of all, too final. With the pills, I could stop after swallowing the first two or three, if I suddenly changed my mind and decided that I wanted to live. But there was no changing my mind once blood was gushing from my open wrists and spilling on my shiny white kitchen floor. Undoubtedly, my father wouldn't be around to keep me from jumping off the roof like Ruby's father. And there was certainly no recanting truth that had been spoken to my mother who honestly believed that the truth was in a lie.

I paused for a moment and actually realized what it was I was contemplating here.

"Suicide, Tonya?" I questioned myself aloud. "Overdosing with birth control pill, Tonya? Are you crazy? Have you totally lost your mind?"

Deciding that I had in fact lost my mind, at least temporarily, I went for a walk. And almost walked to my death. A death I no longer wanted.

So after the man called me crazy, jumped back in his car, and sped off, I went home. An hour later, I answered a knock on my bedroom door and found Satin standing in the hallway.

"How are you?" Satin asked.

"Lousy," I said, and rushed into her arms.

I sobbed heavily on Satin's shoulder for some time, and she didn't say a word. She was quiet and distant, as if she were afraid to get personally involved with what I was going through, like she was consoling some hysterical stranger that she just happened to sit next to on the subway.

"Satin, I'm sorry for everything."

"I know, Tonya," she said. "But we still have to talk, and you may not like what I have to say. Robin--"

"I don't want to hear about her," I said.

"I know you don't, but I need to discuss her with you. My relationship with you is destroying what I have with her."

"Did she go to New Orleans with you?"

"Yes, and for the first time in weeks, Robin was able to make me smile. Not only that, but I was sleeping, eating, talking, dancing. I was doing all of the things I used to do before we got involved. Robin noticed the change in my attitude, and she asked me if the problems that we were having in Baltimore had anything to do with my seeing you?"

"You didn't tell me that you were having problems."

"It wouldn't have made any difference if I had."

"How do you know? Maybe I could have helped."

"The only way that you could have helped was to make up your mind, something you've been refusing to do for a long time."

"What did you tell Robin?"

Satin's head dropped to the floor. "In all the time that Robin and I have been together, I've never lied to her. If she asked me a question, no matter if I was right or wrong, I'd answer her as honestly as I could. But that night I didn't. I lied straight through my teeth. 'No. Tonya and I are just friends,' I said. And what's worse, she trusts me enough to believe what I told her. There I was lying right to her face and she believed me." Satin raised her head and looked at me as if I was to blame for her lying to Robin.

"I felt so guilty that I made up some excuse to get her to fly back three days before me. In those three days I thought about you and Robin. And I had to admit to myself that just by hiding how serious my relationship with you actually is, I was lying to her. I've been lying to her since the day I met you." Satin's eyes narrowed and her voice lowered. "I don't like being a liar. But that's what I am."

"Come on, Satin. We can work this out."

"I know. That's why I came to see you today. My life has been in limbo for too long, and I simply cannot go on this way anymore. I'm tired of the lying, I'm tired of the fighting, and I'm tired of you keeping me at arms lengths."

"I don't want to stop seeing you, Satin."

"I know, Tonya, but you don't want to stop seeing Malcolm either."

"Malcolm and I aren't together anymore," I said.

Satin paused and a little hope flashed in her eyes. "What? What happened?"

"He figured us out, and he doesn't want anything to do with me."

"It's not a question of him wanting you. The question is, do you still want him?"

My eyelashes batted, openly displaying my guilt of wanting, needing, and loving Malcolm.

The hope in her eyes faded. "That's what I thought."

"Satin," I said, wiping my tears and straightening up. "Don't give up on us."

"There is no us, Tonya. Not as long as you want Malcolm."

"I love him, Satin. I love him so much."

"I know you do. So just let us go," she pleaded.

"I can't. I love you, too."

"But not enough to leave Malcolm."

My eyes cut across the room. No, I don't love you enough to leave him. And I don't love him enough to leave you. So where does that leave me?

Satin turned away. "I'm going to go now."

I walked up behind her and put my hand on the door and whispered, "Don't leave me, Satin. I need you. Please, don't leave."

The sadness in my voice accomplished just what I had hoped. It stiffened Satin with guilt, pity, and confusion. She turned to face me, and when I looked into her eyes, I saw myself a few weeks ago, too confused to leave, too afraid to stay, and paralyzed by both. But I knew that her confusion and fear would only last a few seconds, and then she'd be gone. If I wanted to keep her in my life, I had to do something drastic. And I had to do it quickly.

I pressed my nervous lips passionately against hers, and the pleasure that her lips bestowed upon mine was felt all over my body. The level of arousal that was taking control of me was too intense for me to deny myself the pure satisfaction her touch was fully capable of giving. I wanted to feel her close to me. My body craved to feel her soft hands and precious lips everywhere. I wanted her, and I hoped that she still wanted me.

I unbuttoned her shirt and took her breasts into my trembling hands. They were as soft as a whisper and more erotic than the first time that I'd laid my eyes upon them. Wanting to taste more of her, I weaned myself from her lips and lightly kissed her neck, her shoulders, and finally I placed my mouth around her exquisite breast. She let out a moan and put her hand on the side of my face.

Backing her over to the bed, I removed her blouse, put my hands down by her waist, slowly moved them up her sides, and then I caressed her breasts again. She cried another soft moan, took a deep breath, and tilted her head back. The provocative arch in her back, and the sensual way in which she squirmed under my touch pressed upon me not to stop there. But could I follow through with what my hands and lips were promising? Could I perform acts that would kill my mother and cause the rest of my family and friends to shun me? What about Nikki? She's right down the hall. I can't stop now, though, I thought. I've left Satin standing on the edge too many times before. It would be wrong of me to do it again tonight.

I was scared to death, but I slid my frightened hands down her long, smooth body and began to undo her pants. My palms were sweaty and the zipper kept slipping through my fingers. Somehow, I got her zipper down and the sight of her red silk panties made my heart pound hard and fast. Sweat ran down my back and face. Droplets of the salty water leaked into my eyes, causing them to burn. I wiped my forehead with the back of my hand, and that's when I noticed that I wasn't just trembling anymore, I was shaking. I was also becoming quite ill. My stomach was doing somersaults, and I was getting dizzy. I felt as if I was going to vomit and faint all at the same time. I can't get sick. Not now. I've got to do this! If I want to keep her in my life, I have to go through with this.

My breathing hastened as I grabbed the sides of her pants. I yanked at them, but they didn't move. I tugged on them harder, but still I couldn't get them to come down. What could they be caught on? I wondered. I snatched at them again. It took three more pulls before I realized that it was Satin who was preventing me from sliding off her pants. She grabbed my hands and held them tightly. Then she mouthed something and shook her head. A bead of sweat ran down her forehead, over my nose, then splashed on her stomach.

"No," she said. "No."

No? What the hell do you mean--no? After all of this. No?

"What's wrong?" I asked. "Don't you know how much I want you?"

"I want you, too," she whispered. "But not like this."

"Not like what?" I questioned, shrugging my shoulders.

"You're not thinking clearly. You're upset and confused."

"No, I'm not. I know what I'm doing."

"Listen, Tonya," she said as she buttoned her shirt. "If we made love tonight, tomorrow, when you're not so upset, you'll regret it and blame me, just as you did the first time. You'll say that I took advantage of you. And if I let you make love to me, that's exactly what I'd be doing."

"If Robin--"

"This isn't about Robin. It's about you and the way you are feeling right now."

"You don't want me."

Satin closed her eyes as if she were in pain. "I told you it's not that. I want you. Just not this way. Not under these circumstances."

"Circumstances say that I want you now."

"Circumstances say that you're only doing this because you think that you've lost Malcolm, and you can't stand the thought of losing both of us. No, Tonya, I won't make love to you while you're like this. I have to go."

"Why are you hurting me?"

"The last thing I want to do is hurt you. That's why I'm leaving. If I stay, there's no turning back for you, and that will hurt you more than anything."

"Satin--"

"Look at you, Tonya. Look at you! You're sweating. You're shaking. The thought of making love to me terrifies you."

"I'm more terrified of you leaving me."

"Making love to me won't make me stay."

"What will? What more do you need?"

"Something that you are clearly not ready to give--an open relationship."

"Give me time," I cried.

She shook her head. "I can't, Tonya." She started for the door.

"Please, don't go, Satin," I begged. "Don't leave me. Please, Satin.

Please!" I ran over to her, hugged her from behind, and I sobbed into her back.

Tears fell from my eyes, splattering on my bare feet. My heart sagged as the weight of her rejection and soon to be desertion of me collected painfully inside of it. She wasn't even gone, yet the height of emptiness that consumed my room, my mind, and every inch of my body lengthened as if she had departed from my life a year ago. I was so emotional that I found it impossible to speak, to move, or to even breathe. All I could do was cry. And cry I did. I cried my ass off.

There was a bang on my door. "Tonya!" Nikki shouted frantically. "Are you okay?"

I sniffled, cleared my throat, and as best I could, answered, "I'm fine, Nikki."

"Are you sure?"

"Yes," I cried.

"Tonya." she called again.

"I'm fine, Nikki."

Without warning Nikki swung open the door. She saw me standing there with tears streaming down my cheeks, shaking and clinging to Satin's arm.

"What's going on?" she asked, glaring at Satin.

Satin smoothly walked away from the door. Nikki got in Satin's face. "What'd you do to her?" she asked.

Satin licked her full lips, stared Nikki directly in the eye, and said in the most serene voice imaginable, "None of your business."

Nikki's entire body tightened with anger, and she shoved Satin. Satin stumbled backwards, and after she regained her balance, she backhanded the hell out of Nikki. She fell against the wall, and after feeling Satin's stinging handprint on her cheek, Nikki lunged at Satin, but I jumped in between them. "I'ma hurt you, bitch!" Nikki threatened.

I forced her out of the room. "Get out, Nikki!" I screamed.

"What? You're taking up for her!"

"I'm not taking up for anyone. I just want you to leave."

"All right." Nikki stood on her tiptoes and pointed. "To hell with you and that bitch."

I heard her slam the front door a few minutes later. Satin wasn't the least bit affected by Nikki's attack on her. She went over to the mirror and straightened her clothes. "I've got to go, Tonya."

I started crying and begging again. I was weeping so badly that I began to vomit. Unable to leave me in such a delicate state, Satin cleaned my face, walked me over to the bed, and lay down with me. I rested my distressed head on her breast and held her close to me. Before I passed out, I heard her ask in a sorrowful whisper, "What are you trying to do to me, Tonya?"

Just love you, I thought. I'm sorry that I don't know how. But that's all I'm trying to do.

An hour later I awoke with dried tears on my face, a headache, and a letter clutched in my fist.

> *Tonya,*
>
> *You seem to have this grave misconception of me that makes you think that I'm made of steel, that I'm some kind of android with no emotion, no feelings. Well, contrary to what you may believe, your words and actions affect me deeply. And I'm hurting just as much as you are. If not more.*
>
> *As I'm writing this letter, I have to wonder if you realize how lucky you are that I'm a nice person. An enormous part of me wants you so badly that I can taste it. And as I recall, you taste very, very sweet.*
>
> *So I'm putting you on notice right now. I am not made of steel. That being the case, I want you to know, understand, and believe me when I say that next time I won't be so nice. And that's not a*

threat; it's a promise.

Satin

Besides having a headache, I was hungry as hell. I sat in the kitchen eating but not tasting a peanut butter and jelly sandwich and drinking a glass of milk, staring out at the moon as it shined brightly through the small window over the sink. A vision of Satin tilting her head back as I fondled her dark brown breasts appeared on the opposite side of the table under the moon's white light. I must have been out of my mind, I thought. God only knows what Nikki's thinking now.

I finished my glass of milk and got up from the table. Nikki was standing in the doorway. My heart shook at the thought of what she was about to say. I placed the plate and glass in the sink and then tried to leave, but she blocked my path.

"I can't believe you chose her over me."

"What are you talking about?"

"You let her slap me."

"I didn't let her do anything. And besides, you pushed her first. I was just breaking it up."

"Yeah, after letting her get the last lick."

"'Last lick'? How old are you? Talkin' about some 'last lick.'"

"I want to know what the deal is with you and Satin," she demanded with curled lips.

"Leave me alone."

"No. I've left you alone long enough. Satin comes over and within a few minutes you're bawling your eyes out. Now, I'm not leaving anything alone anymore, not until you tell me what the hell's going on?"

"Evidently, I don't want you to know or else I would have told you."

"Talk to me, Tonya."

"Talk to me. Talk to me. Talk to me." I banged my fist on the kitchen counter. "Will you people just leave me alone! I don't feel like talkin'!"

"Tonya, tell me what's going on."

"I can't."

"Why?"

"Because it's none of your damn business!"

Nikki's face turned red hot. "It's every bit of my damn business when I hear you crying," she said and shoved me on the shoulder, nearly turning me around. "It's every bit of my damn business when I see you all hugged up on her." She shoved me in the middle of my chest with both hands. "It's every bit of my damn business when I come back and find you two in bed together!" She pushed me again but this time hard enough so that I fell against the kitchen sink and onto the floor.

She saw us! ran through my mind so fast and hard that I couldn't get up. "We weren't in bed together," I lied.

"Yeah, just like you weren't in the shower getting ready to kiss Meyoki."

"What?" I asked still sitting on the floor with my eyes big as saucers.

"I saw you and Meyoki in the shower. I came down to check on you, to make sure that you were okay, and I saw her walk over to you. And I saw you waiting for her to kiss you."

Nikki's words made me feel as if someone had kicked me in the stomach and knocked the wind out of me. I felt like a fool. Here I'd been trying to keep her from knowing something that she'd known from the start. Here I'd been trying to keep her from thinking that I was using our friendship to sneak cheap peeps and cope feels when she knew all along that I wouldn't take advantage of her like that. Here I'd been going through this alone and I didn't have to.

Nikki held out her hand for me, and I saw that for years she'd been holding it out like that with her words, smiles, laughter, and quiet. Holding it out and telling me to put my hand, worries, and fears in hers, and trust her enough to know that she would never judge, betray, or abandon me. I reached up and touched her fingers then grabbed her hand. Nikki helped me to my feet, and then I fell into her arms and cried for all the years I spent not being able to cry about my truth to my best friend.

"I can't believe you knew all this time and didn't tell me," I said after I'd calmed down.

"Tonya, you couldn't tell yourself so I knew that you didn't want to hear me tell you. So I was just waiting for you to come to me."

"I wanted to, Nikki, but in my mind, coming to you meant that..."

"That these feelings you had for Meyoki and have for Satin are signs of some mental disorder," Nikki finished for me. "I'll tell you what I told Meyoki that day."

"You spoke to her?"

"Yes. When she came out of the shower, I was standing there. She was so hurt and angry with you that she trembled."

"What did you say to her?"

"I told her that instead of getting angry with you she should be trying to show you how wrong you are about yourself."

So that was where the concern came from in Meyoki's eyes when we were sitting outside of Principle Menefee's office, and that was why she wanted to dance with me at The Gray Mist. "Nikki, does Aunt Josephine know?"

"Aunt Josephine suspects. She asked me about you and Meyoki when you two were suspended. And she asked me about you and Satin after the night you went to the Haven."

"What did you tell her?"

"Nothing. It wasn't my place to."

"So you knew all the time that it was me that Meyoki winked at," I asked.

Nikki nodded.

"You took the heat for me," I said.

"I knew that you wouldn't be able to handle being teased about Meyoki having a thing for you, about you being *funny*, about you being *that* way, about you being turned out."

"You know what, Nikki? I still can't. I don't have what it takes to break the rules, to cross that forbidden line and survive enough to be happy."

"You know what my patients have taught me, Tonya? They've taught me that life ain't about nothing but issues. And more often than not these issues involve loving somebody that don't love you, or at least not in the way that you think he should, or she, which ever the case may be. But in any case, people can only love you as much as their law allows. The thing with that is, though, not too many people can honestly brag about being the authors of their own laws. And most people don't find out that someone else has written their law until someone comes into their lives and they suddenly find themselves fighting tooth and nail to live by it. Most of my patients come to me because they've found this out, and they desperately want to write their own laws so that they don't die wishing that they had fought more, screamed more, cussed more, fucked more, loved more.

"So don't think of loving Meyoki or Satin as breaking some rules that you didn't have a hand in making or crossing some line that you didn't draw. Think of it as writing your own laws a sentence at a time; drawing your own line an inch at a time. Think of it as following your heart because life is too short for denials and too damn long for regrets."

25

Confiding in Nikki brought me back from the dead. So I thought it was only right that I did the same for the little girl sitting alone in my studio.

When I got to AAI, I found a week old letter from Dr. Zimmerman that stated that he'd be back within the next two weeks. I didn't have much time. I took the dark green plastic bag off the little black girl and looked at her. I mean, really looked at her. And I saw something I hadn't seen when I first sculpted her. She was adorable! I leaned closer to the pretty, little face. "Who are you?" I asked, almost expecting her thick lips to whisper her name. She looked sad. The kind of sad that stains a little girl's face when she wants her mommy and daddy. "I'll bet your parents are worried sick about you."

I went back to the main library downtown and did some detective work of my own. In the microfilm department I signed out reels of the *Baltimore Afro-American Newspaper* for July 1979 through July 1981. I carefully scanned reel after reel, page after page for two days, but there was no mention of her. On the third day, I found her on the front page of the late edition for Saturday February 9, 1980. She was Tiffany Hill, a little nine-year-old black girl, who disappeared several months before Hazel Cherrylane vanished. A pretty, dark-brown darling with a short, silky afro and a big, bright smile. The story next to her picture read:

> GIRL ABDUCTED WHILE MAKING SNOWMAN
> On Wednesday February 6, 9-year-old Tiffany Hill
> was abducted while making a snowman in the front
> yard of her West Belvedere Avenue home. Eyewitnesses
> have stated that a black man driving a blue Ford
> Pickup lured Tiffany over to the curb, snatched

her inside the vehicle, then sped away.

That's right, I thought to myself. I remember now. My parents were really upset about it. I remember hearing my mother say to my father that it was a damn shame that children weren't safe building snowmen in their own front yards. There was a big candlelight vigil for her in the black community. Somebody named a community center after her the year that I enrolled in AAI, the year I decided to forget that I wasn't the person that everyone else and me needed me to be.

By the time I got back to my studio rain was coming down in sheets. I sat on the radiator in front of the center window. I could see Tiffany's reflection in the pane. And to my surprise I could also see the faces of people on the street, even as they shielded themselves from the rain. No one seemed to be hiding anymore.

While I was sitting there looking at the rain-drenched faces, Dr. Zimmerman pulled up, got out of his car, and waved to me. He was wearing a pair of blue jeans, a black T-shirt, and...sneakers! He didn't have an umbrella but he didn't run out of the rain. He walked slowly, as if he wanted to feel every drop of water falling from that gray sky.

He walked through my door with his arms out stretched. He had a full beard and mustache, a beautiful tan, and was at least fifteen pounds thinner. His fingernails had grown and his hair was combed back so that you could see the round bald spot in the center of his head.

"You look good," I told him as we hugged. "Smell good too."

"That's because I haven't had a cigarette since I left." He took a deep breath. "Haven't had a beer either," he said, patting his flat stomach.

"What about your porno?" I asked.

"You can't give up everything all at once," he laughed.

"So your trip went well, I take."

"Unbelievably well." He stepped back to get a look at me. "You look stressed. I hope my little project isn't the reason for those puffy eyes."

"Not exactly, but I do have to talk to you about that."

"I know."

"What do you mean you know?"

"I mean that I know that she isn't Hazel Cherrylane."

"How?"

"The police contacted me back in June and told me that the DNA didn't match."

"June! Why didn't you tell me?"

Dr. Zimmerman walked over to Tiffany. "Because I was hoping that she'd help you discover what the people in Kuwait helped me to discover."

"Which is?"

"That you don't need to be here any longer, and neither do I."

"I don't understand. What are you talking about?"

"I'm talking about me hiding in this school, making you sculpt the things that I didn't think I could, and taking credit for it as your mentor. I'm talking about going to Kuwait and being able to sculpt and paint some of the most creative pieces of my life almost without any effort at all. I went over there with all of the arrogance of a privileged, white, American male, looking down my nose at what and who I thought these people were, at how backwards and wrong I thought their customs and culture were. But the minute I stepped off the plane, I saw that these people were nothing like the people we see portrayed on the news. And the more time I spent with them breaking down the myths, the better my sculpting became."

His eyes were starry and he talked as if he was far away from AAI.

"You're going back, aren't you?"

"As soon as I get things squared away here. I have to go back so that I can reclaim my work and become the artist I used to be before I got into the mentoring business."

My head started hurting. I was losing everything. Malcolm, Satin, Dr. Zimmerman. Where was I supposed to go without him? I'd been with him since I was eighteen. Everything I knew I knew because of Dr. Zimmerman. Every commission I'd ever gotten I'd gotten because of Dr. Zimmerman.

Dr. Zimmerman looked around the room at all the different sculptures I'd done since he'd been gone. He put his hands on my shoulders. "I know it sounds scary, but I want you to leave AAI, Tonya, and spread your own wings. You can't do it here because just as people see me as Tonya Mimms' mentor, they see you as Dr. Carroll P. Zimmerman's mentee. I want you to explore who you are and what your work can be without AAI and Dr. Zimmerman. I want you to go out and discover and be the artist you were meant to be. The art world would love it if I remain your teacher and you my student for the rest of our careers. But we can't be who people want us to be. No matter who it hurts or who doesn't like it, there comes a time when we have to be who we are." He let me go and turned back to Tiffany, and said, "She's living proof of that."

A couple days later, Dr. Zimmerman brought Mr. and Mrs. Hill to the studio to see their daughter. They were an attractive couple in their early fifties, well dressed, and very polite. They were huddled in such a way that if one of them let go, the other would fall to the ground and lay there forever. Their faces were still with grief and their eyes were weighed down with tears.

Mrs. Hill couldn't speak without crying so Mr. Hill spoke for them. He said in a quivering voice, "They tell us that you found our little girl."

"No, sir. I didn't find her. She found me," I told them.

He swallowed his tears. "Can we see her?"

"Sure. She's been waiting for you."

I stepped aside, and when Mr. and Mrs. Hill saw the face of their dead little girl, their lifeless faces came to life, and they sobbed with relief, closure, and more grief than either one of them could handle. The scene was too intense for me, and I figured that they needed some privacy, so I went out into the hall. Dr. Zimmerman followed. He stood with his hands in the front pockets of his jeans. I still couldn't get over him wearing jeans.

"How are the Cherrylanes?" I asked.

He shook his head. "Not good. On the one hand they feel as if they've lost their daughter a second time, and on another they're hoping that their little girl is alive somewhere. But they're happy for Mr. and Mrs. Hill."

Mr. and Mrs. Hill stayed in my studio for about twenty minutes. When they came out, they were still very upset. Mr. Hill thanked me and then he and his wife carried each other down the hall. Dr. Zimmerman had to take Tiffany back to the police station so I told him that I'd have her ready by the time he got back from driving Mr. and Mrs. Hill home.

I sat down in front of her. "You don't have to say it. I'll say it myself. I was wrong. But you still don't understand. It's easy for people to accept you not being who they wanted you to be. You brought happiness and closure to people's lives," I looked at Hazel's picture. "And hope for another life. Who I am only brings misery and hopelessness."

I took the lid off the pink case I brought for her. I refused to send her back into that brown cardboard box.

"So I guess this is goodbye," I said to her. Then, "No. This is until next time. Even if next time isn't until years to come."

In my mind I know that it isn't impossible, but in my heart, I know that I saw Tiffany smile.

Dr. Zimmerman left for Kuwait at the end of August. I drove him to the airport late one evening.

Before boarding his plane, Dr. Zimmerman turned and said, "Ila liqa' Insha' allah."

"What does that mean?" I asked, smiling and crying.

"Until we meet again, God willing."

"Same to ya," I managed through my tears.

The next day I moved my studio into a first floor apartment on Auchentoroly Terrace. The front room was large with two tall, lean windows that let in an enormous amount of natural light and also faced Druid Hill Park, which was directly across the street. It had a hardwood floor, which I planned to lay a cement slab on top of because it supported my larger sculptures better. It had a small kitchen, and two bedrooms, both of which I'd have to use for storage.

I could have moved into one of my parents' buildings but I wasn't ready to explain things to them yet. I'd been there less than a week when a short, small, light-skinned woman named Nzinga knocked on the door. She had a head full of silky salt and pepper twists, happy brown eyes, and a beautiful gap between her smile. She had a light voice and a contagious laugh. She owned a small art gallery called Umoja above a Laundromat on Preston Street, not too far from AAI. She said that she knew of and had great respect for my work and was wondering if I was interested in doing a series celebrating the lives of African American women. I said yes.

I was so excited about getting my first commission that I sat right down and did some preliminary sketches. What I put down on paper were seven sculptures that would be carved out of mahogany, walnut, and Spanish cedar. The pieces would depict a pregnant African woman walking through a village many, many years before the Middle Passage; a Negro woman screaming as she stood naked and shackled on an auction block; a Mulatto woman searching for her identity; a Colored woman on her knees scrubbing a floor; a black woman with an Afro standing with a raised fist; and an African American woman with her arms around herself. All the pieces would speak of the extraordinary beauty and pride these women bathed in as a result of knowing who and what they were: Beautiful, Strong, Vulnerable, Intelligent, Deliberate Women. That was what this exhibit was going to be about for me--having pride in knowing who and what I was and having the courage to one day speak about it to someone other than myself.

At the thought of that I set my charcoal pencil down on another blank piece of paper and was consumed by a sketch of what would be a clay sculpture of two black women wrapped in a white sheet. Their coal-black skin and desires would glisten against the ivory cloth, giving their bodies and their love an almost blinding glow. Their bare feet would be planted firmly on the marble base, which would be shaped like the 16th musical note.

I wanted to get sculpting on the project right away, but something inside me said that I needed to take care of a few things first.

26

I had rehearsed my speech several times before leaving. Had practiced it on the drive over. Knew it word for word. Where to pause. When to motion my hands downward after making a vital point. I even calculated how long it would take to complete the damned thing. Twenty-three minutes, ten seconds. I was ready. But when it came time for the live performance, I got stage fright. I don't think I was even speaking English. Words and phrases flew out of my mouth, slammed against the walls, and landed in a scrambled pile at my feet.

Malcolm stood in the middle of his living room with his arms folded as I tried over and over to tell him how it was. I finally ended up saying something stupid like, "I didn't mean to sleep with her, Malcolm."

"Like you didn't mean to sleep with me the first day we met!" he said.

I guess I deserved that. But did it have to hurt so much?

"I only slept with her once."

"Once, twice. What does it matter, Tonya?"

"It matters a lot. I don't want you to think that--"

"That you've been lying to me. That you've been using me. That you knew all along that this would happen sooner or later whether it was with Satin or some other woman. That I'm hurting because you're afraid of who you are."

Malcolm pointed his index finger at me with each sentence as if to nail me to the wall and drive a stake through my heart the way my sleeping with Satin had driven a stake through his.

"You know what I want to know, Tonya?" He asked almost whispering the words. "I want to know if during your lying, sneaking, hiding, and denying, did you think about me?"

"Of course I did, Malcolm. That's why--"

"No," Malcolm said, jabbing his index finger into his temple and then his chest, "I mean, did you *think* about *me*? Not about the social and self-acceptance you'd have by being with me. Not about the feelings of normalcy and validity. Not about the freedom from isolation, invisibility, and contempt. Not about the freedom from being called a homo! Freak! Lesbo--"

"Stop it!" I yelled.

"Butch!"

"Stop!" I screamed over his screaming. I closed my eyes so that I couldn't see the hatred on his lips. I started crying, begging. "Stop! Please stop!"

"No, I won't stop. Not until you tell me that you thought about me just once, just *once* while you were being a coward!"

And upon hearing the word "coward", something snapped inside me. No. Something broke inside me. Something that had been holding me down under water it seemed. Now I was moving rapidly and wildly to the surface. And when I reached the top, I took in great gulps of air that seemed to free me even more.

The next thing I knew, I was standing in the middle of Malcolm's living room screaming, shouting, "No, no, no!" I opened my eyes and yanked my hands from my ears. "No I didn't think about you! I was too busy thinking about my mother who blames herself for every piece of unhappiness that enters her daughters' lives, holds herself personally responsible for all of her daughters' shortcomings, who wants grandchildren from both her daughters. My father who has a hard enough time as it is trying to accept who I am. My sister who can't wait until my shit hits the fan so that I will lose somebody close to me. My aunt who told me, when I was seven, that women ain't supposed to run with other women. I was too busy thinking about how hard it is being black, being female, and being gay on top of it all!"

Whoa! Whoa! Whoa! I thought as the "being gay on top of it all" echoed throughout Malcolm's place. And that's when I actually heard it.

Not when it came out of my mouth, but when it bounced off the walls, ceilings, and floors inside Malcolm's place. Whoa! Step back a little, Tonya. When exactly did I become comfortable saying that about myself? When did that go from being a rumor buzzing around in my mind to a spoken-from-my-lips fact? And why don't I feel the need to deny what I just said about myself? And why would I feel comfortable saying it to him? But, then again, why wouldn't I? From the beginning Malcolm has made me feel free and safe enough to do anything. Follow him into the woods, fly, make love on a hill, take him to my studio, take him home to my parents. So why wouldn't I feel free and safe coming out to him?

But Malcolm wasn't aware of nor did he care about this major hurdle I had gotten over ironically enough with his help. So he screamed, "None of that gives you the right to mess up my life." He banged his fist into his chest. "None of that justifies you messing with my heart!"

And in the moment that it took for his words to make me feel like the coward that I truly had been, Malcolm had gone to the nearest wall and began to repeatedly smash his fist into it.

I stood stark still, covering my ears again, yelling, "No, Malcolm! No!"

He kept hitting the wall until pieces of it fell onto the floor. But it wasn't until Malcolm's fist went through the wall that I began to understand that anytime you make a man angry enough to smash his fist through a wall, then you've really hurt him. My first instinct was to turn and run. Get away from his words, his pain, his screaming, and the sound of his fist pounding out chunks of plaster. I didn't want to be the cause of it. Didn't want the blame. I just wanted to run and hide from it all. Disappear from his life as suddenly as I had come into it so that his pain would leave and he could take his arm out of the wall.

Malcolm busted his knuckle open and soon the hole in the white wall was circled and filled with blood. Malcolm raised his bloody fist to pound the wall again but as he reared back, he caught a glimpse of tender flesh and bone. Malcolm turned around to face me. Sadness settled on his shoulders, causing his arm to drop and his six-foot frame to droop. And the next thing I knew, my man Malcolm was standing there crying like a little boy. It wasn't a hysterical cry or anything, but a gentle, cantankerous kind of weeping, almost as if it hurt too much for him to cry.

To see this man weeping was the most frightening and agonizing thing I ever wanted to witness. But I didn't run or close my eyes, and I uncovered my ears so that I could hear it. I stood there looking him in the eye so that I wouldn't deny him the right to face the person who had caused him pain beyond his wildest imagination. I wanted his yelling, his crying, pounding the wall, his bleeding, and the bloody hole in the wall to be like the scar on Aunt Josephine's knee that reminded her not to run. I wanted all of the manifestations of Malcolm's anger and hurt to become an ugly scar on my mind that would remind me never to run, so that I would never cause anyone this much pain ever again.

After it all was indelibly embedded in my mind, I eased over and took Malcolm in my arms.

"If my father could see me now," Malcolm sniffled, shaking his head and wiping his tears.

I held his hand so that he could let his tears fall on me where they belonged.

"I didn't mean to hurt you," I said. "I just didn't know how to keep it from happening."

"I believe that you didn't mean to," Malcolm said into my shoulder. "I just wish that you hadn't."

I kissed his forehead. "You're gonna need stitches."

I wrapped Malcolm's swollen and bruised hand then drove him to the emergency room. We sat there with our heads against wall staring at the ceiling for hours. The towel that I'd wrapped around Malcolm's hand was soaking wet with his blood. I guess it was about one o'clock in the morning when a nurse called him to the back.

"I can make it home from here," he said.

"Are you sure?"

"Yeah," he said.

I sighed and handed him the key to his place. "You take care."

"You too." He turned, walked through the automatic doors then stopped. He waited a moment before turning around and saying, "Hey, Tonya."

"Yeah?" I asked.

"It ain't that bad," he said, smiling that beautiful gap-tooth smile of his. "You look like you need somebody to tell you that."

As the doors closed behind him, I thought about how much I did need somebody to tell me that, but I didn't expect him to be that somebody. How, I wondered, through all of his pain, anger, and blood, how could he think about me enough to smile and say that?

I walked out to the parking lot and thought back to what Malcolm had said about my work, about how I had been choosing between something that had meant the world to me since I could breathe it and feel it, and men who didn't understand that. But in actuality what I'd been doing was choosing between my thoughts and feeling and those of the people close to me and using my work to pretend that the decision I made in high school was my own. Sculpting myself into believing that the choice I made was the best thing for everyone. But there were times, like tonight in Malcolm's place, when it was all too painfully and bloody clear that it wasn't the best thing for anybody, especially not for me.

I can't live my life like this anymore. I don't *want* to live like this anymore.

With that, I put my Jeep in drive and before long I was parking across from her house, but the same urgency that brought me there restricted me to my car. The house was dark and her car was parked in the driveway. She was home. But was she alone?

I didn't want to cause any problems so I figured the best thing for me to do was to leave. But just as I was about to pull off, Satin opened her front door and walked wistfully underneath the hanging branches of the weeping willow. She was wearing a light blue robe. She was so pretty in the moonlight.

Shaking, I got out of the car and slowly walked toward her. Patti Labelle singing *"Sleep With Me Tonight"* was quietly coming out of her window and into the yard. Satin smiled as her tea-colored brown eyes verified that it was in fact me coming up her walkway. My heart cried as the smile on her face let me know that she hadn't forgotten me.

"Hi," she said, wrapping her arms around me as we met under the willow. Her body was still soft and her perfume still whispered my name. I wanted to stand under that tree and hold her all night.

"Hi," I said back.

"How have you been?" she asked.

"Okay, I guess. What about you?"

"Okay, too," she smiled. Oh, how I missed her smile.

"What are you doing here?"

"I'm not sure."

I had no intentions of making love to her when I came. But the tantalizing smell of her perfume, her sweet seductive voice passing through the darkness, and the perfect setting made it impossible for me not to. People often say that you can't miss what you never had. And that's probably true for some, but not for me. I missed never being able to feel her touching me without some obstacle in my way to hinder my pleasure. I missed never waking up in her arms the morning after. And I missed never having the chance to please her in a way that only I could.

Satin was talking, but her words weren't registering to me. Her words were lost in the dream that I had of myself enclosed in the comforts of her embrace. As I watched her mouth form sentences I could not hear, I moved slowly toward her lips. She tried to ignore my growing closeness by talking faster and louder, but as I stood just breathing room away, she had no choice but to end her trivial conversation and listen to what I was not saying. Then without caring about how unhappy this kiss would make my family, without caring about the wedding that this kiss would prevent me from having, without caring about who saw us and would call us dykes or funny, I kissed her. Tongue and all. I didn't hold back. I guess that's what made this kiss different from the rest. It left me feeling as though I had never been kissed before.

"No," Satin protested as she made an attempt to push me away.

"Why?" I asked. "Because I'm too confused? Because I'll regret it later and blame you? Because the circumstances are wrong?" I kissed her again. "I know exactly what I'm doing, Satin. The only thing that I will regret is leaving without showing you how much I love you. And I'll only blame you if you prevent me from doing so. And as far as the circumstances go, well, they are the very things that are telling me that I want you. That I need you."

Of course Satin didn't believe what I was saying right off the bat. She'd been here once too often. She probed my eyes for any signs of uncertainty or nervousness. There were none to be found. Still questioning my sincerity, she reached out and touched my breast. Anticipating a wince, she quickly drew back her hand and scanned my face again for perplexity. But to her surprise, I didn't even flinch.

"Tonya, I meant what I said in that letter," she said.

"I know," I said, and kissed her a third time.

In the dark, under that weeping willow everything black and beautiful about Satin lit up like a torch.

We went into the house. All of the photographs of Satin and Robin were gone.

"I couldn't lie to her anymore," Satin said.

I took Satin's hand and led her to her bedroom where we made love. Finally, after months, years really, of dealing with the aggravation associated with denying and resisting feelings that were stronger than me, we fulfilled each other's needs as Ray Charles crooned *"A Song For You."*

And I must say, the lovemaking was sweet, tender, erotic, and by far the most vibrant of all my past experiences. It was not rushed, and it was performed with great care and understanding. It was wild and exciting, nasty but not at all repulsive. The pleasures that she released from the abyss corners of my soul had me calling her name every second. She touched places on my body that I didn't even know were alive. There wasn't a muscle, a nerve, a pulse or vein on me that was neglected by her. And every part of me would forever remember her touch.

As for my satisfying her, well, I did the best I could with what I'd learned by observing how she caused such unyielding sensations to jolt through me. Starting at her lips I worked my way around, down, over, under, and inside her beautiful body, pausing only to see the rapturous expressions that accompanied her moans of content. My hands memorized every dip, curve, bump, and muscle on her, and I kissed every leaf on that weeping willow and ran my tongue along its roots until I reached the core of its lifeline.

Somewhere around three we fell asleep, but I woke up again at five and found Satin gone. I lay back down and listened to Nancy Wilson singing *"Love Won't Let Me Wait."* I ran my hands over the silk sheets, and I thought back to the first time that Satin had attempted to make love to me, and how ashamed and dirty I felt. Funny how I didn't feel anything except love and completeness now. All of that seemed to have taken place so long ago. I didn't even feel like the same person. I guess because I wasn't.

I eased out of bed, walked over to the curio, and picked Meyoki up off the shelf. I looked into her pretty face and thought, What if...What if I'd believed back then that difference could actually feel like heaven, that being someone that you're not supposed to be could make you feel so free, perfect, and normal?

I went over to the mirror.

"Yes, you are very sexy," I heard Satin say. She was standing in the doorway holding a glass.

"I wouldn't go that far."

"You can go that far and beyond."

We smiled.

"Here," Satin said. "I thought you might be thirsty."

Satin handed me a tall goblet trimmed in gold. It fit into my hand as if she'd sculpted it just for my palm and my fingers. It was the most perfect glass I'd ever seen. Clear and silky. I tilted my head back and closed my eyes the way Aunt Josephine had when Uncle Charlie first gave her that bottle of Coca-Cola. Tilted my head back and closed my eyes the way I had at the dinner table when my mother slapped me and threatened to knock my head off my shoulders. I tilted my head back, closed my eyes, and put the glass to my mouth. Then I drank slowly. The cold, sweet water inside the goblet tasted as if Satin had climbed a mountain and drawn it from a flowing silver spring. I drank half the glass before pulling it away with a long awaited "Ahhhhhhhh!"

Satin had given me something that cooled my throat as much as the spicy chicken in the red sauce had burned it three months ago in that Ethiopian restaurant. The sensation of both made me recall what Satin had said to me, after the first time she'd made love to me. "There are a lot of wonderful things about this life, Tonya. But there are also a lot of difficult things too, and I don't want you to have to deal with any of that if I could help it. But I couldn't."

I sipped the water now, savoring it as I thought how glad I was that she couldn't help it. I looked at Satin, and she was staring at my throat as if she'd never seen one like it before.

"I know that I'm going to come off sounding like an idiot," I said, "but I have to ask you something."

"What?"

"Ahhh...did I...you know."

"Satisfy me? Make love to me like no one before? Did you feed every craving that I had for you? Did you give me fever?"

"Stop," I laughed.

"Yes, Tonya. No one, and I mean no one, has ever satisfied me more." She brought her lips to mine and gave me another kiss that left me knowing that for once I'd made my choice.

"I have another question. Since I've known you, you've always said that you cared about me, but you've never said that you love me. Do you, Satin? Do you love me?"

She smiled, closed her eyes, and tilted her head toward the ceiling. When she was facing me again, I could see an ocean of tears building in her eyes. Then she did something she had vowed never to do. Satin cried. She cried a hard, tear falling, throat-throbbing cry. And I felt her let me inside her for the first time. I closed my eyes so that I could feel her all around me, and it was warm and wonderful. I knew then that I'd been waiting to be inside her all my life.

"Yes, Tonya," Satin said, finally able to stop crying long enough to answer my question. Her voice was cracking and she stared me straight in my eyes. "I love you with all my heart. Always have."

I kissed her tears.

"What about you?" Satin asked. "You love me, I know, but are you ready to deal with all that being my lover entails?"

"To be honest. No. I mean, this is going to kill my mother because she won't be able to see how I'll be happy in a relationship that God and every other 'normal' person in the world condemn. My father...God...my father won't understand the practicality of our relationship. We can't protect each other, can't hold hands or kiss in public without being attacked physically or verbally, can't get married, can't give each other children, and can't put each other on our health insurance. If either of us becomes deathly ill, we don't have the right to make medical decisions on each other's behalf. Employers don't want to hire us. For Christ's sakes, we can't even join the Army. My sister will hate me even more than she does already because my parents will be devastated. Aunt Josephine will be scared for me. Uncle Charlie will just think I'm a freak."

"Then why are you here?" Satin asked.

"Because as hard as it will be for my family to accept my homosexuality, I know that they will not turn their backs on me. My mother won't allow anything to break up her family."

"What if you're wrong?" Satin said, as if she were speaking to a naive optimist who didn't know that she was about to step out into the world and have the throats of her hopes and dreams slashed. "What if this is the one thing that your mother believes should come between her family?"

"Then I'll simply have to accept that because my family's approvals and opinions are not worth me spending the rest of my life without you, wondering what if..."

At the crack of dawn, Satin walked me to the door. I'd decided to tell my family as soon as possible. No sense putting it off any longer than I'd already had. Besides, Satin deserved someone who wasn't ashamed to be seen dancing in public with her, someone who wasn't ashamed to tell her family about her, someone who wouldn't hide her in the corner of her life like a dirty little secret.

We kissed for a good fifteen minutes then Satin eased away smiling. I had managed to undo her robe and was guiding her back into the living room when she stopped me. I gave her an evil grin as she retied her robe.

"You're not slick," she said.

I hunched my shoulders. The smiles gradually cooled from our faces as we stood staring quietly at each other.

"You have a difficult day ahead of you," Satin said.

"No more difficult than the last ten years," I said.

"Remember, you're not alone. That's easy to forget when no one in your family understands that this isn't something that you choose to be; it's something that you've always been but was afraid to be."

I kissed her again. "I'll be back."

She smiled her bright, unforgettable smile. "I'll be waiting."

I stepped outside and a sun as orange and bright as the center of a spring cantaloupe warmed my face with rays that said, "Good morning." The weeping willow was shimmering in the light breeze. I breathed in the day, held it, and tasted it then exhaled. Through the closed front door I heard Phillip Bailey singing *"I Know."* I listened to a few beats then started down the walk. As I moved, I heard a beat other than and very different from the music coming out of Satin's house. PAT-PAT! PAT-PAT! It sounded like hands slapping on thighs covered in thick jeans. PAT-PAT! PAT-PAT! Sounded like somebody just learning to *hambone* and didn't know how to put the shoulder and chest to it yet. It was light but steady, like someone just learning to make a rhythm and follow it. This slightly off beat melody was coming from my high-top Converse sneakers. The same old ugly, clay-splattered sneakers I was wearing when I first met Malcolm. PAT-PAT! PAT-PAT! My sneakers were beating my song, and what a delightful song it was. PAT-PAT! PAT-PAT! PITAPATA! PITAPATA! PITAPATA! PAT-PAT-PAT! went my sneakers.

And as if Malcolm's words were spoken with this day and this bluesy beat in mind, I heard him say, "It ain't that bad."

No, it ain't, I thought, following my music, completely unafraid of where it would lead me. Not bad at all.

About the Author

Odessa Rose is a native of Baltimore, Maryland. She has B.A in English from Coppin State College, and a master's degree in Literature from the University of Maryland at College Park.

She is a devoted wife and mother of two sons; a member of the Black Writers Guild of Maryland, Ronald E. McNair Post-Baccalaureate Achievement Program and Alpha Kappa Mu Honor Society.